EVERYTHING I NEED

A JOURNEY'S END BILLIONAIRE ROMANCE

ANN CHRISTOPHER

The Queen's grandson. A beautiful American doctor. An unforgettable royal love story…

Long-distance romances never lead to happily-ever-after. Or do they?

The road to true love never runs smooth. Especially when an awkward British billionaire with family issues finds himself smitten with a workaholic pediatric surgeon from small-town Journey's End.

But Anthony Scott refuses to give up on his thrilling new relationship with beautiful but guarded Dr. Melody Harrison. Even when the frequent goodbyes and ongoing loneliness threaten to break both their hearts.

Long-distance love affairs often crash and burn. But not always…

If you love hot and emotional contemporary romance, pick up the steamy conclusion to this two-part romantic saga today!

1. No Ordinary Love **(Baptiste & Samira #1)**
2. Beyond Ordinary Love **(Baptiste & Samira #2)**
3. Everything I Hoped For **(Anthony & Melody #1)**
4. Everything I Need **(Anthony & Melody #2)**
5. Untitled **(Nick's Story #1)**
6. Untitled **(Nick's Story #2)**

ALSO BY ANN CHRISTOPHER

JOURNEY'S END Small-Town Contemporary Romance Series
"Book" 1: *A JOURNEY'S END* Novella
Book 2: *LET'S DO IT*
Book 3: *ON FIRE*
"Book" 4: *LET'S STAY TOGETHER* Novella
Book 5: *UNFORGETTABLE*

Billionaires of Journey's End Contemporary Romance Series
Book 1: *NO ORDINARY LOVE*
Book 2: *BEYOND ORDINARY LOVE*
Book 3: *EVERYTHING I HOPED FOR*
Book 4: *EVERYTHING I NEED*

DEADLY Romantic Suspense Series
Book 1: *DEADLY PURSUIT*
Book 2: *DEADLY DESIRES*
Book 3: *DEADLY SECRETS*

IT'S COMPLICATED Contemporary Romance Series
TROUBLE
RISK
JUST ABOUT SEX
SWEETER THAN REVENGE

The Davies Family Contemporary Romance Series

Book 1: *SINFUL SEDUCTION*

Book 2: *SINFUL TEMPTATION*

Book 3: *SINFUL ATTRACTION*

Book 4: *SINFUL PARADISE*

The Warner Family Contemporary Romance Series

Book 1: *TENDER SECRETS*

Book 2: *ROAD TO SEDUCTION*

Book 3: *CAMPAIGN FOR SEDUCTION*

Book 4: *REDEMPTION'S KISS*

Book 5: *REDEMPTION'S TOUCH*

Boxed Sets

DEADLY Series

IT'S COMPLICATED

SWEET LOVE

BELLA MONSTRUM Young Adult Horror Series

Book 1: *MONSTRUM*

Single Titles

CASE FOR SEDUCTION

THE SURGEON'S SECRET BABY

SEDUCED ON THE RED CARPET

To Richard

ACKNOWLEDGMENTS

Special thanks, once again, to:

Caroline Linden, for the brainstorming sessions and research help;

My copy editor extraordinaire, Martha Trachtenberg, for her eagle eyes;

Earthly Charms, for the gorgeous covers; and

Mom, for answering my medical questions. And for being a great mom.

© **Copyright 2018 by Sally Young Moore**
ALL RIGHTS RESERVED

This is a work of fiction. All characters in this book have no existence outside the imagination of the author and have no relation whatsoever to anyone, living or dead, bearing the same name or names. All incidents are pure invention from the author's imagination. All names, characters, places and incidents are products of the author's imagination or are used fictitiously. Any resemblance to actual events or locales or persons, living or dead, is entirely coincidental.

Except for use in any review, the reproduction or utilization of this work in whole or in part in any form by any electronic, mechanical or other means, now known or hereafter invented, including xerography, photocopying and recording, or in any information or retrieval system, is forbidden without the prior written permission of both publisher and Author copyright owner of this book.

For information, contact:

Blue Iris Press LLC

7350 Montgomery Road #36476

Cincinnati, OH 45236

www.BlueIrisPress.com

ISBN-13: 978-1-948176-18-7

Excerpt from *A Journey's End* © 2013 by Sally Young Moore

Dear Readers:

Welcome to *Everything I Need*, the second part of the sexy and emotional saga between Anthony and Melody! Please note that this book picks up in real time where *Everything I Hoped For* ends, so you'll want to read that one first if you haven't already.

Happy Reading!

Ann

1

"That's everything, I think." Anthony Scott emerged from the bedroom, passed through the living room to deposit his overnight bag in the foyer by the front door and came back to sit on the sofa in front of the crackling fire. "All packed."

Melody Harrison watched the proceedings from her kitchen, where she poured herself a cup of tea, and tried not to freak out now that they'd reached Sunday evening and the end of their first weekend together as lovers. Easier said than done, especially with an unexpected mass of anxiety tightening her chest and creeping steadily higher. The moody silence, which had grown worse all afternoon after they finished decorating the Christmas tree they'd cut together and returned his rental car, also didn't boost her flagging morale any.

"How much longer until Baptiste picks you up for the airport?" she said.

His best friend, Jean-Baptiste Mercier, a Parisian billionaire with his own plane, had recently begun dating her best friend, Samira Palmer, here in small-town Journey's End in Upstate New York.

Anthony checked his watch. "Fifteen minutes," he said, his upper-class British accent sounding more clipped than ever. Like a pissed-off Benedict Cumberbatch as Sherlock Holmes complaining that Mrs. Hudson had moved his violin.

Her heart sank another couple notches.

"You okay?" she asked brightly, stirring her tea.

He frowned. Avoided eye contact. "'Course."

Melody worked hard to feel reassured. Unfortunately, she never quite managed it beyond about 30 percent. The thing was, he didn't look okay. He didn't look okay at all as he rested his elbows on his knees and absently rubbed his hands together, his grim and downturned profile something that you might see on a man walking the last several steps to the lethal injection chamber.

Do not freak out, Mel, she told herself as she joined him in the living room, settled in the armchair and set her mug on the coffee table. *Do not get clingy. So Anthony's a little sour right now. So what? Do not make a mountain out of a molehill.*

Good advice, but she was pretty sure that the mountain was already there. The longer he didn't look at her, the more she felt as though Kilimanjaro had been inserted into the middle of her living room.

Suddenly he glanced up. They looked at each other long enough for her to feel a jolt of turbulence from his cornflower blue eyes. His jaw tightened. He quickly blinked and turned away, at the setting sun on the other side of her sliding glass doors, but the damage had been done.

She felt profoundly unsettled. As vulnerable as a squealing and furless newborn panda.

And *this,* sports fans, was why she should have stuck to

her vow to focus on her status as both a spinster and a pediatric surgeon and to avoid romantic entanglements. Failing that, she should certainly have waited to get to know Anthony better before she leapt into the horizontal boogie with him, but she'd divested herself of both her panties and most of her good sense within a few short days of meeting him, hadn't she?

Yep. She was a regular genius.

Now here she was. With her heart in her throat and no real idea what to expect next as he returned to London and they officially embarked on their committed long-distance relationship.

Desperate for something to do with herself, she reached for her tea. Blew on it. Sipped it. Tried to figure out how she'd wound up here on this glum Sunday night, where the darkness and chill inside far exceeded anything going on outside and this man's moods were now, evidently, at the center of her existence.

Well, actually, she knew exactly how she'd wound up here.

She'd met Anthony several days ago, at a gala celebrating the merger of Baptiste's French winery with one here in Journey's End in the Hudson River Valley. After a rocky initial meeting, she and Anthony had discovered they shared some serious chemistry. They'd spent some time together while he was in town. At the end of last weekend, he'd gone back to his London home. He and Melody had talked and texted religiously while he was there. Then he'd surprised her back here in Journey's End this past Friday. Emphasis on *surprised* because he'd caught her on a blind date with someone she'd met online.

That had gone over well. Not.

A blowup had ensued, followed by some spectacular sex.

Then Anthony had filled Melody in on a pertinent detail or two from his past. Like the fact that his father was a Texas oilman and Anthony had a trust fund in the neighborhood of a billion dollars. Oh, and Anthony's grandmother on his mother's side? The Queen of England. As in, *the* Queen of England. True, he was her youngest grandchild and about as likely to accede to the throne as Melody was, but he was still a prince of England.

Had Melody seen any of that coming? No, she had not. Was she, as a black woman with her own life and career on this side of the pond, prepared for the possibility of press intrusion into their fledgling relationship? Was she prepared for the scrutiny (and public judgment) of her appearance, including the burn scar she bore on her face and neck, which dated from a childhood accident in the kitchen? *Hell* no. The thought made her cringe.

And yet...

Was she prepared to say good-bye to this man? To wish him a great life without her?

She watched him absently crack his knuckles, her innards softening to caramel goo.

Absolutely not.

So she and Anthony had decided to be exclusive and continue seeing each other. See what happened.

And what was happening at this particular moment was that Mr. Anthony Scott looked as cold and forbidding as he'd been when they first met. There was something about seeing him in a sweater, jeans and leather jacket, with his blond hair brushed and shot through with golden streaks, that made her heart ache. This morning, they'd been naked in bed together, her fingers running through that silky hair and his body thrusting deep inside hers. Now he sat over there, a million miles away on her sofa, and she couldn't muster the courage to go sit beside him, much less reach for his hand.

Yet they thought they could make a run at a successful long-distance relationship when they couldn't breach the brick wall that had sprung up between them while they were in the same town and the same room?

Yup. They were off to a *baaaad* start.

She could almost laugh if it wasn't all so doomed to failure.

She and Anthony were going to crash and burn, and they were going to crash and burn *big*.

Guaranteed.

Don't think like that, Mel, said a quiet little voice in the back of her head.

Be brave. Take a chance.

She took a deep breath and decided that she wasn't going to let this whole thing go down in flames on account of her unmitigated cowardice. Hadn't she survived a horrible childhood burn and all the corresponding surgeries, pain and negative attention from staring people? Hadn't she gotten into and then clawed her way through Harvard Med, for God's sake? Couldn't she act like a mature adult and try to reach across their divide?

You bet your ass she could.

She cleared her throat. "You sure you're okay? You've been awfully quiet."

"I'm fine," he snapped, staring down at his hands as he rubbed them.

"Clearly," she muttered, putting her mug back on the coffee table with a distinct *thunk* before moving over to sit beside him on the sofa.

His head came up. He nailed her straight on with those unwavering blue eyes, frosty now.

"Meaning?" he asked aggressively.

That tone made her hackles rise.

She nailed him with her own unyielding stare. Screw it. This relationship had nothing if they didn't master basic honesty and Communication 101.

"Meaning you're starting to remind me of the night we met. When you were being a *jackass*."

He looked startled.

"And since I'm sure that's not your intent, and I'm pretty sure something's on your mind, why don't we talk about it? Give you a chance to practice talking about your feelings."

Whoa. She hadn't meant to be *quite* that forceful.

Neither of them spoke for several beats. The silence turned brittle.

"You probably wouldn't want to hear every thought that's popped into my head this afternoon." His wry smile never came within a mile of his eyes. "I believe you've complained about my being too blunt with my words at times?"

Fair point, not that she wanted to concede it just now.

"Well, it turns out that I prefer your bluntness to your cold shoulder. Imagine my surprise."

"I'm not giving you the *cold shoulder*," he said, incredulous. "If anything, I'm lost in my thoughts. Is that illegal in the States now?"

"Spill, Anthony."

He hesitated. Heaved a rough sigh.

"Have it your way. If you must know, I'm wondering if we'll be able to make a go of it after all, because this is all shaping up to be much more difficult than I'd expected."

Melody absorbed this information like a punch to the solar plexus.

He *what*? Was this the end already? Was he about to dump her now that he'd screwed her?

"I've also been wondering if you'll be on another blind date with some other bloke as soon as my plane goes wheels up tonight—"

"I will *not*—" she began, outraged.

"—but I've dismissed that possibility because we've given each other our word and I believe we trust each other reasonably well." His gaze, filled with sudden sensual appreciation, skimmed her up and down, making her skin sizzle. "Besides that, we quite enjoy each other in bed, don't we, darling? We've given each other a lot to think about and a lot to remember each other by until we meet again on Friday, haven't we?"

Melody opened her mouth, feeling a little breathless—

Anthony's lips twisted with unmistakable bitterness.

"I'm wondering why the bloody hell I'll have to spend the week in exile across the ocean, going to meetings most of the time and alone in my drafty cottage the rest of the time while, meantime, you're out having fun with Baptiste and Samira or here in your cozy little apartment with your Christmas decorations, a blazing fire, river views and your amazingly comfortable bed that has the added bonus of having your incredible body in it."

She gaped at him, her head spinning.

"I'm wondering if I could possibly skive off my meetings and just stay here, but my grandmother would have my head. And *then* she'd never let me hear the end of it. My life wouldn't be worth living."

"Anthony…" she said when he paused to catch his breath.

"I'm wondering what you've done to me to turn me into this complete nutter in such a short period of time, because I don't lose my head—about *anything*—nor am I a clingy person." He paused thoughtfully. "*Now,* of course, I'm wondering if it was a mistake to confess my looming nuttery and if you'll use that as an excuse to run in the other direction."

"Anthony—"

"I'm wondering what I've ever done to get lucky enough for a woman like *you* to cross my path, much less give me a chance, and I want to kiss your feet that you haven't written me off now that you know all about both sides of my family. The fact that you've actually met my father and are still even speaking to me qualifies you for sainthood in my book."

She had to laugh.

He watched her, his avid gaze crisscrossing her features. Then he cursed, took her face in his hands and kissed her hard. He eased back to end the kiss, leaving her stunned and hopelessly aroused as he rested his forehead against hers.

"Mainly I'm wondering if it's physically possible for me to survive without seeing your smile or kissing you between now and Friday," he said gruffly. "Aren't you glad you asked?"

Melody paused to smooth his hair and rein in her answering confession, which would include gems like *I want to stow away on your plane* and *I am literally now incapable of thinking about anything but you.*

He wasn't the only one up on a ledge about the future of their relationship outside of the four walls of her apartment this weekend. That was for damn sure.

She let out a shaky laugh.

"You have all that up there?" she asked, tapping his temple. "No wonder you look so pained all the time. There's no room for any fun thoughts."

Crooked smile from Anthony. "You've no idea."

He let her go and sat back, idly twisting her one of her corkscrew curls and setting off frissons of pleasure every time he brushed the side of her neck.

They stared at each other.

"Can I tell you something?" she asked quietly.

His expression softened, as did his voice.

"You can tell me anything, darling."

As always, his use of the endearment made her feel as though her skin glowed.

She stole another quick kiss, lingering over his tender lips because they were so delicious. When they broke apart, she noted, with great satisfaction, that his eyes were glazed.

"I work at the hospital," she said. "*All* the time. I eat. Sometimes I sleep. When I can't sleep, I read my medical journals." She pointed to where they were piled high in a basket. "Sometimes I have a glass of wine. Sometimes I meet up with Samira, but not so much now that she's with Baptiste. And that's it. That's all there is to me."

One corner of his mouth curled.

"Sounds pathetic, to be honest. I never realized you were such a loser."

"Well, I am," she said, managing a quick laugh before her swelling heart filled her throat. Her smile slipped away. It was much too hard to think clearly when he looked at her like that, all steady warmth. "So the next time you feel like I'm having too much fun without you, just remember that I'm either in the OR trying to patch some kid back together or sitting here wishing you were with me."

He hesitated. Ran his hands over the top of his head, ruffling his hair.

"Melody—"

His phone vibrated. They both stiffened.

At that glum moment, Melody would have been happier to hear Jack from *The Shining* chopping through her front door with an ax.

He pulled his phone out and checked the display. "It's Baptiste. He's on his way."

"I know," she said.

To her everlasting dismay, she felt her chin wobble and discovered that she was perilously close to tears. She'd already cried once in front of him (the other day when one of her patients had suddenly died) and had no intention of doing it again. Ever, if she could help it.

The man was going home to London. They'd known this moment would come. No big deal whatsoever.

So she plastered a bright smile on her face and jumped up.

"Did you forget anything? I'd better make sure you grabbed all your stuff."

She hurried into the bedroom, giving herself a swift mental kick in the ass along the way. What the hell had gotten into her? She met a new man and all of the sudden she carried on as though life was a Shakespearean tragedy every time he left her side? Was *that* where this was going?

No freaking way.

Her life did not depend on a man. Her happiness did not depend on a man.

She wouldn't let it.

Tomorrow she would go back to work at the hospital like she always did. Normal life would resume. The birds would still sing in the trees and her curly hair would still refuse to behave. Her entire life had not changed because of this relationship.

Okay.

Focus, girl.

She did a lap around her ultra-neat bedroom with her usual brisk efficiency and noticed it right away: the telltale patch of red plaid under the edge of one of the white decorator pillows on the bed. Anthony's flannel pajama bottoms. He'd be sad if he got back home and they weren't in his overnight bag, wouldn't he? She snatched them up and headed for the bathroom. And there was something else: Anthony's toothbrush in her holder, along with his travel-sized bottle of funky British mouthwash and tube of toothpaste. She grabbed those, too.

Men.

And to think he'd claimed he'd packed. How was it "packing" when you forgot pretty much everything you'd brought with you? Was it a vision problem? Maybe she should hold up a couple fingers and ask him how many he saw—

Anthony appeared in the bathroom doorway, startling her.

She shook her head, disbelieving, and snorted out a laugh as she held the items up for him to see.

"You forgot half your stuff, you silly goose."

But Anthony was evidently in no mood for teasing.

She watched the storm roll in and settle on his face, dimming the vivid cornflower blue of his eyes the way an afternoon rain throws Miami beaches into shadow.

His jaw tightened.

"Why are you getting rid of my things?"

2

The sudden rough edge to his voice caught her by surprise. So did the look on his face, as though he planned to call the local authorities if she didn't put his stuff back *now*. A negative electrical charge in the air made nerve endings tingle all up and down her arms and across her scalp.

She froze, baffled.

This whole situation demonstrated, in stark detail, the problem with sexing someone up first, then trying to build a relationship later. The sex, at least for her, kicked the intensity level up to eleven, but the parties involved still didn't know each other well enough to understand whether the inevitable bumps in the road were normal or if they led to hidden sinkholes that could ruin everything.

"Why're you looking at me like that?" she asked. "I'm *not* getting rid of your stuff. I'm making sure you pack it so you don't miss it when you get home."

His eyes flashed. "Why can't my things stay where they were?"

She blinked, bewildered. "I didn't realize you wanted them to."

"Well, I do," he said flatly.

She held her hands up. "My mistake."

He grumbled something indistinct.

"What the hell is going on here?" she asked. "Why am I getting the feeling that your toothbrush is not the real issue?"

"Because you've completely missed the point." He barked. "Some women *want* the man to leave something behind. Some women *want* the man to feel that there's a place for him."

"A thousand pardons."

"Besides. You need the reminder."

"Of what?" she said, still baffled.

"My pending return."

The lingering belligerence in his tone didn't sit well with her. Nor did the *additional* reference to the fact that she hadn't kept the faith the last time he left town.

She crossed her arms, beginning to fume.

"Stop throwing that blind date in my face. And don't bark at me. I'm not one of your soldiers. And you're not General Patton pledging to return to the Philippines."

A flicker of grudging respect crossed over his face. "It was General MacArthur."

"Close enough."

They watched each other, the silence turning wary until a light bulb went off over her head. She snapped her fingers as all the puzzle pieces fell into place.

"Hang on. I know what you're doing. You're picking a fight with me."

His expression became guarded.

"Pardon me? Why on earth would I do that in my last ten seconds with you before I have to leave for the week?"

Look at his face! She was definitely on to something.

"It's part of the separation process. It's easier for people to let each other go and say good-bye if they're angry with each other. I learned about this whole thing during med school."

A dull flush climbed up his neck and resolved over his cheekbones. He cocked his head, squinting at her. "Are you *analyzing* me?"

Meeting his stony expression head-on shaved a year or two off her life. This man gave intimidating a whole new meaning, and she'd been yelled at and humiliated by some of the most fearsome professors Harvard Med had to offer.

Yet she wasn't scared. Not at all. She was exhilarated.

"Am I wrong?"

His jaw began to flex in the back. Maybe that was why it took him so long to speak.

"I hope I haven't reached quite *that* level of insanity and dependency over a woman I didn't know existed two short weeks ago."

The words hovered between them, lingering in the air like a blast from a skunk's tail.

Worse? The veiled implication made her wince. It was all buried in those staccato syllables, something to the effect that she thought a *bit* too highly of herself, or maybe that she read way too much importance and/or permanency into any plans he may have for their relationship.

Whatever it was, it cut far too close to the bone of her sparse dating life and forgettable previous relationships with men. It made her want to duck her head and mumble an apology for letting her narcissistic side run wild.

Then she remembered: she didn't have a narcissistic side.

He *was* picking an argument. No matter how he tried to dodge and deflect when confronted with the truth. This behavior was a known psychological phenomenon.

Funny thing, though. She still wanted to hit him.

Actually, she wanted a lot of things at the moment.

She wanted him to march his arrogant self out of her apartment and not let the door hit him in the ass on the way out. She also wanted him to stay here forever so she could employ more of her previously undetected intuitive skills and uncover all of his secrets.

Mostly she just wanted a reaction from Mr. Cool and Aloof.

"Tell you what," she said with a sweeping gesture toward the bathroom door. "Why don't you wait for Baptiste in the lobby? Have a great flight."

Seething now, she took a determined step or two away from him.

He made a strangled noise behind her, the only clue that she might have hit a nerve.

Bingo.

She turned back, triumph surging through her as they glared at each other.

One glimpse of those flashing blue eyes revealed everything she could have hoped to know. Honestly, it was like looking into a funhouse mirror of her own emotions. A reflection of everything she felt about him.

She infuriated him.

She fascinated him.

She amused and unraveled him.

He didn't want to leave her.

This thing between them terrified him.

What if it didn't work out?

And, worse, what if it somehow *did*?

This was all too much, way too soon.

Yet he had no intention of backing away from any challenges she might present.

His expression turned determined as he looked her up and down. Hot. Possessive.

There was no mistaking his intent.

She started to shake her head and remind him that Baptiste was probably pulling into the parking lot this very second. The circumstances weren't exactly conducive to her relaxing and enjoying herself. Plus, they'd already had sex roughly eight hundred times in the last twenty-four hours and her intimate lady parts were sore and wonderfully sated. There was a limit to how much her body could take and how many times she could cream and come for him.

Enough was enough.

She started to open her mouth and tell him that now was not the time. But she got exactly nowhere.

Because that was the thing about Anthony Scott.

He had his rough edges and arrogant moments, sure.

But when he looked at her like *that*?

There was only *this*.

She reached for him, palming his scratchy cheeks and pulling his face down for her urgent kisses. He was right there with her, running his hands down to her ass and hefting her as his mouth slanted over hers. She hopped up, wrapping her legs around his waist and reveling in his earthy scent and the size of his erection as he ground against her. His skilled mouth nuzzled, licked and nipped, his tongue growing more insistent and sweeping deeper once he gripped a handful of her hair and tilted her head the way he wanted it.

Just the way *she* wanted it.

She crooned and mewled, choking out little sounds of encouragement that he didn't seem to need as he plunked her on the marble countertop next to the sink.

There was a tiny pause while they stared at each other in mutual astonishment. God only knew what all ran through his mind when he stared at her with such dark intent, his expression vaguely troubled, but she could only manage a single flustered thought:

What is this man doing to me?

Then he unleashed all his passion with a low growl and thinking became impossible.

Never had a quickie been quite so quick or so relentlessly thorough. While she propped her hands on the counter behind her and tried to withstand the onslaught, *his* hands managed to hit all the highlights of her body in sixty seconds or less. They gripped her hair and massaged her nape. Reverently stroked her face and neck, maneuvering her head this way and that for his kisses and nips. Manhandled her breasts and nipples, rubbing and squeezing jolts of sensation out of her body and making her squirm with growing agitation.

Down below, meanwhile, she held his waist in a death grip between her thighs. If this man thought she was letting him hop a plane to London when he belonged right *here* with her, he damn well better think again. But Anthony didn't act like he was going anywhere. He rotated his hips with sharp thrusts, never missing a beat as he unerringly hit the sweet spot between her legs and made her foolish as she panted and moaned incoherently for him.

Then his hands went to the waistband of her yoga pants.

Ah, God.

She got her sluggish lids open and looked up to see him watching her, a glimmer of something unrestrained and primitive in his eyes as he tugged her pants and panties down. She wiggled to help him, then reached for his belt and started to unbuckle it. But he took over with an impatient rumble and freed himself much faster than she could have managed with her shaky hands.

And there he was.

As a medical professional, she'd seen her share of penises and wasn't one to wax poetic about their various forms and uses. But *this* one was particularly fine, ruddy and thick with a plump head that reminded her of some delicious summer fruit.

Just as she was thinking, *oh, shit, I hope he has a condom nearby,* he reached sideways and opened the top drawer. Staring her in the face, one brow raised to a cocky *say something; I dare you* level, he rummaged around and produced...a string of condoms.

It took her lust-fogged brain a couple of beats to realize that he'd planted the condoms earlier and meant them to stay with her along with his pajama bottoms and toiletries, marking his place and reminding her of his existence until his return.

She registered his *gotcha* gleam of amusement. She also registered his unyielding stance on the issue (there'd be hell to pay if she dared complain) and, beneath that, the hint of vulnerability.

Bottom line? He'd respect her wishes and pack up all his stuff if she insisted, but he'd receive such instructions as stab wounds of rejection.

As for her?

While she wanted to do many things with this man, sending him away with his eyes a stormy blue rather than the bright cobalt she'd come to know and love was not one of them.

So she sat up straighter, took the condoms from him, tore one off, replaced the rest and shut the drawer with a decisive snap.

His expression softened as he dimpled at her.

Something in her heart turned over.

She watched with a faint feeling of regret as he sheathed himself. She hated these pauses when she was ready to crawl out of her too-tight skin and they had to stop and do the medically safe thing. She didn't want anything between her and that hard dick. It felt unnatural to have a barrier between them, like trying to eat sand or wield the scalpel in her left hand.

He glanced up at her when he finished. Some of her ambivalence must have shown because he studied her for a long beat or two, his face troubled.

But this was no time for deep thoughts or discussions. Not when he put his hands on her hips, slid her off the counter with her yoga pants and panties down around her knees and turned her to face the counter.

And the mirror.

She planted her hands on the cool marble, shivering with anticipation as she braced herself. Doggie style had never really been her thing but, on the other hand, sex with Anthony Scott wasn't like sex with anyone else.

As always, she couldn't wait to get him inside her. Especially now. There was something about the way he loomed behind her, all hard-edged masculinity here in her bathroom among all her creams and lotions. Something about the way they were still mostly clothed, with only his dick and her pussy exposed.

Something about the look in his eyes as they watched each other in the mirror.

He nudged her feet apart, widening her stance. Bent at the knees, getting the angle just right. Thrust home.

They both cried out, undone by the exquisite contact between them. Melody gasped, trying to get her head around the spiraling sensations between her legs and the way her soreness actually increased the pleasure. Anthony also took a moment to adjust, bracing one palm on the counter and rubbing her breasts with the other.

Funny, huh?

Three minutes ago, she would have sworn that she didn't have another orgasm in her, not for at least another two or three days, but now her secret inner muscles began to tighten and clench all around him.

She bore down experimentally, watching his face in the mirror to see what he would do.

He'd hooked his chin over her shoulder so that they were cheek-to-cheek, so she had a perfect view of the way his eyes rolled closed and his features slackened with astonishment.

Astonishment...and gathering ecstasy.

Then his eyes flicked open again and he dragged that hand back and forth between her breasts a final time, abrading her sensitive flesh with the stretchy material of her sports bra.

She gasped. Trembled as his hand slid its way down her belly and lower, zeroing in on her sex.

He cupped her, pressing two fingers to her clit and penning her in until his heavy body blocked her from behind and there was nowhere for her to go and nothing for her to do other than receive the thrill of each delicious thrust.

Then he began to *move*.

And that amazing dick of his—or maybe it was his amazing fingers—led her to hidden pleasure centers that she hadn't known her body possessed. Every surge of his hips generated bolts of electrical pleasure low in her belly, much to her shock. And yet it was no shock at all. Not with Anthony. That was one of the things that was so galling—and so exciting—about him. He knew things about her that *she* didn't know, and he didn't bother showing her the decency of acting surprised about it. It was as though he'd reached inside her, pulled out a handful of flawless ten-carat diamonds, ignored her absolute astonishment and said, *yeah, I thought that was in there.*

He left her feeling so raw and vulnerable.

And so exquisitely undone.

It didn't take long for his face to turn red with exertion or for a sheen of perspiration to cover his forehead. It took even less time for her abandoned cries, punctuated by his sharp grunts of exertion, to reach a helpless crescendo.

The mirror showed her everything. The wild glitter in her eyes and satisfied Mona Lisa smile on her lips, both of which were partially hidden by her spiraling curls. The way his face twisted and then slackened into rapture as he pressed his face to the side of her neck. The way his lips moved as he murmured sweet words to her that she couldn't quite hear.

She could have stayed like that all night.

She could have died like that.

But time was not their friend and Anthony knew it. So he surged those hips a little harder. Stopped pressing her clit and began rubbing it. Over and over again. Unblinkingly held her gaze in the mirror and watched as she blew apart in his arms, shouting his name as she let her head fall back and came and came and *came*.

He quickly followed with a ragged groan, turning to stone as his muscles clenched in a final thrust.

They were still panting, all four of their hands braced on the counter as they leaned into it and tried to catch their breath, when Anthony's phone buzzed. Buzzed again.

Anthony raised his head and met her eye again as he pulled the phone out of his back pocket, his expression full of unmistakable regret.

He hit a button and held the phone to his ear.

"One minute," he said, and no one hearing that polished

voice, so deep and resonant, would suspect that he was still buried to the hilt inside her.

Or that he'd just taken her perfectly serviceable woman's body, turned it inside out, upside down and sideways, thereby ruining her for anything less with anyone else, ever again.

He hung up and put his phone away. Withdrew and left an even *sweeter* ache between her legs. Stooped to pull her panties and yoga pants back up, nipping her ass and nuzzling the small of her back under her top as he came back up. Hugged her from behind as she grinned and squirmed. Squeezed all the breath out of her body as they swayed together for a minute, his lips resting on her temple. Left her standing there, dazed and undone, while he got rid of the condom and came back to wash his hands and splash water on his face.

Then he grabbed her hand towel, dried his face and rested his palms on the counter, matching her stance as he leaned into it again.

They stared at each other in the mirror, neither smiling.

Nor was there anything to say. The moment was too heavy for that. Far too important.

This was it, then. The moment of truth, arriving much too soon.

So they thought they wanted a long-distance relationship? Thought they were up for the challenge of trying to see each other as often as they could when they lived on opposite sides of an ocean that was nearly thirty-five hundred miles wide? Thought that maybe the grandson of the Queen of England could make a go of it with a black woman who lived in Upstate New York? A woman who had an unsightly burn scar on one side of her face? Oh, and they wanted to do it all without the press finding out?

Yeah. Good luck with that.

She could almost hear God's raucous laughter.

Well, they'd soon see, wouldn't they?

One way or the other, they'd soon see.

At last, after a long pause, during which he catalogued her features and focused on her eyes before dropping to her lips, he opened his mouth.

Her entire body waited on high alert.

"Friday," he said.

She barely heard his hoarse voice over the relentless thumping of her pulse in her ears.

He cleared his throat. "I'll see you on Friday."

Lobbying a final pointed look at her, he walked out without another word.

She heard his footsteps echo through her apartment and stop in the foyer. The creak of leather as he grabbed his overnight bag. A long pause. And then the quiet opening and closing of her front door as he returned to his regularly scheduled life without her in London.

"Friday," she told her reflection in the mirror, trying both to sound upbeat and to ignore her trembling chin.

3

What the fuck am I going to do now? Anthony wondered half an hour later, staring blankly out at the rain as it streamed past his window on Baptiste's private plane and ignoring the book about the Nuremberg Trials open on his lap. Excess energy made him feel wired and jumpy. He wished he could jog for an hour or so or, better yet, spend some time doing the butterfly in the pool at his gym back home. Twenty laps should do it. But since he was pent up on the plane for the rest of the night, he had to satisfy himself with cracking his knuckles. One at a time. The ritual had always calmed him back when he served in Afghanistan.

Crack. Crack-crack.

He heard the exaggerated clearing of a male throat and glanced around. A frowning Baptiste sat facing him across the aisle, his paperwork and a glass of wine sitting on the table in front of him.

"That's very annoying," Baptiste told him in his French accent. "How many more knuckles do you have?"

Anthony grimaced and dropped his hands. As this was Baptiste's plane and his mate was kindly giving him a ride back home to London on his way to Paris, he couldn't very well tell him to fuck off. Well, he *could,* but it would probably end badly for Anthony, who had no real desire to descend the thirty thousand feet without a parachute.

But his overflowing energy was still there.

It made his leg jiggle. When he realized what he was doing and forced himself to stop, the energy zinged back to his hands. So he ran them over the top of his head, back and forth, back and forth. He tried his best to erase all the simmering anxieties from his brain, but that was the thing about simmering anxieties, wasn't it? They simmered.

As did the unanswerable question.

What. The fuck. Am I going. To do now?

Some sort of delayed reaction had settled in, frying his brain and leaving him shell-shocked and stuck. A bomb seemed to have gone off and he had more of an idea about how to handle a wildebeest stampede in Botswana than he did the shrapnel generated in the middle of his life by one Dr. Melody Harrison.

What the fuck. Am I going. To do now?

Now, suddenly, he was in a relationship. One that felt like the most important of his life.

Just like that—*boom!* A fully formed relationship.

A few short weeks ago, he'd been minding his own business, happily single and doing his best to fend off the blue-blooded matchmaking mamas of the world, like Mrs. Carmichael, who tried to pawn off her daughter Annabella on him every chance she got. Had he known Melody Harrison existed? No, he had not. Had he felt that his life was missing anything? No, he had not.

Yet *one* look at Melody's picture…

He turned away from the window and glared at the top of Baptiste's head.

"This is *your* fault, you duplicitous foreigner."

Baptiste idly flipped a page in his file and scribbled something, never bothering to look up.

"And what have I allegedly done this time?"

"You sent me that link to Melody's bio."

Baptiste shrugged and scribbled again.

"I wanted you to have another pediatric surgeon for your medical foundation. Where is the harm?"

Where was the—?

"A woman like *that*?" Anthony said, incredulous. "You introduce me to a woman like *that,* a brilliant and beautiful Harvard-trained pediatric surgeon who has a mouth on her and isn't afraid to stand up to me and my bullshit, and you don't expect me to have a violent reaction to her? Why don't you French ever *think*?" He tapped his own temple. "You know your actions have consequences. You know I'm susceptible. You know my game isn't up to scratch."

"Eh." Baptiste sipped his wine, still poring over his paperwork. "Your game is adequate enough, judging from the mark on Melody's neck earlier."

Anthony's lips twitched at this unexpected reminder that he *had,* in fact, made a few inroads with Melody. Just like that, his brain shifted to some of the thrilling moments they'd shared over the weekend. Moments when she'd been hot and wild in his arms, her skin flushed and dewy and her long curls damp as they trailed across his chest and lower. Moments when her face had twisted, her eyes had rolled closed, her back had arched and her delicious musk had saturated his senses.

Moments when he'd lost his bloody mind and left it back in Journey's End, a town he hadn't even known existed several short days ago.

Maybe his game *was* a bit better than he gave himself

credit for. But his unexpected success with Melody over the weekend only intensified his misery now.

"I don't want to leave her," he said, slumping back against his seat as the growing ache of loss and longing took hold in his gut. He rubbed his face, trying to put his fears into words. "What if she forgets me when I'm gone? What if she decides I'm not worth the risk? What if someone more suitable swoops in and steals her away before we can get this relationship on solid footing?"

He dropped his hands in time to see Baptiste look up and gape at him.

"The Queen is your grandmother. You're a prince of England. Your father is a billionaire. *You* are a baby billionaire. Who the fuck is more suitable than *you*? I'd really like to know."

"Don't you get it?" Anthony said, aghast that he had to bother explaining his situation to Baptiste, of all people. The man had been through every major milestone with him since boarding school. He knew the score. "My position is a liability. Not an asset."

"Yes, I'm sure," Baptiste deadpanned. "The luxury. The adulation. The connections."

"Yes, and also the press intrusion, security issues and lack of privacy."

"You've done all right so far," Baptiste noted mildly. "I don't see any paparazzi or burly bodyguards. Your face hasn't been splashed on any tabloids lately."

"The clock is running out on that, I'm afraid. When I get my title and/or when the paps get wind of Melody, all bets are off."

Baptiste didn't say anything to this, but his expression fell.

That was agreement enough, as far as Anthony was concerned.

They sat in a pensive silence for several beats.

Then the flight attendant appeared.

"Did you gentlemen decide on whether you'd like the filet mignon or the mahi-mahi?"

"I'll have the filet. Medium-rare, please," Baptiste said.

"Not really hungry," Anthony said glumly.

Baptiste gave him a withering look of absolute disdain before focusing on the flight attendant.

"He'll have the same. And bring him some of the stout. He'll like that."

Anthony doubted he'd be able to choke it down right now. "Not thirst—"

"Melody likes this particular stout," Baptiste added.

Wait, she did? Anthony perked up.

"Worth a try, I suppose."

The flight attendant and Baptiste both stifled a laugh at his expense, which did nothing to boost Anthony's flagging morale. He watched the flight attendant head back to the galley, his mind shifting to other concerns.

"The thing is," he said quietly, "Melody has a life. A growing career. I *want* her to thrive. Whatever she does. How can I subject her to my world?"

"Ah. So you make Melody's decisions for her now? She has no say?"

Anthony had to snort at *that* unlikely image.

"Of course not. But how could she possibly know what she's getting into with me? I'm positive she's never had photographers lurk in the bushes to ambush her or rummage through her rubbish to see what they can discover about her. Or a friend sell a fun childhood story to a tabloid and destroy a lifelong relationship for five thousand pounds."

"So let her go, then," Baptiste said. "Set her free to find, I don't know, another doctor like her. Think of all they'd have in common. She'd be much happier, I'm sure."

Anthony knew his mate was just having a go at him. But the banked amusement in Baptiste's voice, his friend's shrewd assessment of Anthony's worst fears and his own sudden flare of jealousy at the idea that Melody might yet take up with someone else all formed a toxic combination that threatened to transform Anthony into a pale and scrawny British version of The Incredible Hulk, rampaging around the cabin and causing destruction and chaos.

He thought of all the things *he* had in common with Melody. Their shared traumas and desire to help people. Their laughter, quiet understanding and the occasional exhilarating flares of disagreement.

The *passion*.

His skin tightened with renewed longing. Worse, his leg jiggled anew with a fresh adrenaline surge.

Let Melody go? When he felt more of a connection with her than with the last dozen women he'd dated combined?

"No," he said flatly, glaring at Baptiste for having the temerity to raise the topic.

"Then your choice is made. You should be happy you've met her." Baptiste said with a disbelieving laugh, having made his point in spectacular fashion. "Why so morose?"

What a stupid question.

"It's what I do best. I'm happiest when I'm miserable. You know that."

"Enjoy this time with her," Baptiste said, still laughing. "You're under the radar for now. See what happens. Why make more of it than that until you have to?"

Anthony resisted a strong desire to lunge across the cabin and throttle his best friend into oblivion. Something about his glowing face and pending parental happiness set Anthony's teeth on edge, especially when juxtaposed with his own looming uncertainty about whether Melody—or, indeed, any woman—could handle a relationship with him and his teetering tower of baggage.

"Says the man who took *one* look at Samira and abandoned his entire life in France, refusing to go home for weeks, "Anthony said sourly. "The man who, if I recall correctly, called me on more than one memorable recent occasion and had to be talked down from a very high ledge because *he* was unsure about where *his* relationship was going. Two months ago, you didn't believe in love or long-term relationships, yet now you're so syrupy sweet you should sign up to write greeting cards for the lovesick."

Beaming and incandescent with happiness, Baptiste raised his wine and toasted him.

"C'est la vie."

Disgusted, Anthony gave him the finger before slumping back in his seat.

Chuckle of amusement from Baptiste.

"Your grandmother is lovely and the rest of your family isn't so bad. Not even Tony."

Anthony snorted.

"It's true. I like your father very much."

"Yes, well, perhaps you should see about him adopting you. I'm sure he'd love having a son who actually wanted to spend time in his presence."

"You should give him more of a chance."

Anthony scowled at him as the flight attendant returned and distributed their drinks.

"I don't want your advice about my *father*. Tell me how you're making things work so well with a decent person like

Samira. *You're* no catch. Everyone knows that. You go through women the way babies go through nappies."

"*Went* through women," Baptiste clarified. "And I'm going to tell you what my buddy Daniel recently told me: you have to figure out your own shit and suffer the way the rest of us have suffered. You don't get to weasel out of it by copying what worked for someone else."

"Fucking *brilliant,*" Anthony said bitterly. "Why do I bother with you at all, then?"

"Because of the plane," Baptiste said, chuckling.

"It *is* a very fine plane," Anthony said, raising his glass to him. "Cheers."

Baptiste grinned and toasted him. "*Santé.* To your health."

They sipped appreciatively. Anthony silently put another ten thousand or so points into Melody's growing pro column for her taste in stout; this one was quite good.

"I think you need to chill down," Baptiste finally said.

Anthony blinked. "*Chill down?* What does that mean?"

"Relax. Don't worry so much."

"Chill *out*. Or maybe just *chill*. Actually, I don't think people say that much anymore."

"Yes, *chill*. That's what I said."

"Easy for you to say. Your life is all settled now, isn't it?"

"It will all work out for you if it's meant to be," Baptiste said. "*My* history isn't the greatest, God knows. And my parents were horrible. No question. Yet Samira got over all that. She still wants me. Perhaps you should view this period as a test to see how suited Melody is to your situation? If not? Bid her adieu."

"I've already told you, I'm not bloody bidding her *anything,*" Anthony said. "And you're minimizing my dilemma. The troublesome members of *my* family are all still alive and kicking. While *yours* are all conveniently dead and therefore unable to complicate your life."

"Not necessarily." Baptiste shuddered dramatically. "You'd be surprised how long a shadow my mother casts from her grave."

Having met Baptiste's mother, an unlamented woman who'd showed as much warmth to her son as five-star restaurants showed to rats in their kitchens, Anthony had to agree. He laughed.

His amusement didn't last long, though. Not with the physical distance opening up between him and Melody and the uncertainties growing. And that had led him to his temporary loss of sanity this evening.

There was no other way to describe it, was there? All he'd known was that he'd felt the slow creep of dread up his throat as he watched the clock and realized that zero hour had arrived.

And then when she'd tried to give him back his belongings…

It wasn't that there was anything special about a tube of toothpaste, for God's sake. It was just that it seemed critically (and also inexplicably) important for him to leave something behind with her. Something to hold his place until he could return.

Whatever.

So he'd picked a fight with her, a fact that seemed abundantly clear in hindsight.

He had *not* expected the lovely Dr. Harrison to read him like that.

To disarm him. To inflame and enthrall him.

But that was what she did, wasn't it? He couldn't stand the idea of leaving her and not witnessing some clever thing she might do or say. Was driven mad by the possibility that their circumstances might keep him, one way or the other, from learning everything he possibly could about this fascinating woman.

The upshot?

A surging wave of emotion had overtaken him to the point where he'd pounced on her. Just taken her up against the counter like a rock star and a groupie shagging in the bathroom of some drug-fueled club.

The best sex of his life.

Hers, too, from the look of it.

He regretted nothing. Maybe he should, but he didn't.

He clenched his fists, his hands all but trembling with the remembered feel of her vibrant body, and shook his head at himself.

What the bloody hell had happened to him since he met that woman?

"It was…" He wasn't in the habit of baring his deepest personal feelings to Baptiste, who'd never been known for his sensitivity and who, along with their other boarding school friend, Domenico "Nick" Rossi, had always been keen for a laugh at Anthony's expense. But, on the other hand, he also wasn't in the habit of meeting a woman who blew his mind in the best possible way. And if Baptiste couldn't understand Anthony's current turmoil, who on earth would? "It was surprisingly difficult to leave her earlier. I don't know how you manage it with Samira."

Baptiste sipped his wine again, shooting him a steady look of quiet empathy that went a long way toward soothing Anthony's frayed nerves.

"I haven't really handled it. And now you understand why I hadn't gone home in so long."

Oh, Anthony understood, all right. He understood perfectly.

"Perhaps I owe you an apology for giving you so much shit, mate."

"Not at all." Baptiste unleashed that dazzling smile of his, all sparkling eyes and Gallic charm. "I enjoy knowing how terrible you feel. That's enough for me."

"Well, you've always been a prick."

"Perfectly true," Baptiste said, laughing as he finished his wine and picked up his pen again. "I cannot continue to hold your hand. I have work to do before we land. If we're finished...?"

Anthony wished that they were, but another embarrassing confession—there seemed to be no end of them tonight—refused to stay silently inside his mouth.

"I want a real chance with her. D'you understand? It would be one thing if we lived in the same town and spent time together and she decided that I'm an unmitigated arse and she never wants to see my face again. That's fair. I'd have no one to blame but myself." Even at this early stage, it seemed abundantly clear that *he* wouldn't be the one putting the brakes on things. He was already so far gone that the idea seemed laughable. "But if this distance thing ruins it, or the press finds out and makes her life unbearable..."

He trailed off, both possibilities making him quietly insane.

Baptiste nodded. "Yes, well, you can sit there and wallow in nightmare scenarios that haven't happened yet, or you can look at it the right way."

Anthony pricked up his ears. "And what's *that,* pray tell?"

"It will have to be a very special woman to take you on. And who have you ever met that's more special than Melody?"

Anthony froze, stunned by this sudden jolt of clarity and equally stunned that it had come from Baptiste, of all people.

"Well, other than Samira, obviously," Baptiste added. "Samira is the *most* special. But Melody is a close second."

Anthony barked out a startled laugh, his black mood lifted. Just like that.

What would he do without this man?

"You're my brother," he told Baptiste. "You *know* that?"

"Yes, yes," Baptiste said idly, flapping a hand as his ears turned red and the flight attendant returned with their dinners. "Let's eat. You Brits are so exhausting."

4

Dr. Muhammed turned the light off with a decisive click, swung the high-powered lamp away from the examining table and looked at Melody with that determinedly upbeat and gentle expression that had never boded well for Melody during the entirety of their decades-long relationship.

Melody's heart sank as she waited for the verdict.

"I think we've done as much as we can do, Mel," Dr. Muhammed said. "Your skin doesn't have the elasticity we'd need for any additional procedures. I'm sorry."

Melody knew what this meant—she was a medical professional and she'd been dreading this conversation for half her life, after all—but she had to ask the question anyway.

"So this is as good as it's ever going to get?" she asked, touching the thickened skin of her jawline.

Kindly smile from Dr. Muhammed. "This is the best I can do for you at this point, yes."

Translation: this was as good as Melody's face would *ever* look because Dr. Muhammed was the best plastic surgeon in the business. From here on out only a wizard with a magic wand could improve Melody's appearance.

Melody nodded and slid into her role as Good Little Patient. She kept her chin up, blinked away even the whiff of tears or a wobbly chin and plastered a smile on her face, infusing it with as much cheerful indifference as she could muster. Meryl Streep might be the best film actress of her generation, boy, but she had nothing on Melody when it came to inhabiting a persona here at the hospital, where bad news was frequently the order of the day.

"It's fine," she said quickly. "I understand."

The rational scientific part of her did understand. There was a limit to what modern medicine and even the best experts could accomplish. Melody had come to the end of the road following years of painful skin grafts, surgeries and the occasional infection complication. No big deal. The world was littered with better people than Melody who had slammed headfirst into nastier brick walls than this.

Was this fatal? No. Was Melody in pain? Not anymore, thank God. Did the scar affect her quality of life? Not unless you counted her epically expensive ongoing search for the best makeup concealer on the market.

Plus, Dr. Muhammed had warned her the last time that they might be nearing the end, so Melody had had some inkling that she needed to get her mind right and temper her expectations. That being the case, she shouldn't have entertained *quite* so many daydreams about, for example, taking impromptu selfies with her friends without worrying whether her bad side was showing.

Oh, but there was much more to Melody's incipient glumness than that.

Why? Because when she should have been wallowing in the afterglow of the best sex of her life, she'd instead foolishly spent a good chunk of last night, after Anthony left, looking him up online. That was demoralizing enough to send her shaky self-esteem plummeting to the depths of the nearest gutter. Why? Because it raised the unanswerable question:

What could a wealthy and handsome war hero prince of England possibly have in common with a fledgling pediatric surgeon from Upstate New York?

More to the point, what could he want with *her* out of all the women in the world, any one of whom would happily line up for princess auditions?

Yeah, she knew the undamaged part of her face was pretty. She had nice eyes. And she was smart and accomplished enough to hold her end of the conversation at a dinner party.

But, come on. *Her?*

It was one thing when Anthony was there with her, looking at her with those rapt blue eyes. At moments like that, when they laughed or had sex together, it seemed plausible that they enjoyed each other enough to generate a foundation strong enough to support some kind of a relationship.

But it was something else entirely to know that he was far away doing God knew what back in his regular world while she was here in hers.

Then there was his insane wealth.

She'd researched the castles, palaces, mansions and cottages where he'd grown up and realized that even the least of those put the lovely upper middle-class house where she'd grown up to shame. And it absolutely blew her mind to realize that his royal ass had probably never touched the seat of a non-luxury car. His suits and shoes? Probably all custom, whereas her clothes were all Macy's sales rack with the occasional secondhand store designer steal thrown in. Plus, she spent her days off cleaning and vacuuming her place and wishing she had a housekeeper. He probably *had* a housekeeper. Or several.

Just to throw the final nails into the coffin of her postcoital glow last night, she'd continued with the Anthony Scott online research and read everything she could about his varied and extensive dating history. Not Hugh Hefner territory, mind you, but still active enough to give a regular, un-Botoxed and un-augmented woman like herself a moment's pause.

Anthony's past loves included a steady stream of English roses, models, actresses and assorted others with flawless faces and nary a bad angle for a nearby camera to snag on. No scarred or black women, though, although there *had* been a shot of someone whose skin was slightly darker than all the others', so perhaps she'd been ethnic.

Or simply the victim of a heavy-handed spray tan.

Each new piece of information had been a pinch to Melody's ego, yet she'd sat at her computer for hours like some sort of twisted emotional Augustus Gloop from *Charlie and the Chocolate Factory,* bingeing on every tidbit she could discover about her new boyfriend (their mutual exclusivity made Anthony her boyfriend, didn't it? She'd have to verify that before she embarrassed herself), no matter how obscure the tidbit and no matter how sick it made her.

Last night's bottom line?

It wasn't pretty, folks.

In addition to the whole distance thing, the money thing and the British royal family member thing, each of which was more than enough for the average woman to digest, Anthony had spent his life dating anti-Melodys. Not a science-y or bookish girl in the bunch.

Had all the research been a bad idea? Well, yeah. The worst. Duh. But it had been her first opportunity to research

Anthony after learning he was a prince. How could she pass that up? She couldn't.

Now here she was, paying the painful price. Her only comfort? The grim knowledge that she wouldn't be the last curious little cat to succumb to a nosy impulse only to regret it later.

So her morale had already been hovering somewhere below sea level when she arrived at the hospital this morning.

And now *this*.

"You're allowed to be disappointed, Mel," Dr. Muhammed said.

Melody stiffened her spine.

"What's to be disappointed about? We've both treated people who've been burned way worse than I was. We've treated kids who get into terrible accidents and suffer through surgeries and treatments and then die anyway. And kids who turn up with some terrible disease and die before their second birthday."

"Mel..."

"My scar is not a tragedy. It's a blip, if that. Especially when I think about where I started out and how far I've come. How far you've brought me. Hell, I wouldn't even be a surgeon but for you. And now I get to work here at the hospital with you? Practice with you?" Melody shook her head in true amazement. "I have nothing to be disappointed about."

Dr. Muhammed rubbed Melody's thigh the way she always did, her repressed smile demonstrating a wealth of quiet emotion and pride.

"You're strong and stoic. That's why you've always been my favorite patient. Nothing gets to you."

Wow. See? Melody was a much better actress than she gave herself credit for. She felt the edges of her smile slip and propped them back up with a couple of two-by-fours and some duct tape.

"I'm no saint. I'm just trying to keep things in perspective."

"And you're shaping up to be a phenomenal doctor. I'm so proud I had anything to do with it."

"Thanks," Melody said with a flush of pleasure.

"I can refer you to a colleague of mine in LA for another opinion, if you're interested. He might be willing to try—"

Melody held up a hand to stop her.

"I seriously doubt that anyone other than Hermione Granger with her wand can do anything that you can't do. And I don't know how I feel about someone else cutting on my face at this late date."

"Up to you. Why don't you think about it?"

"Eh," Melody said, shrugging.

Dr. Muhammed nodded. Tapped Melody on the thigh, which was her permission to hop down from the examining table.

"Why don't you make an appointment in six months or so? We'll keep an eye on things and see how you're doing."

"Great," Melody said, the strain of keeping her plucky smile in place making her cheeks ache. *Do not cry, Mel. Do. Not. Cry.* "And thanks. For everything."

They came together for a hug and a squeeze. Melody kept her gaze lowered as they pulled apart, hurried out of the examination room and reception area as quickly as she could and blew out a breath as she hit the medical office building's main corridor for the long and winding walk to the hospital.

Time to see her own patients.

Do not cry, Mel. This can't hurt you. Nothing will hurt you if you don't let it.

She would *not* fall into a funk about her face.

She would *not* mope around like a lovesick Cinderella, wondering when and if Anthony would follow up his *got home safe* text with a phone call. She had more dignity than—

Her phone buzzed in her pocket.

Oh, was that Anthony?

She locked down her impulse to jump and squeal, but the girlish simper proved impossible to control.

She dodged a technician pushing a cart and darted into the nearest waiting area, her heart doing a sudden flamenco dance as she pulled out the phone and her ear buds—

Oh, for God's sake.

The display revealed the self-assured grin of her slightly older sister and only sibling, Carmen.

Otherwise known, in Melody's mind, if no one else's, as Princess Perfect.

She made a derisive sound. Poor Anthony. If and when he ever got a load of Carmen in all her gorgeous perfection, he'd be sorry he hadn't held out for the better sister, wouldn't he?

The phone rang a couple more times while Melody wrestled with her ambivalence.

On the one hand, she and Carmen theoretically loved each other and liked to touch bases when they could. They'd been playing phone tag for a week or more while Carmen lived the perfect life of a New York City dermatologist to the ladies-who-lunch Upper East Side crowd and counted her money and Melody, meanwhile, had struck up her new relationship with Anthony.

On the other hand, Melody's time was short at the moment, her morale was temporarily low and nothing would smack it down faster than a few passive-aggressive comments from the woman who, more often than not, bested Melody in everything while also getting on her last nerve.

It was bad enough that the caller wasn't Anthony, but *Carmen*? *Now*?

Melody cursed and tried to think of a way out of answering.

Familial duty won by a nose by the fourth ring.

"Hey, girl," Melody said, keeping her voice upbeat. "I'm about to run patients. How are you?"

"You won't believe this," Carmen said with the breathy excitement that always presaged her latest triumph, from being named captain of the high-school cheerleading squad (Melody had never made the team) to being led past the velvet rope and dozens of envious gawkers into the latest hot Manhattan club. "Leonard got an endorsement from the outgoing senator."

"He did? That's great!" Melody said with genuine pleasure. Leonard was Carmen's politically ambitious lawyer boyfriend. While Melody had always felt he was sort of a douche who wasn't quite right for her sister, Carmen had always fawned over him as though he was a young Jack Kennedy looking for his future first lady. And if Carmen was happy, Melody was happy for her. Generally. "Is he excited?"

"He's thrilled. Trust me. We've got a fundraiser tonight. Wait'll you see my dress. It's Stella McCartney. Royal blue. You'll love it."

"Awesome," Melody said, checking her watch and wondering if she had time to swing by the coffee bar for a little pick-me-up. She could probably manage it if they wrapped up the conversation quickly, which seemed like a real possibility. Only five or six more details about Princess Perfect's mesmerizing exploits before Carmen remembered that a conversation should be two-sided, asked a pro forma question about Melody's life and announced she had to hang up before listening to any answer that took longer than a sentence or two. "Make sure you send me a pic."

Hah. Good one. Carmen never went to the bathroom without sending out several status updates.

"And we got approved for the apartment," Carmen continued. "Upper West Side. Six blocks from the park. But the kitchen needs a redo. So that's a pain in the ass. But they're saying they can do it in eight weeks or less, which'll give me a chance to get mine listed. Not that anyone ever brought in renovations on time, but anyway..."

Melody stifled a yawn. "Well. Better to get it done before you move in."

"I know, right? Leonard is having the plans drawn up, so that's not on my plate. Thank God. And in a complete segue...I think he's about to propose!"

Leonard had been about to propose for roughly the last five years and two presidential administrations.

"Yeah? Did he drop a clue, or...?"

"Yeah. The clue is we're buying this expensive-ass apartment together. He's going to want his personal life settled before the primaries. And people love a love story. But I may have to rethink my plan to have a summer wedding. We'll never be able to get anything for next summer."

"Mmm-hmm," Melody said absently, rubbing her growling stomach.

"So, listen. I gotta go. Patients," Carmen said.

Melody rolled her eyes. See? "No worries. Talk to you soon."

"Hang on," Carmen said, belatedly remembering her manners. "How're you? You good?"

"I'm good. Don't let me keep you—"

"Anything new or are you still reading your medical journals every night and carrying on about being an old maid?

You gotta sign up for some of those online sites and really get out there. You can't just sit around and wait for someone like Leonard to fall in your lap. You don't want to be the last single girl standing. Even Carrie Bradshaw got married."

Ah, there it was. The obligatory *I'm better than you* comment.

Telling Carmen about Anthony was never a real possibility. Her relationship with Anthony was still evolving and new. Far too important for Melody to share with anyone other than Samira at this point, especially someone who didn't wholeheartedly wish her well.

"Nope," Melody said brightly. "Nothing new here. And I'd better get to my—"

"Hold up." Carmen snapped her fingers. "Wasn't your appointment with the plastic surgeon today? How'd that go?"

Melody opened her mouth, but hesitated a bit too long.

"Oh, no." Carmen lapsed into her tragic voice, the one that was so doom-laden it should be reserved for cataclysmic events such as the destruction of home planets in sci-fi movies like *Star Trek* and *Star Wars*. "How're you feeling? Are you okay? Oh, my God. I'm so sorry. I know you were hoping they could do more for you."

Melody started to get that bristly feeling all up and down her arms. This level of sympathy and despair was *not* indicated. Her face looked pretty good, all things considered, especially when she thought about where she'd started from all those years ago.

"I'm fine," she said briskly, starting to mean it. She *was* fine. Not some pockmarked zombie lurching toward the nearest hospital to have one side of her rotting face surgically reattached. "I knew this was coming. I've already made peace with it. So, listen, I'll talk to you next—"

"Mel." Exasperated sigh from Carmen. "You don't have

to be so strong all the time. It's okay to open up a little. I'm here for you."

"I know," Melody said tightly. "I'm open. I'm not sure what you think I should do. My situation is what it is. I'm moving on. What else can I do?"

"You're so brave. I don't know how you do it. And, honestly, your face looks amazing. The scarring isn't that big a deal. With the right makeup? You can hardly even see it."

Mel froze. Well, *that* was complete bullshit.

Melody didn't look like Frankenstein's monster, but she damn sure wasn't packing Cindy Crawford's strategically placed beauty mark, either.

"You *can* see it," Melody said flatly.

"Honestly, Mel, it's not even that big of a deal."

Just like that, Melody slammed into her daily (weekly? Monthly?) limit of her sister. Time to end this whole convo before things got any worse.

"You know what? I can't get into it. I gotta go. So you have a good week."

"What's wrong *now*?" Carmen asked, years of exasperation coming through loud and clear.

Melody had hoped to end the call without shots being fired, but that was clearly optimistic to the point of foolishness. She took a quick glance around to make sure no one was within earshot when she let her sister have it.

"First of all, you're being condescending. Second, it kills me how it's always the beautiful women with perfect skin who march around talking about how great I look. What would *you* know about it? If I look great, it's because I spent forty-five minutes painting the right makeup on my face. But no matter what I do, people still stare at me. When people stare at people like *you,* it's because you're beautiful. Not the same thing at all."

Heavy silence from Carmen's side of the line.

Followed by a harsh sigh.

"I can never win with you," Carmen said quietly. "Sometimes I wonder why I keep trying."

Melody's shoulders slumped. She suddenly felt terrible. Carmen might not get her words right sometimes, but her heart was generally in the right place. It wasn't Carmen's fault that she had a perfect face, nor was it her fault that Melody had had a tough morning.

Melody took a deep breath and geared herself up to do the right thing. If there was one thing in the world that she hated, it was apologizing to Princess Perfect.

But right was right.

"Sorry, Carmen," she said gruffly. "Didn't mean to jump down your throat."

"You're beautiful either way, Mel. You know that, right?"

The fervency in her sister's voice went a long way toward soothing Melody's raw feelings. Melody wanted to believe her. Wanted to be like all the other women out there whose worst skin flaw was the occasional monster zit on the tip of her nose. But her head was still too full of the doctor's words from a little while ago and the flawless images of all the beautiful women Anthony had loved before.

And the freaking scar would still be there when Melody stood in the mirror to brush her teeth tonight. And every night for the rest of her life.

"Thanks," she said, blinking back a couple of unruly tears before any of her passing colleagues saw her and decided she was cracking up. "Gotta go. Talk to you soon."

"Mel..."

"Bye."

Melody hung up, cleared her throat and squared her shoulders, determined to get her morning back on track before it was too late. But seriously, was this shaping up to be a day from hell, or what? Not even nine a.m. and she was already sick of herself and her self-pitying tendencies.

Enough was enough. Time to get her head back in the game and—

Her phone buzzed just as she was about to stick it back into her pocket and remove her ear buds. Her heart galloped into high gear, then sprinted even faster when she checked the display.

Anthony!

She veered back into the waiting area, sat by the window and hit the button.

5

The picture resolved and there he was, sitting on the edge of his navy duvet-covered bed and looking extraordinarily handsome in a dark suit, white shirt and pale blue tie that perfectly complemented his coloring. His hair was perfectly brushed and gleaming and his cufflinks were in place.

He looked every inch the prince, as unattainable to her as a magic carpet ride to London.

But she was *so* glad to see him.

Her heart skittered and kept on skittering despite her stern warnings to keep her feelings in check at this early stage of the game and not wear her heart on her sleeve.

"Hi," she said, keeping her voice quiet as she held the phone up to her face.

He dimpled.

"Hi," he said, his voice husky. "I have a minute before I leave. Just wanted to say hello."

Evidently he had *not* gotten the memo about playing it cool. Though he looked a bit tired after his overnight flight, his bright eyes crinkled at the corners and sparkled at the sight of her.

"You made it safe and sound, I see," she said, although he'd already texted her earlier that he'd landed. "How was your flight? Did you get some rest?"

"I'm good, but I'm wondering about you." His roving gaze touched every part of her face and lingered on her eyes. His expression darkened. "What's happened? Has something upset you?"

"What? No. It's fine. I'm fine." She tried to look more upbeat, a task made nearly impossible by all that unsettling intensity leveled straight at her. "Are you on your way to your library speech? Have you got your small talk ready to go?"

He cocked his head, squinting at her.

"I have. I plan to discuss the ongoing rainy weather, the need for childhood literacy and, if I'm feeling particularly daring, a documentary that they're running about Winston Churchill on Sky TV tonight. I'll be dazzling as ever. What's wrong, darling? How did your appointment go?"

The *darling* always got her.

As did the realization that this man could see past her best poker face and would continue to resist her efforts to sweep her feelings under the rug, where all inconvenient feelings belonged.

"It's really no big deal," she said, putting a bit more effort into her carefree smile. "Just that... my appointment didn't go that well. That's all. We can talk about it later when we have more time."

He slowly nodded.

"We could do that. Or we could talk about it now so I can offer my support. That way, maybe *you'll* feel better and *I* won't spend the rest of the day fretting about how you are and kicking myself for not being there when you need me."

He waited.

She floundered. Opened her mouth. Shut her mouth. Smoothed her hair.

Let out a shaky laugh.

"Yeah, okay, first of all, I'm fine. I'm not falling apart here."

He bowed his head. "Of course not."

"I've made it through med school and my residency. I'm not some snowflake who melts at the first sign of trouble. I'm a tough cookie."

"The toughest. Only could we speed up this whole disclaimer process a bit? Before I have to go?"

"And I don't *need* you. I don't *need* people. I soldier through and get along just fine on my own."

His jaw tightened.

He paused just long enough for her to think, *huh, maybe I went too far that time* before a disquieting gleam of amusement appeared in his eyes.

"You seemed to need my cock a great deal when I had you against the sink last night," he said silkily. "Or did I misread the signs?"

Melody all but gagged on her efforts to muster up a biting retort that never came, her face going up in flames.

"And we did agree that we're building something together," he continued. "I'd hoped you would take that as seriously as I do."

"Fine," she snapped, taking a furious glance around to make sure no one was within earshot as she hunkered over her phone. "If you must know, there's nothing more my plastic surgeon can do for me. And she's the best. So this is as good as my face will ever look. I know this isn't a tragedy, but I'm a little disappointed. Happy now?"

He went very still and absorbed her outburst in silence,

his smirk receding in favor of an expression that was solemn but otherwise unreadable.

"I'm sorry you're disappointed about that, darling," he said quietly. "There are other experts."

She sighed and tried to get a handle on her feelings.

"I know, but...honestly, it's almost a relief. I couldn't stand the thought of another surgery. So now I know. Time for me to move on and focus on other parts of my life."

"Are you okay with that?"

She gave it some thought and came up with a surprising answer.

"It'll take a minute, but...yeah. I think I am."

"Good."

A question popped into her mind. Her initial impulse was to bury it since it came along with a lot of emotional significance. But since she was responsible for holding up her half of their burgeoning relationship, she decided to go ahead and ask it. Get it out there so she wouldn't have to wonder.

"Does it matter to you?" she asked nervously, smoothing her hair with her fidgety free hand. "I mean...maybe you thought I'd look like a regular woman one day."

His brows contracted.

"A *regular woman,* did you say?"

"Maybe you were hoping my face would get better. That's all I mean."

"Better?"

"It's a simple question," she said defensively. "Why're you looking at me like that? Stop scowling."

His lips twisted. He muttered something and shot a disbelieving look at the ceiling before focusing on her again.

"You're right, aren't you? I really am a terrible communicator. Now seems like a good time for me to practice."

She winced, not at all certain she wanted him to practice expressing his feelings. Not with *that* look on his face.

"You're *not* a regular woman. You're the most extraordinary woman I've ever met. Maybe *you* don't know that, but *I* certainly do. So it seems significant that you also don't look like any other women I know."

Melody gaped at him, her heart skipping more beats than it hit.

"I don't want your face to look better. Whatever *that's* supposed to mean. In fact, I'm scrunching up my brain right now, trying to think of a way that you could look any more gorgeous than you already do, and I'm coming up blank. Well, you could be naked. *That* would do it."

She barked out a startled laugh.

"I don't think you get it, so let me spell it out for you. I've been pinching myself hourly since we met. I can't believe my good fortune and I really can't believe that you're giving *me* a chance. My only hope is to up my game and make you fall madly in love with me before you come to your senses and realize you could find someone so much more suitable. Someone with much less baggage coming along for the ride. I view this all as a race against the clock to marry you before my time runs out."

"Anthony."

They stared at each other.

He looked as startled to have said something like that as she was to have heard it. A vivid flush ran up both sides of his face and concentrated over his cheekbones.

She opened her mouth—

"You'll have to excuse me, darling," he said quickly, standing. "I can't be late for my speech."

And he hung up on her.

Melody's phone rang just before midnight that night, the witching hour when her lids began to droop and she faced the monumental decision whether to grab another glass of chardonnay and continue reading her medical journals on the sofa or forgo the wine and continue reading in bed, hoping that boredom and exhaustion would kick in enough to allow her to sleep soundly until her alarm went off at the butt crack of dawn.

It never worked out that way, though. Usually she fretted over her patients, tossed and turned for a while, then slept for three or four hours before waking before the alarm to fret some more.

The life of a young surgeon, people. Nothing but glamour.

Last night had been particularly tough. After sleeping soundly inside the wonderful cocoon of Anthony's arms, her fluffy bed without him had seemed as welcome and inviting as a yoga mat out on her windswept balcony.

As for tonight, she'd been stretched out on the cushions when the phone rang, lounging beneath her cashmere throw, but now she popped up, fluffed her hair and wished she had her lip gloss on hand. Her heart rate spiked into the target rate for Olympic athletes, which was not conducive to a restful night. The adrenaline surge this late at night would make sleep all but impossible.

She didn't care even a tiny bit.

She just wanted to talk to Anthony again.

She hit the button. The picture resolved to show him lounging on his belly in bed with weak sunlight sparking streaks of gold through his tousled hair. He had a rumpled pillow bunched up between his crossed arms and his chin resting on his forearm. His bright eyes seemed more aquamarine than cornflower for some reason; she found the color changes endlessly fascinating. And a five o'clock shadow had appeared across the hard planes of his cheeks since she last saw him, making him seem sexy and real. Not at all like the unapproachable royal whose pictures were splashed all over the Internet.

This was the man she was beginning to know, although the starched and sophisticated prince who'd called earlier also worked for her, she had to admit. Watching his eyes crinkle at the corners as he checked out her lacy camisole, she felt a powerful pang of longing for him.

She supposed she'd better get used to it. They'd be spending far more nights apart than together, wouldn't they?

"Hey," she said.

"Good morning, darling."

He spoke in the rusty early morning voice that made her belly swoop. She felt renewed stirrings of longing for him. Spiraling desire.

"I hope you brushed your teeth before you called me," she said, determined to keep a simper from exploding across her face. It would be nice if she could maintain *some* dignity where this man was concerned, even if it was only a microgram or so.

He laughed. "I'll try to remember that in future."

"See that you do."

"Before I forget to ask, how're you coming on your nickname for me? Not very fair for me to walk around calling you *darling* all the time, exposing all my feelings, while you can't even be bothered to call me the generic American *babe*. How d'you suppose that makes me feel?"

"Funny you should mention that. You'll be happy to know that I actually have given a lot of thought to your nickname.

I've already rejected *Tony,* because you don't look like a Tony and that's your father's nickname, and also *Junior* and *AJ* because they both reference your father. I know he's not your favorite person."

"Smart girl," he said darkly.

"You're the future Earl of Stockbridge, so I could call you *Stocky,* like your friends do—"

He winced. "Only if you never want me to speak to you again."

"But that seems like a dig rather than a term of endearment," she said, laughing. "I don't like *baby* and I hate *babe,* so those are out, and my parents call each other *honey,* so that's out. I'm out of ideas. The whole process is exhausting."

"I'm hearing a lot of excuses and no workable nicknames."

"I'm going to have to wait until inspiration strikes one day."

His lips twitched with repressed amusement. "You could call me *God.* You did a lot of that when we were in bed last weekend, as I recall."

Something about the dry deadpan and the wicked glimmer in his eyes just killed her every time.

She ducked her head and lapsed into an embarrassing and unstoppable grin while her cheeks burned with all the heat of a red-hot fireplace poker.

"How nice of you to throw that in my face."

He smirked. "Well. I *did* notice."

"Noticing is fine. I take issue with your mentioning it."

"Ah. Sorry."

Sure he was. He looked exactly as sorry as a raccoon who had knocked over a garbage can outside a restaurant and was enjoying a late supper.

They beamed at each other for a delicious moment or two.

Until his amusement slowly faded away.

"So, listen..." He paused to clear his throat. "I meant to ask if I needed to apologize when we spoke before. But you got me sidetracked with all your nonsense talk about *a better face*."

She frowned. "First of all, I never talk nonsense. Every time I open my mouth, butterflies of wisdom flitter out. It's a thrilling phenomenon."

He laughed.

"And second, why would you need to apologize?"

His smile receded once again, leaving only naked intensity as he carefully gathered his words.

"I, ah..." He adjusted his pillow. Tugged on his earlobe. "I might have lost my head a bit before I left. In the, ah, bathroom."

"Oh," she said, startled. *That.*

She frowned, waiting.

"I didn't hurt you, did I?" he asked.

The suggestion was so ridiculous (when Eagles fans screamed their fool heads off at their Super Bowl parade, no one ran through the crowd asking individual people if *they* were okay, did they?) that she couldn't stop an incredulous laugh.

"No," she said. "You didn't hurt me. I thought I'd made that clear in the moment, but I'll have to do better next time."

His expression shifted to unmistakable satisfaction and sensual male knowledge.

"Just wanted to check. That's never happened to me before. I wouldn't want to go overboard and scare you off in the first month of our relationship. Not when it seems so promising."

A couple of puzzle pieces clicked into place, giving her a new understanding of the intriguing Anthony Scott.

"Oh, I get it," she said, nodding sagely. "As an upstanding military man, you're kicking yourself for losing control. And you're planning to keep a tighter grip on your emotions from now on. Hit me with that famous British stiff upper lip."

Anthony tensed and stared at her with frozen disbelief, a faint frown wrinkling his forehead. "Where do you manage to hide your crystal ball? I've been wondering."

She made a dismissive sound. "I'm not clairvoyant."

"I'm not convinced," he said flatly.

They watched each other without speaking for a beat or two and she *did* begin to discern a couple of his emotions. Admiration and respect were there on his face. Wariness. Maybe a little frustration. The slow smolder of his desire woven throughout everything else.

"Why can't we just be who we are with each other?" she wondered aloud. "We had a moment together in the bathroom. You didn't want to leave. I didn't want you to leave. Those feelings rose to the surface. We enjoyed each other. No children or small animals were harmed. Why isn't that okay? Why do we have to dissect it?"

"Ah. Now I see that you don't understand me at all."

"Enlighten me then."

"I don't get carried away. Well, not unless I'm having a panic attack in an elevator. I don't lose control. My emotions don't rise to the surface."

That made sense. She'd seen enough of his patented look of cool-eyed disdain to believe him.

"So where do they go?"

Incredulous laugh from Anthony.

"I ignore them. I put them aside. What else? My whole life, I've been trained to soldier on. I do what's expected of me by my higher-ups." A new edge crept into his voice. "I don't question authority and I *don't* get tied up with American women I just met thirty seconds ago."

A ringing silence followed this announcement. Melody tried to analyze the implications for their blossoming relationship, while Anthony blinked and looked vaguely appalled that he'd had so much to say on the topic.

Then Melody pressed a hand to her chest.

"Oh, no," she cried on a fake sob. "So this is...so this is *good-bye*?"

Anthony burst into startled laughter, which was exactly what she'd hoped would happen. She could almost see the gathering storm clouds drift away from his head.

"No, this isn't *good-bye,* you terrible woman. Though it should be after *that* performance."

"I like it when you laugh," she told him. "You should do it more often."

He gave her a pointed look. "I seem to be doing it quite a bit lately."

"And how do you feel about that?"

"Delighted."

He treated her to another dimpled grin, the kind that made her heart thump and her blood sizzle. The urge to grab his face and pull him in for a kiss damn near took her out. She privately decided that it was a good thing they were on separate continents. Otherwise, they'd spend all their time in bed doing X-rated things rather than talking and getting to know each other.

"I think you should lighten up," she said. "We don't have to analyze and judge everything, do we?"

He gave her a disbelieving look. "Have we met? I don't do *light*."

"You're going to start. We're having fun together. Let's leave it at that."

Anthony frowned thoughtfully. "That all sounds very casual. We're not casual."

"There you go with another label. All I'm saying is, we have to pace ourselves. Just see what happens. You can't freak out every time you show a little emotion and I can't have a heart attack every time my phone rings."

He leaned closer. "Are you telling me you look forward to my calls?"

Oh, shit. Unforced error.

"My lips are sealed on that topic," she said, her face burning again.

"I repeat: you are a *terrible* woman."

"So how did your library speech go?" she asked pointedly, laughing.

"It was perfectly adequate," he said glumly, propping his head on his hand. "Only five or six people fell asleep, and only one of them snored outright. It could have been so much worse. They usually post clips of these things online, if you ever need something to put you out for the night."

"I saw it."

He perked up. "You did? What did you think?"

Melody, who had no problems with public speaking, decided not to mention the way he'd fidgeted with his cufflinks, kept his head ducked as he consulted with his notes or all but sprinted off the stage when the speech was over.

"I thought you seemed a little uncomfortable," she said gently. "Don't you like giving speeches?"

"Like?" He made a face. "I neither like nor dislike it. It's what needs to be done, so I do it."

"Right, but do you *like* it?"

He blinked, clearly taken aback. "What possible difference does it make?"

"Your personal happiness doesn't matter?"

There was a long pause before his brows contracted.

"My grandmother is a hundred and ninety-two years old. She can't handle these engagements like she used to. She's trying to scale it back a bit, so it's all hands on deck with me and my cousins. This business isn't about personal happiness."

Melody shrugged. "Maybe not for her and the heirs, but she's the monarch. What about *you*?"

Anthony cocked his head and squinted at her with genuine puzzlement.

"Why are you planting seditious thoughts in my head? You Yanks just can't help yourselves, can you?"

"*Seditious?* I just asked whether you enjoyed giving speeches or not. It's a simple question."

But the look on his face as his gaze slid out of focus and settled, unblinking, on something off in the distance, told her it wasn't simple.

It wasn't simple at all.

"Don't get moody again," she said, wishing they were in the same room so she could nudge his shoulder or smooth his forehead with a kiss to snap him out of it. "I have something to show you."

He blinked and refocused, looking a little shaken.

"What is it? Sexy lingerie? Your naked body with melted chocolate smeared in strategic places? We did agree we'd be having phone sex."

"No, and don't get any bright ideas, either," she said, laughing as she got up and carried the phone down the hall to the bathroom. "I have to wind down and get some sleep in a minute. Otherwise I tend to make nasty mistakes when I'm cutting on all the little children."

"I know you do, darling. I didn't mean to keep you. I just wanted to catch you before you went to bed. I'm off to christen a new ship today."

She stopped walking to gape at him. "You get to christen a ship? Seriously? With a champagne bottle and everything?"

"Well, they rig the bottle on a rope so you can pull it and the bottle smashes against the ship, yes."

"Is that as much fun as it sounds?"

"Not hardly. Though it is nice to meet people and talk to them."

"And will there be a speech, too?" she asked innocently.

He shot her a quelling look. "You're on very thin ice with me. You know that?"

"This'll make up for it," she said, gesturing to the sink with a flourish. "Ta-da!"

She held the phone over the counter so he could see that she'd placed his toothbrush and toothpaste in a place of honor. While hers sat in the best little plastic decorator cup that Target had to offer, she'd placed his in a sparkling crystal tumbler, which was part of a set she'd bought a couple years ago when she discovered the delights of bourbon. She'd also taken the time to make a sign that said *Anthony's Toothbrush* and used her colored markers and shaky drawing ability to decorate it with a crown and several stars and arrows so there could be no question about placement or ownership.

"What did you do?" Anthony scrambled up to a seated position and laughed his head off as he leaned in for a closer look. "Hang on. Put the phone back again so I can see. Look at that crown! You didn't tell me your art skills were so solidly at the primary school level—"

"Hey!"

"But why do *I* get the special glass? There's room in your cup for my toothbrush."

"I want to keep your toothbrush in the style to which it's become accustomed," she said solemnly.

"Thank God you fully appreciate my position. I'll expect a curtsy next time I see you. Watch some online videos to make sure you do it properly."

"Sorry," she said in her sweetest voice. "I'm American. I don't do royalty."

"Ah, but you did this royal, didn't you?" His eyes began a slow burn as he pointedly looked her up and down. "Multiple times. And very well."

"Oh," she said, heading for her bed so she could stretch out on her side and prop her head on her free hand. "You remember that?"

"Remember?" Humorless laugh as he slumped back against his headboard. "It's all I think about."

Much as she wanted to keep her feelings on lockdown, they kept turning sideways, slipping through the bars of their cage and running free.

"I know the feeling," she said softly.

Sharp inhale from Anthony.

"I can't decide whether video chatting with you is a good thing or not. I mean, it's good to see you every day. But it's torture to see you every day."

Torture.

Good word for the way she felt. The thrill of seeing him versus the pain of not being able to touch him. For instance, he had a very fine chest, well-defined with ripples in all the right places and a dusting of golden hair that trailed south to parts she didn't want to think about now. Not if she wanted to relax and get some sleep. He also had broad shoulders and sinewy arms that liked to hold her tight and not let go. A delicious morning scruff that scratched her in sensitive areas and drove her wild. Cornsilk hair. Satiny skin.

Desire tightened inside her, making her secret inner muscles clench for him.

"Sweet torture," she said.

"*Sweet* torture." He tipped his head. Considered. Nodded with unmistakable satisfaction. "Good term."

"Glad you agree."

He mirrored her posture, lying on his side and propping his head on his free hand. "I've been storing up, you know. All the things I want to say to you when we're together again. All the things I want to do with you."

"Yeah?" she murmured. "That sounds promising."

His gaze smoldered as he looked at her.

"I'd planned to promise not to lose control again. But now..."

"But now?"

Wry smile. "I don't believe in making promises I can't keep."

She couldn't have stopped the delight from spreading across her face even if she'd wanted to.

"Good."

They watched each other for a moment, the silence drowsy and peaceful. She kept telling herself to say good night and hang up, but she was so lost inside those bright blue eyes that she didn't want to get herself out of there.

"Do me a favor," she finally said.

He nodded. "Anything."

"Think about what you'd like to do instead of making speeches. If you were a regular guy, I mean. I'd love to hear about it. Okay?"

A shadow flickered across his face, but he nodded again.

There was a pause.

"Do *me* a favor," he said.

"Anything," she said, reining in most of her smile.

"Keep my side of the bed warm for me."

"I can do that."

He opened his mouth again, looking miserable. Hesitated.

"I *miss* you," he said, his voice husky.

Those three words shouldn't have the power to make her so unreasonably happy, but they did. She felt her heart swell until, honest to God, it felt as though it bumped up against her ribcage.

If he ever said *I love you,* she'd probably spontaneously combust.

"I miss you, too," she said.

6

That Friday night, Anthony laid onto Melody's doorbell for a good long ring, impatience getting the best of him as he adjusted his grocery bags and reached for his phone to call her. She had, of course, just buzzed him up, but maybe she'd fallen back asleep and didn't realize he was there.

She had the flu.

The ruddy fucking *flu*.

The news had hit him hard. Rarely had he felt such a sickening combination of disappointment and anxiety. He'd lived all week for the moment when he'd see her again on Friday, and now *this*?

"Don't come," she'd said last night when she called to tell him.

The sound of her hoarse voice, in between fits of a hacking cough, had shaken him. If she'd taken a cheese grater to her vocal cords and then dipped them a couple of times in battery acid, they couldn't possibly sound any worse.

"I have the flu," she'd continued, sniffling. "That's what I get for hanging out at a hospital with sick children and all their nasty little germs."

"But…"

He floundered, struggling to make sense of a God that could be this cruel. Melody sounded miserable, as though she'd marched up to death's door and started pounding on it, demanding entry. And he'd *lived* to see her again. Touch her. Hold her. Kiss her. Never mind the sex, although that was certainly on his mind as well.

For the first time in his life, he was packed! Early! His overnight bag was by the door, waiting to be thrown into his car in the morning.

To make matters worse, if they didn't connect this weekend, they wouldn't see each other again until after Christmas due to their mutual work commitments. He hadn't begun to grapple with what the holidays with his grandmother and the rest of the family at Sandringham would be like when Melody would be in Journey's End with Baptiste and Samira, all of whom would probably have the time of their lives without him.

"But…all you hospital workers take the flu vaccination, surely," he'd said, his disappointment demanding that he employ some magical thinking to rectify the situation. He raised his voice so she could hear him over another prolonged fit of coughing. If she kept on like this, she'd probably bring up one of her lungs in a moment, poor thing. "It's probably not the flu at all."

"The vaccine doesn't work on every strain of the virus."

He began to feel surly.

"Well, what about those antiviral medications that you take first thing when you turn up sick?"

"I took it this morning. It hasn't kicked in yet."

There it was. Just the sliver of hope he needed.

He brightened. "You'll probably feel back to yourself on a good night's sleep."

"It's going to take longer than that," she said, coughing and then gasping as she tried to catch her breath. "My fever's still a hundred and one. And I don't want to risk it and make you sick."

"But…" Honestly, he knew he was being an arse, but he needed to see her and bask in her presence for a little while. At this point, he'd settle for flying back to Journey's End and standing outside her window so they could put their hands up to the glass the way visitors did with their family members in prison. "Who's taking care of you? Samira?"

"I can't expose her. She's pregnant and she's meeting Baptiste in Paris this weekend anyway. And I don't need anyone to take care of me. I'm a grown woman and a medical professional. I'm fine."

"Do you have juice? Some nice chicken broth? Are you forcing fluids?"

"I'm fine. But my head is killing me. I've got to lie down again, okay? I'll call you later when I feel better."

"But—"

"Bye."

She'd hung up. She hadn't called back, though there had been one sorry excuse for a text that consisted entirely of a little dead face with Xs for eyes.

That had done nothing to allay his fears. He'd struggled with indecision, remembering back to when he'd served overseas and spent time with some of his boys when they'd been injured. The flu couldn't be any worse than some of those bedside scenes although it was, admittedly, a great deal more contagious.

The bottom line? He didn't give a fuck. He'd go and hope for the best.

So he'd hopped his prescheduled commercial flight and now here he was.

He supposed he *might* be in for a bit of trouble for ignoring her wishes, but he'd face that bridge when he came to it.

He raised his hand to knock again—

The door abruptly and violently swung open to reveal a snarling Melody.

Ah. The bridge in question.

"What are you doing here?" she cried in her maimed voice. "We agreed you weren't coming."

"We did no such thing. You told me not to come. I heard you out and then I ignored you."

"I don't want to make you sick, Anthony. That's the *one* thing that would make me feel worse than I already do," she said, then clapped a handkerchief over her mouth and lapsed into a coughing spasm.

Her moment of speechlessness gave him the cover he needed to study her closely. He didn't like what he saw. Her complexion was bright with fever, her eyes glassy. Her body threw off a perceptible wall of heat that felt a bit like walking too close to a campfire. Though her forehead was sweaty, she wore blue flannel pajamas with…yes, those were puppies on them. And a huge and fluffy purple nightmare of a robe that made him wonder if she planned to spend the winter in Winterfell. As for her hair, she had it piled on top of her head like a curly black haystack, and there were fuzzy slippers on her feet that appeared to have rabbit heads on them.

She looked, in short, as though Typhoid Mary had mated with the children's section of some department store.

But she was upright with attitude, alive and kicking, and he'd never been so glad to see anyone in his life.

"I told you I'd be back on Friday," he said. "It's Friday. Here I am. Cheers. Are you going to let me in?"

"No, I'm not going to let you in! And why would you

want to come in, anyway? You want a piece of *this*?" she said, waving a hand up and down her body.

"Don't worry. I've thought of everything." Adjusting the groceries again, he reached into his pocket, pulled out a surgical mask and put it on, hooking the elastic behind his ears. "I'll be fine. I've had my shot. And I never get sick anyway."

Incredulous snort of laughter from the patient.

"Well, guess what, genius? *I* wear masks all day. *I* never get sick. And look at me now. Go stay at the hotel. I'll be fine."

He sighed, struggling with his exasperation and his growing affection for this maddening woman as she tried to look formidable while huddled, shivering, inside that hideous robe.

She didn't honestly think she'd get rid of him, did she?

"Dr. Harrison. I realize that you physicians make the worst possible patients, but I'm here to take care of you and you're not going to stop me in your weakened condition. Look at you. You're barely conscious. Kindly step aside."

A glare-off ensued. He emerged the victor when another coughing fit overtook her, forcing her to double over at the waist. She gave up and waved him inside with a flourish, shutting the door behind him.

"You're just not that smart, are you?" she called after him.

"I've been accused of worse," he said, dropping one of the bags on the coffee table.

She pointed to a tub of disinfecting wipes. "Will you at least wipe down some of the surfaces before you touch anything? The whole place is radioactive. It's like Chernobyl up in here."

He chuckled as he hurried to the kitchen and put his bags down, surveying the scene.

She had a fire going in the fireplace and a half-drunk glass of cranberry juice and some crackers on the coffee table, so that was good. She'd made herself a nest of pillows and blankets on the sofa, so that was also good. But a quick peek at the stove and in the cupboard revealed no chicken broth or soup, so that was bad.

She looked shaky and miserable as she watched him, and that was awful.

He'd felt protective before, of course. Of his mother. His first pet, a golden retriever named Kermit. Of the boys in his unit overseas. But *protective* didn't begin to cover the way he felt about this woman who was so sick and so proud and who touched his heart so deeply. And there was no point reminding himself that this was all very new between him and Melody or that she'd be good as new in another few days. None of that mattered to his knotted gut at this moment.

What was the word for when you would happily sacrifice a limb or two to make someone feel better? That was the word he needed.

"How do you feel, darling?"

She slumped onto the sofa and reached for one of the blankets, her expression falling.

"My head hurts."

Knowing what it cost her to admit that much of a weakness, he figured she had to be half blinded by pain. Something along the lines of a sword through the temple.

"Would you like a cold compress?"

"I'd like a new head," she said, resting on the pillow and closing her eyes.

She fell into a restless doze, shivering and pulling the blankets closer, then throwing them off all in the space of about five minutes while he warmed up her broth and raided the pantry shelf where she kept her first-aid supplies. She muttered, then cried out.

He hurried back, his hands full of all the things he'd need, and sat on the coffee table facing her.

"Wake up," he said quietly. "Time for some medicine and a little to eat."

She didn't stir.

"Melody?"

Nothing.

His heartbeat tripped and stumbled. She was far too still all of the sudden.

"Melody," he said, shaking her shoulder.

She startled awake, staring at him with glazed eyes. When she went to sit up, the effort seemed to be too much for her and she slumped over again.

"I'm tired," she complained.

"I know," he said soothingly, his breath coming a lot easier now. "Let me help you."

"I don't need help. I'm fine," she said, eyes still closed.

He felt his lips twitch with a repressed grin.

"I know," he said, scooting over to sit by her hip, helping her up and holding the mug for her.

"What's this?" she asked, sniffing hopefully. "Smells good."

"Broth from the Chinese buffet around the corner. When did you last eat?"

"Not sure. What day is it?"

For pity's sake.

"You should be thanking God I'm here. Take a sip for me. It's not too hot."

"I'm not hungry," she said drowsily, drinking deeply.

He pressed his lips together, determined not to laugh at

her. When she'd finished most of that, he put it down and reached for the orange juice.

She made a face. "You should have gotten cranberry."

He snorted back a laugh. "Don't drink it too fast. You need to take some paracetamol."

She shot him a sidelong look. "Speak English."

"I'm trying. When did you last take some?"

"Dunno." She scrunched up her face, thinking hard. "This morning, maybe? Or was it lunchtime?"

"Pathetic." He handed her a couple and watched her take them. "Don't they teach you to write these things down when you go to Harvard Med?"

She glared at him. "No one likes you very much. I feel like I should tell you."

He grinned behind his mask. She watched him with her bleary eyes, her lips curling into the beginnings of a smile.

"That's not true," he said quietly. "I can think of one person who likes me very much."

"Who?" she asked, shifting around so she could lean against his side, wrap her arms around his waist and press her burning face to his neck. "Anyone I know?"

He greedily gathered her closer with a huge sigh of relief, breathing deeply for the first time in what felt like years. But when he went to kiss her, the mask blocked him. So he yanked it off and tossed it aside.

He kissed her forehead. Burrowed his fingers into her hair and massaged her scalp for the pleasure of hearing her coo. Massaged her temple.

Reveled in the thrill of being back where he belonged. The feeling of...of...*rightness* damn near overwhelmed him. Maybe he was a half-British, half-American lesser royal who couldn't quite figure out where he fit in or what he should do with his life.

But he could get this one thing right, goddammit.

He could figure out what this one special woman needed and give it to her before she thought to ask for it.

She eased back enough to look up at him.

"You're insane. It'll be your own damn fault if you turn up with the flu. You know that, right? And don't come crying to me if you get sick."

"Wouldn't dream of it," he said, kissing her forehead again.

"And don't expect me to take care of you, either. I only take care of sick people when I get paid for it."

He choked on a laugh. "Noted."

She was smiling when she pulled back and looked up at him again.

"I'm *so* glad you came."

That might have been the moment, out of all the moments, when he fell irrevocably in love with the amazing Dr. Harrison. It was definitely his reward for putting himself in harm's way and well worth the potential risk to his health and well-being.

"Did you honestly think I'd let you suffer here by yourself?"

"Well, yeah. We're just getting to know each other. You didn't sign up for a whole medical drama this early in the game."

"I signed up for *you*. If you turn up sick, then..." He shrugged.

She studied his face, looking vaguely troubled.

"What?" he said, giving her hair a playful tug when the moment got too heavy.

"I'll bet Annabella Carmichael isn't sick," she said darkly, laying her head on his chest. "You might want to rethink."

He had to laugh. The idea of him either a) being with

Annabella, or b) going to such great lengths if *she* turned up sick, stretched his imagination to the breaking point.

"I'm good with my choice, thanks."

Melody coughed again, covering up her mouth.

That reminded him.

"Here. I brought you something for that," he said, shifting her aside so he could reach for the grocery bag on the coffee table.

"If you brought me some honey-lemon cough drops, I'm going to marry you," she said hoarsely. "Just so you know."

He bit back a grin, reached into the bag and produced…a bag of cherry cough drops.

"Too bad. Thanks for playing," she said, starting to take them from him.

"Not so fast."

He cocked a brow at her, reached into the bag again and came back with a bag of honey-lemon cough drops, which he opened for her.

"Thank you!"

"I consider this a binding contract," he warned her as she took one and popped it into her mouth.

"Don't worry. I probably won't make it through the night, so you'll be free to marry Annabella, your true love."

He scowled, grabbed one of her pillows and placed it into his lap. "You. Put your head down. Get some sleep."

She eagerly stretched out again, settled in and sighed with unmistakable satisfaction as he stroked her hair. She fell asleep in no time.

He found the remote and watched TV, delighting in a *Law & Order* marathon. He could never get enough of that show, especially the courtroom half of each episode. He was just beginning to doze off, head lolling, when his phone buzzed.

He snatched it out of the back pocket of his jeans by the

second ring, soothing Melody when she stirred restlessly and taking a quick glance at the display.

It was his father, Tony.

Fuck.

He hadn't spoken to the old man in several days. Tony had shown up in town and dropped the bombshell announcements that he'd had a heart scare and that he wanted to mend his fences with Anthony. Since Anthony had enough bitterness toward his father to fuel at least a civil war and possibly even a world war, he didn't think peace between them was possible. Besides. There wasn't enough lumber, nails and workers in the world to get *these* fences mended.

But the old man had seemed hopeful and had wanted to stay in touch. Now *this*.

Anthony struggled for a moment, wanting to send the call directly to voice mail and then most likely delete it without listening. He couldn't do it in the end, though, a clear sign that he'd let the old man fuck with his head, something that Anthony had sworn he'd never let happen again.

Cursing, he hit the button.

"Yes, hello," he said wearily.

"What the hell's going on?" the old man barked, his Texas accent a little twangier than usual, no doubt due to the—ah, there it was. The unmistakable slurp that meant he was well into his bourbon. "Why haven't you called me back?"

"What is it?" Melody mumbled, popping up and rubbing her eyes. "What's wrong?"

Anthony scowled. Yet another reason to dislike Tony: waking up convalescents.

"It's nothing," Anthony told her. "Go back to sleep."

"Is that Miss Melody?" Tony boomed in Anthony's ear. "You cracked that nut yet? You weren't doing so hot on that front the last time I saw you, were you, boy?"

Melody groggily focused on the phone and frowned at it. "I can hear you, Tony."

Tony laughed. "Why does she sound funny? Put her on the phone."

"No," Anthony said. "She's got the flu. She shouldn't have to deal with you tonight on top of everything else."

"I'll talk to you next time, Miss Mel," Tony shouted in Anthony's ear, forcing him to hold the phone out. "Take good care of yourself. I know the boy's useless in that department."

"Anthony's taking *great* care of me, you terrible man," Melody grumbled to additional laughter from Tony as she slowly stood and grabbed her orange juice. "I probably won't make it through the night regardless, but that's not Anthony's fault. I'm taking a shower. I think I probably smell. Bye."

"Bye, Miss Mel," Tony called. "I'll catch you the next time."

Melody managed a limp wave.

"One second," Anthony told his father, then covered up the phone and anxiously focused on Melody, who was now drifting her way toward the hallway and looked as though the slightest thing, like, say, a carpet fiber that was slightly taller than the others, might trip her up and take her out. "I'm not so sure that's a good idea. Why don't you wait until I can help—"

"Screw you," she croaked. "I'm a grown woman. I can manage a shower."

She disappeared around the corner. He waited for a beat or two, braced for the thud of her body hitting to the floor, but heard only the faint sound of the shower.

He breathed easier.

"Yes, all right, I'm back," he said into the phone. "We need to make it quick. I want to check on her."

"This is an interesting turn of events, I must say," the old man said thoughtfully. "I never took you for the nursemaid type."

"Yes, well you've never taken me for much of anything other than a worthless waste of tissue, have you?" Anthony got up, went to the drink cart and poured himself a whisky. "To what do I owe the pleasure of the call?"

"I don't deserve such a bad rap from you," Tony said sadly. "Have I been one of those cuddly fathers who tells you your shit don't stink, or that you're a winner just because you showed up to every soccer practice even though you never kicked the ball during a game? No, I have not—"

Anthony snorted.

"—but I've always wanted the best for you. That's the truth."

"Yes, well, I certainly felt my *best* when I walked in and found my girlfriend Amanda sucking your cock when I was back in college," Anthony muttered.

Tony sipped again. Smacked his lips. Chuckled.

"You know, I forgot about that little, ah, incident."

"Yes, well there have been so many coeds for you, it's probably hard to keep track."

"Time for you to get over it, don't you think?"

"Is that the sort of thing one normally gets over, do you suppose?"

"It wasn't my finest moment, I admit."

"No," Anthony said. "Nor was your cheating your way through your marriage with my mother, making the resulting divorce as nasty as possible, then skipping her funeral following her premature death when I was only thirteen. In fact, I don't believe I've ever experienced *any* of your finer moments."

"I'm not discussing your mother with you right now," Tony said, using the icy tone he always employed whenever his ex-wife came up. "But if you think about it, it was best for you not to be with a little college girlfriend who was so free and easy with her affections. I mean, but for me, you might not be with Miss Melody right now, and we can all agree that she's a damn sight better for you than Amanda ever was."

"What do you *want*?" Anthony snarled, stalking down the hall to listen at the bathroom door (he heard the comforting sound of Melody splashing around in there) and back to the living room again. "I don't have time to play twenty questions with you."

"Fine. Got a little bad news for you, son. It's for your best, but I don't expect you to like it."

Anthony froze, a nasty suspicion flickering to life in his mind. "What is it?"

Tony sighed. "I'm not releasing your trust fund to you just yet."

Outrage tightened its grip on Anthony's throat, making speech impossible for several long seconds. "You *what*?"

"You heard me."

Anthony worked his mouth, trying to force the words out.

"That trust comes to me when I'm thirty-five. Which I will be *next year*. And when it does, I won't have to scrape by on my stipend from the crown or the measly interest income checks you send my way every six months."

"Yeah, but as your trustee, I'm not handing the funds over just now. Not when you're drifting along with no purpose and no goals, christening ships and opening supermarkets for your grandmother. That's no life for a grown man like you. You don't need to be under her thumb."

"Well, I bloody well won't be under *your* thumb, either, if that's what you're thinking. I've told you I'm not an oilman. I'm not moving to Houston."

"You don't have to move to Houston," the old man said

easily. "Don't get me wrong. I wish you would, but all I want is for you to get yourself sorted out. Find your own path."

"And what *path* is this, pray tell?" Anthony demanded.

"No idea. You'll figure it out."

"And under your grand scenario, when *will* you release my money?"

"Not real sure," Tony said slowly. "I was thinking we could revisit the issue when you turn forty."

Anthony stiffened, his fingers reflexively tightening on the phone until it was a wonder he didn't crack the case in two.

He thought about his decades-long plan to come into his money next year, come out from other the yoke of his father's tyranny and come into his own. He'd never been sure what *coming into his own* would look like, but he'd known that next year was the year when he'd get it all sorted out. And *it* (whatever *it* turned out to be) would, of course, be separate and apart from anything his father did or anything his grandmother did. *It* would magically catapult him to a place where he was something other than Anthony Scott, future Earl of Stockbridge, whose importance was tied to the royal blood dripping through his veins via an accident of birth, or Anthony Scott Jr., son of an oil tycoon.

He could, for once in his life, just be Anthony, a bloke like any of the others he'd served alongside while overseas. Free from the galling knowledge that his grandmother and the taxpayers paid his bills on the one hand and his narcissistic and overbearing excuse for a father held the purse strings to his future on the other.

Most of all, and this had weighed especially heavy in his thinking in the last couple of days, he could be the rough equivalent (not *as good,* clearly, but less *not good enough*) to a self-made woman like Melody, who had a brilliant career in front of her.

And now *this*.

Five more years of being beholden to others and knowing that his future, whatever it might turn out to be, was not yet his own.

His dreams smashed to rubble beneath his unsuspecting feet.

"You can't do this!" he yelled on an overwhelming surge of frustration. "It's *my* money! My mother left it to *me*!"

"Calm down, son," the old man said soothingly. "This'll do you some good. You'll see."

"Don't you patronize me," Anthony snarled. It dawned on him that he no longer heard the water from the shower, so he reined it all in and tried to get a grip on his temper. The last thing he needed was for Melody to walk in on him throwing his mobile through her sliding glass doors. "You don't get to hold on to my purse strings and justify it by telling yourself you're being a good father. You don't have my best interests at heart. You never have. You're just angry that my mother got half your fortune in the divorce and then passed it along to me when she died. You can't stand the fact that she might have got one over on you or that I might not need to dance to your puppet strings any longer."

Tony laughed bitterly.

"You've never danced to my puppet strings a day in your life, boy. If you had, you'd be here in Houston, working hard to learn the business so I can focus on my golf game and take a spa day every week. And if you were so interested in not being a puppet, you might want to think about cutting the strings your grandmother's got running through your arms and legs."

That flared Anthony up again.

"Don't you bring her into it! You can't stand the fact that she and I are close and I want to do my best for her, can you? You never could."

There was a deathly silence.

It went on for so long that it gave Anthony the chance to take several deep breaths, stop fuming and decide that he might have gone too far this time.

"Be mad all you want, AJ," Tony finally said. Anthony could practically hear his shrug. "Don't make me no never mind. As long as you recognize that half of your anger is for your own damn self. Because you're a grown man who doesn't have a thing of his own. Not one thing that wasn't handed to you from someone else. Not one thing earned through your own hard work. Not an apartment, let alone a house. Not a car or a career. Probably not even the drawers covering your ass right now."

Outrage washed over Anthony again, but the bitter sting of truth was far worse.

"Don't you *dare*—"

"But cheer up. These extra five years will help you get it all figured out. I hope you make some progress real soon. You wouldn't want me to decide you need additional motivation and cut back on your interest checks, would you?"

"Are you *threatening*—"

"Bye, son," Tony said cheerily. "Talk soon."

And he hung up first, denying Anthony of even *that* satisfaction.

Anthony cursed. Hurled his phone against the sofa cushions.

"What'd I miss?" came Melody's hoarse voice behind him.

7

Shit.

Anthony wheeled around to discover Melody standing there wearing a wry expression and a fresh pair of flannel pajamas in a red and green plaid. She probably wore them for the Christmas season, but he had to fight back the hysterical urge to tell her that the pattern was called Royal Fraser and was, in fact, his grandmother's official plaid.

She'd smoothed her wet hair back into a ponytail and looked refreshed and rosy, although her high color was probably still due to the fever, and she brought a fragrant cloud of fresh-scented lotion with her.

At the sight of her, a large portion of his anger receded.

"Nothing, darling. Feel better after your shower? You didn't pass out and drown yourself, I see."

"That was a loud *nothing*," she noted darkly.

He grunted something noncommittal.

She rolled her eyes and reached out a hand. "Come on. You can tell me in bed. I'm barely alive here. I don't have the energy to drag it out of you while standing up. Grab your whisky. You look like you need it."

"Best offer I've had all day," he murmured.

He followed orders, took her hand and followed her to her room, where the nightstand lamp infused everything with a cozy glow. He watched while she sank into her side of the queen-sized bed and burrowed under her delightfully luxurious white sheets, then quickly divested himself of his clothing and dove in after her.

By then, she was drowsy and pliant, her supple body generating enough heat to put the old radiators at one of his grandmother's castles to shame. He eagerly spooned her up from behind, tightening his arms around her while she settled her luscious arse against his crotch.

His crotch noticed. Beastly thing didn't care that she was an invalid.

She noticed the noticing.

"I hate to waste an erection," she said, wriggling against him in a particularly unhelpful manner.

"Oh, don't worry," he said brightly. He nuzzled her neck, wallowing in the delicious scent of her since that was all the wallowing he'd allow himself this trip. "There's plenty more where this came from. You seem to produce an endless supply."

He kissed her cheek, delighted with the way it plumped with her smile. Then a thought hit him.

"Hang on. Don't go to sleep just yet. I'd meant to make you a hot toddy."

"Hmm. First of all, hot toddies are disgusting. Second, there's no empirical evidence that they do anything to help with the flu."

"'Course they do. They make you so drunk and sweaty that you no longer care that you have the flu. That's worth something."

"True," she said, laughing.

His mother snuck into his brain. He typically posted sentries at the borders of his thoughts and counted on them to keep her from getting too close. That way lay madness. But sometimes, especially when he was tired or upset, his mother tiptoed right up to the other side of the gate and insisted that he acknowledge her.

"My mother made a wildly effective hot toddy," he said. "I've never been able to recreate it."

There was a pause.

"Is she the reason you know how to take such good care of me?" Melody asked quietly.

"I suppose she is."

"Tell me about her."

Anthony's heart swelled.

"She was a wonderful nurse. Right there with the popsicles and the hot broth. And she'd let me climb into her giant bed, which had a whole mountain of pillows. And of course there was a telly to watch. I never had one in my own room. I remember this one time when I had a nasty stomach thing. She stayed with me all day. Made a fort with the linens. But then Granny had a state dinner that night, so my mother had to get ready. The maids came in to do her up. When it was all said and done, Mum wore this amazing white dress, all glittery, with one of Granny's borrowed tiaras." He paused, the memory getting to him. "She looked like an angel."

The growing tightness in his throat and ache in his chest forced him to slow down. Take a breath.

"She sounds like a wonderful mother."

"She was the *best* mother. She kept my cousins running around, making sure I wasn't lonely as the only child, but I always had the feeling that it was the two of us against the world. We would sneak out on adventures to Harrod's or to the zoo. The park. A movie. We had the best Christmases. Hot chocolate with peppermint sticks in them. Gingerbread men. Figgy cakes. We'd make gifts for my cousins when I was little—she was very crafty and creative—and then she took me out to buy them things with my allowance when I got older. Our last Christmas together, she taught me to wrap the presents. You should see the way I do them up with fancy paper and satin ribbons. They're like works of art."

"Sounds amazing."

He felt the smile slide off his face as his story came to an end.

The end of his old life.

The end of his childhood and those days of absolute happiness.

That was the problem about opening the door to his mother's memory. He always slammed headfirst into the end the way she'd skied headfirst into the tree that wound up killing her.

"Three months later, she was dead," he said bitterly.

"I'm sorry." Melody reached back over her shoulder to cup his face. "I'm so sorry. I know you miss her."

"Yes." He cleared his gruff throat. "At the holidays, especially."

She nodded.

They didn't say anything for a while. He lay there, trapped in his moody memories.

"What happened with your father tonight?" she asked sleepily, now rubbing his forearm where it lay across her waist.

He cleared his throat, all the anger surging back to him.

"Mum left me everything in trust with my father as

trustee. I'd thought it would all come to me on my thirty-fifth birthday next year, but he's decided to wait until I'm forty because he thinks the delay will be *good for me*."

He couldn't quite keep the bitterness out of those last three words.

"Oh, no," Melody said, her voice infused with just the right amount of horror on Anthony's behalf. Her empathy instantly made him feel better. "What's he trying to accomplish?"

"Not sure. He was yammering on about me doing things on my own. Becoming my own man. Whatever *that* means."

"Hmm," she said thoughtfully.

"What?"

She opened her mouth. Hesitated.

"I'd like to remind you that I'm at death's door. So don't bite my head off."

"What?" he asked warily, a nasty feeling of dread tiptoeing up his spine.

"Why are you *really* so mad at your father?"

"Isn't that enough?" he cried. "That's he's trying to extend his financial reign of terror over my life?"

"It's enough, but I don't think it's all."

Christ.

That arrow zoomed through the air and hit him in the dead center of his chest.

And with zero warning or anesthetic.

"There you go with the ruddy crystal ball again." Sudden agitation forced him to let her go and sit up against the pillows, flapping the linens over his lap. "It's a terrible habit. Why don't you leave me a private thought or two?"

She turned over to face him, her eyes heavy-lidded but surprisingly understanding.

"That's not how I roll. You should know that by now."

"Have you tried to roll another way?"

"Anthony."

The quiet reproach was the worst possible punishment, much like his grandmother's raised brow. It made him batshit crazy. He could deal with a lot of things, but knowing that either of those women might think one iota less of him was not one of them.

He flapped the linens again. Smashed the pillow behind his head into a more comfortable position.

Melody waited patiently. He half hoped she'd fallen asleep, but a quick glance down at her revealed only her steady brown gaze.

"He cheated on Mum. Repeatedly. No one was off limits. The nannies. Her friends. His friends' wives. He wasn't discreet. He didn't think to save her feelings, much less the tabloid embarrassment." He crossed his arms. Noticed that his left foot was jiggling under the covers and forced it to stop. "A preadolescent boy already spends a good chunk of his time wishing his father was out of the picture so he can have his mother to himself, doesn't he? And when you add in the fact that the father has made the mother sob herself to sleep on more than one unforgettable occasion?" Anthony tensed with renewed fury. "There's no more vindictive or unforgiving force on earth than a young boy."

Melody shrugged. "Maybe. But you're a man now. And you're smart enough to know there's more to it than you probably ever saw. Your mother wasn't an angel and I'm betting your father isn't a demon, either."

"I'm not so sure about that," he snapped, catching himself gritting his teeth in back. "And what would *you* know about it, anyway, having only met him for thirty seconds when he was at his charming best?"

"I know I don't like the look on your face when you talk about him," she said implacably. "Seems like it hurts you more than it hurts him. But, hey. What do I know? I'm probably delirious with fever."

"Does the fever also make you meddlesome?"

"*Meddlesome*. Now there's a word we don't hear much on this side of the pond."

He snorted.

"If being *meddlesome* means I want the very best for you, then yes. I'm meddlesome." There was a weighty pause. "Maybe your father is also meddlesome."

"My father doesn't know me well enough to know what's best for me," Anthony muttered. "He wouldn't know what was best for me if it marched up and bit him in the arse."

"If you say so," she said sleepily.

She closed her eyes, leaving him to marinate in his dark thoughts for a moment or two. Her beautiful face slackened into peaceful relaxation as her breathing evened out.

He frowned down at her, then felt some of his storm clouds begin to drift away.

Just looking at her made him feel better. It was as though she wanted to model serenity for him so he could calm down a bit. He reached out to smooth some of those spiral curls away from her temple, categorically unable to keep his hands to himself when she occupied the same room.

What was best for him.

What did that even mean? He'd come home from overseas alive and with all of his limbs. Wasn't that best? He belonged to a family that had the honor of serving the people of Britain and the privilege of living in the stateliest homes in the land—for free. Wasn't that best? Who the hell wanted to hear a prince whine about having to give boring speeches or the fact that his free bachelor pad on the grounds of Kensington Palace wasn't quite to his tastes?

So he had to wait a few more years to come into the fortune his mother had left him. Big deal. He'd put his head down and continue to do his duty by his family and his country the way he'd always done. The way his grandmother had done every day of her life since she ascended the throne all those decades ago.

What was best for him.

Please.

Did anyone anywhere on the planet even know what that—

"Did you think about my question?" Melody asked quietly, her eyes still closed.

He stiffened and played dumb, which seemed like the best idea at the moment.

"What question?"

Her lids flickered open and she nailed him with those all-seeing brown eyes.

Reproach...reproach...*reproach.*

Until he couldn't stand it any longer and fidgeted uncomfortably.

"Yes, well, I don't see the point. At all." He cleared his throat. Adjusted the pillow. Surprising how difficult it was to crack open the door to his back-burnered dreams and let a little sun shine through. "But as you're insisting on this pointless discussion...I'd wanted to be a human rights lawyer. That was my plan going into law school."

"A human rights lawyer?"

"Yes. I actually clerked in the legal department at the UN. And then at a firm in New York that specializes in human rights. Nelson Mandela said, 'To deny people their human rights is to challenge their very humanity.'" He laughed ruefully. "Maybe it's corny, but that meant something to me."

Melody's jaw dropped.

"I suppose I'd been exposed to these issues early on. Mum was always quite concerned with the rights of refugees around the world. Women's rights to education and reproductive rights. That sort of thing. After she died, I thought that I might, ah, sort of continue in her footsteps."

He found himself holding his breath, waiting for Melody's reaction.

She beamed up at him with the sort of delight he'd expect from women worldwide if he announced he'd discovered a failsafe and inexpensive cure for male premature ejaculation.

"A human rights lawyer? Oh, my God. You'd be wonderful at that, wouldn't you?

He blinked, a bit startled that she didn't laugh him out of the room.

"I would?"

"Yes! With your experience overseas. Your contacts. Your perspectives. Because you've seen immense privilege *and* immense suffering, right? Why aren't you doing *that* rather than christening ships?"

"Well, I…" His thoughts spun as he tried to get his words together. She made it sound so easy. As though he could just hop out there tomorrow and get some political prisoners freed from some dire incarceration in a third-world country. "I'm not licensed, for one thing. I've never taken the bar exam here, nor been called to the bar back home in London."

She frowned. "Why not?"

"My grandfather died round about the time I graduated from law school. Granny needed me. She needed all of us. So I went back home and sort of slid into taking up some of her appearances for her during her mourning period. That continued. Here I am."

"Well, where would you have taken it?"

"Not sure. That was up in the air, which was why it was easy for me to start with the family business. I didn't have firm plans to get back to."

"Well, you can take the bar now."

"No, I can't."

"Because...?"

Rising frustration made him snappish again. Why dabble in hope when he knew very well that his legal dreams were as unattainable as sex with Melody tonight?

"Because I have commitments to my grandmother, for one thing. Because it's been ages since I got my degree, for another. I've probably forgotten everything I've learned. And what would I look like, turning up to some bar review class and studying with all the little twenty-six-year olds?"

"You'd look like a man pursuing his dreams," she said without missing a beat. "A man who was making the most of his life even though it wasn't easy."

"And if, by some miracle of miracles, I managed to pass someone's bar exam, what about a job? I'd need one of those, wouldn't I? You think firms are going to beat down my door trying to recruit a man who's been out of school for years and has never practiced a day in his life? Is that how things work in the fairy world you've concocted in your fever-addled brain?"

She shrugged, her smile tinged with equal parts exasperation and amusement. "I have every confidence in your ability to find a job when the time comes."

"I can't just—"

"Oh, for God's sake!" she cried, the sudden exertion setting off another wave of violent hacking. She hastily covered her mouth and coughed it out, leaving him to feel terrible as he reached for both the water and the lozenges, not sure which to give her.

"So sorry, darling. I didn't mean to—"

She smacked his hands away and glared up at him while she caught her breath.

"You see what you're doing to me?" She coughed again, cleared her throat and accepted a lozenge this time. "You're making me sicker. If I do die tonight, it really *will* be your fault."

"I think that's a *bit* much."

"You've had every advantage in the world," she said, her voice once again sounding as though it had been fed through a trash compactor. "You didn't have to pay for school, did you? Or your expenses while you were in school? And you *have* an income, right? Even though it's not what it would be if your father let you have your trust. You come from the royal family, for crying out loud. People will be dying to hire you. Do you think the average guy on the street out there has those advantages going for him?"

"Yes, but I don't want the advantages!" His voice boomed off the walls. He took a deep breath and dialed it back as best he could. "I want to earn my place. The same as everyone else."

"Then earn it," she said quietly.

He gaped at her, his mind fried.

She didn't really believe that, did she?

That it could be that simple for him? That a firm might want him because he was the best (or could be the best with some training), rather than because his grandmother was the Queen?

And if Melody *did* think that…and if she was one of the

smartest people he knew…did that mean that *he* should also believe it? Did that mean that he really could do it?

"I think people who go after what they want, even when it's tough, are incredibly sexy," she said, burrowing a little deeper under the covers, her expression the picture of benign innocence, as long as you didn't look too closely and notice the glimmer of a challenge in her eyes.

But Anthony noticed.

And he felt the distinctive thump of excitement—of sudden possibilities—at the base of his throat.

That was the thing about being with Melody. When they were together here in the cocooned safety of her apartment (he had to catch himself from thinking of it as *home;* a place he'd only been a few times could not be *home* even if he had shoehorned his toothbrush into a place of honor in the bathroom), it felt normal to talk about his hopes and dreams. To play at being a regular bloke who could go out in the world and do his own thing like everyone else.

But then he thought of Granny's face if he waltzed back home and announced that he'd decided to take his life in a different direction. He thought of the logistical nightmares involved with rearranging his calendar and of his private secretary's incipient conniption fit if he so much as canceled a luncheon appearance next week.

That was the problem with taking advice from Melody, an American woman who had never met Granny, knew nothing about how things worked in the family and had no real hope of ever understanding the duties and expectations that had been placed on his head since birth.

And yet…

An unexpected image tiptoed into his mind. He saw himself dressed in a suit, briefcase in hand, striding up the steps of some federal courthouse on his way to argue some case. He saw himself standing tall and strong before the UN, with unshakable confidence in himself and his mission. It was a heady feeling, the kind to which he could easily become addicted. He saw Melody there with him, cheering him on, her face beaming with pride, and he had a tough time thinking of anything he wouldn't do—any mountain he wouldn't move, any ocean he wouldn't swim—to put *that* look on her face.

To be worthy of this woman? He'd damn well do whatever had to be done.

With some difficulty, he yanked himself back to the present and glanced down at her again.

Her smile was steady. Knowing. Inspiring.

He had the uncanny feeling that she'd just seen everything he had.

"Sexy, eh?" he asked.

"Sexy."

A responsive smile tugged on the corners of his mouth.

"Yes, well, I know you become obsessed with sex whenever you think of me, even when you're on your deathbed—"

She croaked out a laugh.

"But I'd like to encourage you to get a bit more sleep. See if we can't get you to survive the night."

"Works for me," she said, closing her eyes again.

He slid down, put his head on the pillow and gathered her close. When he kissed her forehead, she didn't feel so hot.

"Have you broken your fever?" he murmured against her skin.

"I'm working on it."

"Work very hard. I want you at seventy or eighty percent before I have to leave again."

She snuggled closer, her arms tightening around his waist as she rested her head on his chest.

"I will. I sleep better when you're here."

"You do?" he asked, feeling the sort of pride of accomplishment best reserved for curing diseases and landings on Mars.

But her deep breathing, smooth and even now, was his only answer.

Jet lag caught him around the ankles and tripped him up right about then, and they were still in each other's arms when they woke Saturday morning.

8

The rest of the weekend passed in a blur.

"Well," Melody said late Sunday afternoon as she sat on the end of the bed and watched Anthony pack for his flight. Dressed in jeans and a sweater, she wasn't quite the picture of health yet (her skin was still far too pale, she'd lost a few pounds and her eyes remained a bit glassy), but she did seem a thousand percent better. "Here we are again."

He zipped his overnight bag and looked up at her, straining hard to keep a lid on his surging emotions. They were all over the place, to be honest. Faint anxiety to be leaving her alone after she'd been so sick and her fever might surge again. The relentless ache of loss that settled into his bones every time he went back to London, made worse by the fact that their mutual commitments would keep them apart for two full weeks this time, until they met up in Tanzania at the new year. The glum prospect of Christmas without her.

Growing sexual frustration that had his skin so tight he was fairly certain he would split open like an overripe peach if he so much as sneezed.

"Here we are again," he said quietly. "I know I keep

repeating myself, but you seem so much better. It's really amazing."

"I feel so much better. The antiviral really helped. So did your skilled care. I'm wondering why you never mentioned you were a trained medical professional like me."

That made him laugh.

"No one is more surprised by this turn of events than I am. But I had to come." His heart crept out of his chest and settled on his sleeve again, but there was no stopping it. "You know I had to come."

She nodded, a half-smile playing around her lips. And *that,* right there, was his reward for ignoring her orders and showing up here. The way she glowed when she looked at him, as though he had personally hung every star in the sky, discovered fluffy little puppies and introduced the world to warm chocolate chip cookies.

Honestly, when she looked at him like that, he had to fight the urge to pinch himself and make sure this wasn't all a dream that had catapulted him into the slot of luckiest bloke on earth.

He stared at her, his heart thudding.

"Just make sure you don't get sick," she said. "I couldn't live with the guilt."

"I'll do what I can."

They watched each other, neither blinking. Everything he felt seemed to beam back at him from her steady gaze. He thought about how he'd have to find a way to remember that she'd only been in his life for a short while and he probably could, in fact, sleep without her if he set his mind to it. He thought about how he hadn't touched her bare skin this go around. His fingers flexed with a wave of need. Nothing he could do about that. Nor could he contain the slow creep of heat up his neck and into his scalp as he thought about what he wouldn't give to be inside her in that moment.

And there was *nothing* he wouldn't give.

He exhaled, a long and shaky breath.

His attention dipped to her lush mouth.

Melody went very still.

"Anthony…"

He flicked his gaze back up to her eyes. Waited.

"Don't look at me like that," she said.

Her voice was husky, yeah, but it sounded less like the huskiness of someone recovering from the flu and much more like the need of someone teetering on a sexual edge.

The sound of her voice did *not* help.

He took another shaky breath. Held out a hand.

"Come here," he said.

"*Anthony*. I'm trying *not* to get you sick."

"That's my business," he said in his most velvety tone. "Come *here*."

She was already on her way, standing and hurrying into his waiting arms. She did a little hop at the end and he caught her just as her legs went around his waist and her arms round his neck.

She was warm and solid, surprisingly strong and insistent as she tightened her hold and tried to get closer. They clung together, swaying, and it was the sweetest torture imaginable.

"I'd give anything to kiss you right now," he said, agonized. "You have no idea."

"I think I have a pretty good idea," she said wryly, running her hands over his hair and scraping his scalp with her fingernails.

He imprinted everything about her in those long seconds, greedily collecting details the way ants collect seeds for the winter. He cupped her head and caught handfuls of her curls, reveling in their silkiness and the faint lemony fragrance of her shampoo. Ran his hands up under the lower edge of her sweater for the pleasure of rubbing her back and sides, noting the smoothness of her skin. Reached lower, for her delicious arse, and thrust against her. It was supremely unsatisfying. No traction. So he backed her against the nearest wall, reveling in her breathless cry of encouragement, pressed his face to her neck and ground against her for several of the most thrilling seconds of his life.

He found himself running increasingly desperate scenarios in his mind.

Kissing was out, obviously, and she wasn't up for full-on fucking, but a hand job wasn't out of the question, was it? What about a blow job? She seemed perfectly willing. Maybe he could go down on her. That could work, couldn't it? He could swing her around to the bed, help her off with her jeans and knickers, and kiss her there until she shouted out his name the way he loved.

Yes! He had a plan!

He started to sweep her sweater over her head, catching a glimpse of her smiling face, rosy now with passion, and that was when he caught himself.

Scott, you fucking wanker.

What the bloody hell do you think you're doing?

He stiffened. Pressed a lingering kiss to her cheek and put her down on her unsteady feet. Backed up several steps, trying to reach the minimum safe distance outside her zone of influence, although he was beginning to suspect that even Saturn would not be far enough. Blew out a shaky breath and ran his hands across the top of his head as he watched her.

"I'm sorry, darling. Didn't mean to lose my head again."

To his astonishment, the little siren followed him. Reached for his belt buckle.

"I don't want to leave you like this," she said, staring him in the face. "And we're not going to see each other again for two weeks."

Whereupon his determination to be a good guy spun off the road and landed, upside down, in a ditch.

But he reached for his reserves of strength and dredged up enough to put his hand atop hers and stop her.

"I'm trying to do the right thing here." His guttural voice sounded as though it belonged to someone else. "Kindly make it a bit easier for me."

"I'm stronger now," she said with a sultry woman's smile that made him want to crawl out of his skin. "It'll be fine as long as I don't kiss you."

"It really won't," he said, tightening his grip on her hand. "You know I can't control myself around you. Why risk it? I don't want to finish you off outright."

A tense stare-off followed. He emerged the winner when she scrunched up her face, backed up a step or two and roughly rubbed her temples with the heels of her hands.

"Sorry," she said, now crossing her arms and huddling inside her sweater. "Maybe I'm the one who can't control herself."

"Don't apologize," he said sharply. "We want each other. That's a gift."

Her lips twisted. She opened her mouth as though she wanted to say something, then turned away at the last second, shaking her head and muttering something with dark humor.

The subtext?

That their passion for each other felt like more of a curse than a gift at times like this, when another good-bye loomed in front of them. No words necessary.

Meanwhile, his own unspeakable words collected in his mouth and backed down his tight throat. He wanted her to know how important she was becoming (had become?) to him. How determined he was to be with her even though the speed with which things were developing between them scared the shit out of him when he thought about it. How it shaved years off his life every time he walked out her door and started another countdown until he could see her again.

It was far too soon to lay all that on her.

Not to mention the reality that being with him would change her life forever. For-ev-er. Hell, if he cared anything about the poor woman, the best thing he could do for her might well be to turn her loose before their feelings grew any stronger and/or that first paparazzo snapped her picture and splashed it on a tabloid somewhere.

But then he thought of the way she'd glowed when she looked at him just now and the way his heart swelled when she was in the room. And holding back any of his emotions or thought processes felt as unnatural and impossible as trying to catch sunshine in a bottle and using it to light the night sky.

He opened his mouth. Hesitated, telling himself to give it more time. Then said it anyway because there was no way to keep it inside.

"This is untenable in the long term. You know that, don't you?" he said quietly.

She tensed and tried to shutter her expression, which was caught somewhere between fear and excitement. "What are you talking about?"

He took a deep breath, fully aware of the magnitude of what he was about to say. Fear was there for him as well, but there was far more swelling happiness. Possibly even euphoria.

"I want you to come to London soon. See how you like it."

She gasped, her eyes widening.

"Don't go putting any carts before any horses, Anthony," she said. "We're just getting to know each other."

Just getting to know each other.

How quaint. Just getting to know each other? What, like kids did these days when they texted back and forth for ages before they bothered to get together, shag and, more often than not, never saw each other again? He could almost laugh.

"Do you actually believe that?" he asked, incredulous.

She froze.

"I want you to come to London soon," he said again. "See how you like it."

"But..." She blinked and smoothed her hair behind her ear. "I can't take time off again anytime soon. I've been sick, and we've got Tanzania coming up in a couple weeks."

He shrugged. "You can come one weekend. That'll give you a taste of it. For a start."

"But...you don't think it's a little soon for that?"

"No," he said levelly. "Do you?"

She stared at him, her gaze hard and searching, then looked across the room with unfocused eyes.

Once again, he sensed her excitement and trepidation.

He could hardly blame her for *that*.

She turned back, her expression suddenly shrewd.

"Does your grandmother know that I'm black?"

Important though he knew this moment was, Anthony couldn't stop himself from stiffening.

Well, Melody had him there.

Much as he'd love to vouch for his grandmother's stellar record of inclusiveness and judging people by the content of their character rather than the color of their skin, she belonged to another generation. And it hadn't exactly escaped his notice that there weren't a lot of brown people rattling around above stairs in the great houses of Britain.

"No," he admitted.

A humorless smile flickered across her face. She squared her shoulders and straightened her spine, thereby stealing a bit more of his heart.

She was nothing if not proud, this one.

Nothing if not strong.

Did she have the slightest idea how much that thrilled him about her?

How she kept revealing the kind of strength and poise that made him increasingly certain that *she*, out of all the women he'd ever met, could survive—hell, *thrive*—in his world?

"Until your grandmother knows the full story, it's irrelevant whether I like London or not. Don't you think?"

No, he didn't think. Because he wanted the lovely Dr. Melody Harrison at the center of his life and it wasn't too soon to start jumping hurdles and laying the groundwork to make that happen.

It wasn't too soon at all.

"You leave my grandmother to me," he said grimly.

9

It was nearly midnight on Christmas Eve before Anthony found an opportunity to drift to the outer edges of the drawing room, sneak out the door and hurry down the corridor and into his grandmother's study to call Melody. Everyone tended to get a bit knackered at Granny's black-tie holiday dinners, so he didn't think his absence would be noticed for a bit. Not to mention the fact that someone was plinking away on the piano and the haphazard chorus of songs was starting to get a bit louder. In a moment, if the past dozen or so years was any guide, Uncle Dicky would treat the assemblage to his "Bell" trilogy ("Silver Bells," "Jingle Bells" and that overlooked classic, "Jingle Bell Rock") sung in his faulty baritone, and all the unfortunates in the room would be trapped until his last off-key note trailed off.

So Anthony had some time.

Breathing a sigh of relief, he sank into the chair behind Granny's desk and, taking care not to knock over any of the silver-framed photos on the end, propped his feet up—

Without warning, the door swung open and Mrs. Brompton, one of Granny's retainers since roughly eighteen-sixty, when they first started gathering the red bricks to construct the mansion here at Sandringham, creaked in, oozing displeasure.

Caught already. *Shit.*

Anthony's reflexes were slowed by the whisky or three that he'd drunk during the course of the evening, so he couldn't swing his feet down as quickly as he normally did. Worse, he clipped the edge of one of his grandmother's precious orchids and nearly sent it crashing to the floor with his clumsiness.

Mrs. Brompton did not approve, as evidenced by the way she drew herself up to her full and spindly height. Her lips, which were thin on a good day, all but disappeared.

"This is your *grandmother's* study," she said icily.

If there was one thing he lived for, other than these phone calls to Melody when they were apart, it was rattling Mrs. Brompton's cage. Childish, certainly, but he had to live for something, didn't he?

He tried to look innocent as he leaned in and rested an elbow on the red box, which housed his grandmother's important state papers and carried her insignia and the words *Anna Regina* embossed in gold.

"This particular study? Right here? How can you be certain?"

Mrs. Brompton ignored the question with dignity, hurried over, rubbed the spot on the desk where the back of his shoe had briefly rested and roasted him with laser strikes of disdain shooting from her eyeballs.

"You won't be so cheeky when she finds you. She wants a word."

He tensed. "What, *now*?"

"Yes. *Now*."

Unbelievable. The old girl hadn't looked twice at him all night and now, suddenly, she needed a word with him?

Well, it could wait, whatever it was. He wanted to catch up with Melody before she sat down to dinner on her side of the pond.

"Do me a favor, Mrs. Brompton," he said, smiling and trying to infuse the request with the same sort of soulful charm that always allowed Baptiste and Nick to get away with murder with their elders and authority figures. "Could you tell her I'll be there in a moment or two?"

Mrs. Brompton was, as he'd always suspected, immune to charm.

"Probably not," she said, staring down her pointy nose at him.

Lobbing a final sniff in his direction, she executed the sort of brisk pivot that would have made her a big hit at a military parade and marched out, the squeaky sound of her footsteps disappearing down the hall.

Anthony heaved another sigh of relief, settled in again and dialed Melody.

Hopefully, her yeast rolls had turned out okay. She was evidently trying a new recipe to take to Samira's dinner and wasn't at all sure—

The call connected.

Anthony couldn't prevent an anticipatory smile of delight from exploding across his face. Until the picture resolved and Baptiste's grinning face came into focus.

"Oh, for God's sake," Anthony said, rolling his eyes.

"Merry Christmas!" Baptiste cried, toasting him with a fizzing flute of champagne in his free hand. *"Joyeux Noël! Feliz Navidad!"*

Anthony had to laugh.

"Yes, all right, I get the point. Merry Christmas to you,

too, you fickle prat. I thought you'd be here with me, like always, but I've been thrown aside for a pretty American face."

"You can hardly blame me for that," Baptiste said with the annoying and self-satisfied smirk of a man who, unlike Anthony, had the pleasure of getting laid often and well by virtue of sleeping in the same bed with his woman every night. "And you can't expect me to listen politely while Uncle Dicky sings 'Jingle Bells' again. It would be fine if he stuck to the first verse, but he insists on singing all four verses. And my friendship for you only goes so deep."

"Can't blame you for that, mate. What have you done with Melody? Why're you answering her phone?"

"She asked me to." Baptiste picked up a delicious-looking little nugget of something and held it up for Anthony to see before he popped it into his mouth and smacked away. "She makes delicious stuffed mushrooms, by the way. With crabmeat. As a Frenchman, I thought I knew about mushrooms, but these are a revelation."

A nasty twinge of jealousy joined the simmering loneliness Anthony had tried to repress all day, making for an uncomfortable combination. On the one hand, he of course wanted Melody to have a delightful Christmas, wherever she was. On the other hand, *he* wanted to enjoy those delicious mushrooms along with everyone else.

"Yes, but what have you done with her?" he asked.

"She's helping Samira with the roast beef," Baptiste said, panning the camera around to the stove.

Melody and Samira, both dressed in lovely red dresses and wearing chef's aprons with kitchen towels slung over their shoulders, were doing something to a roast that looked so amazing that Anthony could practically smell its savory goodness through the phone.

Also in the background? Glasses of wine. Flickering candles. The crackling fireplace. Assorted dishes laid out on the counter, including Anthony's personal favorite, pecan pie, a treat he'd discovered one fall when he'd traveled to New York to visit a school chum.

The kitchen staff here at Sandringham could do many wonderful things in the kitchen, but it had never yet produced a pecan pie.

"Hi, Anthony," the women called, waving and smiling. "Merry Christmas!"

He felt a hard pang in his heart region.

"Hello, darling. Samira. You both look amazing. I'm sick that I can't be there to enjoy the food with you."

"We wish you were here," Samira said.

"How're you feeling?" he asked Samira, who was pregnant. "Well, I hope."

"I feel great. Thanks for asking."

"She's starting to show," came Baptiste's excited voice from somewhere outside the frame. "Did you notice?"

Anthony froze. First of all, he was not in the habit of commenting on the bodies of his friends' girlfriends and, second, Samira looked as slim as ever.

Luckily, Samira put her hands on her hips and stepped in to save him.

"I am *not* starting to show," she snapped at Baptiste. "This is my first baby and I'm not even three months pregnant yet. I probably won't show until the fourth or fifth month. Stop saying that and putting people on the spot."

"You *are* starting to show a little," Baptiste said somewhat defensively. "Certainly, your lovely breasts are—"

"Baptiste!" Samira squawked, throwing her towel at him. It hit the phone, then dropped away. "Knock it off!"

They all laughed. Baptiste turned the phone back around to his own face and sat on the sofa.

"I'll be over here, staying out of your way like you told me to," he told the women. "I will, of course, be available if you need a taster."

"We will bear that in mind," Samira said acidly.

"I'll be right there, Anthony," Melody called.

"No worries," he said.

"So, listen," Baptiste said, lowering his voice and sobering as he turned to Anthony. "Don't get in a funk. I know how you are."

"What are you talking about?" Anthony tried to look bewildered. "I'm fine."

"You don't like Christmas," Baptiste said darkly. "You hate Sandringham. Don't pretend."

Anthony shrugged irritably. "It's fine."

Baptiste's brows crept toward his hairline. "Whatever you say."

"Have you heard from Nick?" Baptiste said, eager to change the subject. "He hasn't returned my texts."

"He was headed for Mustique with some blonde, last I heard—"

Melody appeared in the frame as she sat beside Baptiste.

"Sorry about that," she said brightly. "Samira needed some help seasoning the gravy."

"There's *gravy*?" Anthony asked, feeling himself slide into despair.

"What else are we going to put on the mashed potatoes?" Baptiste asked smugly.

Anthony groaned and collapsed with his head in his hands, to much laughter on the other side of the pond.

"And I suppose your yeast rolls are works of art," he asked glumly when he raised his head again.

Melody raised a plate and repressed a smile. "See for yourself."

Anthony squinted and leaned forward to get a closer look at what was, quite possibly, the most delightful treat he'd ever seen: a fat golden brown roll topped with mounds of pecans and melted caramel goo.

Choked on his jealousy, he looked to Melody for some sort of an explanation.

"Why?" he pleaded, pressing a hand to his broken heart. "What would make you be so cruel to me at the holidays?"

She and Baptiste laughed their fool heads off.

Anthony didn't see anything funny about the whole debacle.

Baptiste shot a glance over his shoulder. "Gotta go. Samira looks like she needs my help with the macaroni and cheese."

"I do *not* need your help," Samira called. "You are not getting a taste of this, so you can stay where you are."

"I'll be right there," Baptiste told her, smothering a laugh with difficulty. "Try to control your impatience."

Samira cursed.

"Not sure it's safe for you over there, to be honest, mate," Anthony said, raising his brows.

Baptiste seemed supremely unconcerned that he might be taking his life into his hands.

"It will be fine. He's all yours, Melody," he said, standing and passing Melody her phone. "Make sure he isn't glum, okay? Talk to you soon, Stocky."

He headed for the kitchen, leaving Anthony to face Melody's faint frown of concern.

"Hey," she said, brightening as she gave him an appreciative once-over. He noticed that she'd ditched her apron to reveal a healthy dose of cleavage where her dress dipped low in the front. His heart rate kicked up. "Where are you? What room?"

"Granny's study."

"Show me."

He panned around the room, trying to see it through her fresh eyes. The blazing fire and mantel topped with a garland dotted with white lights. The stately Christmas tree, which was actually one of the smallest in the house. The silk, chintz and gilt. The framed photos and the red box on the desk.

"I'm speechless," she said, looking a little dazed when he turned the camera back around. "Do you ever get used to all that?"

He hesitated.

How to tell her that, while he certainly appreciated the place's beauty and history, he didn't feel (had never particularly felt, at least since his mother died) at home there any more than one felt at home at the nearest art museum? That none of this was his or any reflection of him but for an accident of birthright? That being in these surroundings where nothing ever changed and yet everything was forever changed by his mother's glaring absence only made him sad(der)?

That he would happily take Melody's cheerful apartment instead and never set foot in this place again?

"It *is* beautiful, I suppose," he said, glancing around. "One does get used to it. But it's a house. A dwelling. The people make a home."

She watched him, arrested. "You're very reflective today, aren't you?"

Something about her keen interest made him fidgety. He tugged an earlobe.

"Something about the season, I suppose."

She blinked, reining in some of that intensity.

"Well...In a complete change of topic, you look *amazing*."

The subtle heat in her gaze went a long way toward soothing some the ache in his chest over being the only one who wouldn't get to partake of their incredible feast. He felt a pleasurable rush of blood to his cheeks.

"Yes, well, Granny loves her black-tie Christmas Eve dinner. My only regret is that you weren't here to enjoy the delicacies with me. We had haggis and fruitcake, among other things."

"*Haggis?* The sheep's gut concoction with oatmeal? I'm sick with envy."

"As I knew you would be. *You* look amazing, by the way."

She smoothed her dress and flashed him a sultry woman's smile. "Partial to Christmas red, are you?"

"I'm partial to *you*."

"How was church? I saw the pictures of you leaving the service with your family. It looked like you might have accidentally smiled in one, but then I thought it might have just been gas."

He had to laugh. "The services are not known for being scintillating. Let's leave it at that."

"So what else did you do all day while I was slaving over a hot stove?"

"Not much. Several of the uncles played cards, but Uncle Dicky is a notorious cheat. We exchanged our gag gifts. I drew Granny this year. Got her a mug. Here it is, in fact."

He grabbed the mug from its place of honor on the desk and held it up for her to see:

I'm the only queen around here it said, with an askew crown perched on the *I*.

"Perfect!" Melody said. "How'd she like it?"

"She loved it," he said, grinning at the memory. "Laughed so hard, I thought she was going to choke on her tea."

"Nice! And what was your gag gift?"

"It was brilliant. A T-shirt that said, 'Introverts Unite—Separately.'"

"That's perfect for you! I wish I'd thought of it."

"Your Christmas gift for me must be at least that good. I'm a size large."

"I hope I can do a *little* better than that." Melody's smile widened conspiratorially. "Would you like to see the gift I almost got myself?"

"Love to."

She held up a printout of a picture of a tabby cat. "This little guy was at the shelter. I saw his picture online. But when I got there to check him out, he'd already been adopted."

"Sorry to hear that. He looks like a very fine cat."

"Yeah, me too," she said glumly. "But there'll be a better pet out there for me. I just have to find him."

"Good attitude. So are you all packed for our trip? You've got your passport in order? We'll be together this time next week, won't we?"

"I'm starting to pack," she said. "I've got my list together."

"And are you excited?"

She all but levitated off the sofa.

"I'm dying to see all the animals. And I can't wait to see the hospital and meet the children. Do they like American candy? I'm thinking I should bring them some—"

"Hang on. Why did *I* not get a mention in there?" he asked sourly.

"Oh, I see you all the time," she said airily.

He glared at her. "You do *not* see me all the time. As you well know."

Her smile slipped away, leaving unmistakable melancholy. "As I well know."

They stared at each other for a beat or two. He somehow resisted the urge to rub the ache in his chest. The constant dull throb there seemed to be a permanent addition to his life these days. All the days when they weren't together overflowed with them.

"So you talked to your parents?" he asked brightly, determined not to be morose. "Your sister?"

She blinked and seemed to make an equal effort to recapture her smile.

"Yeah. My parents are all settled into their condo in West Palm. They have this whole extravaganza every year with a few of the families who also winter there. And my sister is positive she's going to get a ring tomorrow, so we may be hearing wedding bells soon."

"Well, best wishes to her."

"Best wishes to *us* if this anticipated engagement falls through," Melody said darkly. "She has a way of making people's lives miserable if she doesn't get her way."

"Noted," he said, laughing. "I look forward to meeting them all."

As always, the allusion to their shared future made Melody nervous. She ducked her head and smoothed her hair, pointedly avoiding his gaze.

"Hmm. So why did Baptiste want me to make sure you're not glum?"

He hesitated, thrown off-kilter both by her noncommittal stance and by this one central wound in his life that never seemed to heal.

"I'm not that keen on Sandringham at this time of year, to be honest. Too many memories."

"You miss your mother," she said softly.

A sudden wave of grief slowed down his answer.

"I'll be fine." He stared her in the face. "And you're assuming my mother is the only one I miss."

Melody let out a long and serrated breath that did nothing to steady his equilibrium.

In the background, he heard the indistinct voices of Baptiste and Samira and the clatter of cutlery.

"I knew a long-distance relationship was going to be challenge," she said, leaning closer. "As long as I'm busy at work and don't sit down and start thinking too much, I'm fine. But sometimes—" She broke off. Helplessly shook her head. "This is *hard,* Anthony."

"It's excruciating," he said, roughly rubbing his forehead with the palm of his free hand. "It's untenable. As I said—"

Baptiste's cheery face suddenly popped into the frame next to Melody, startling them both.

"Sorry, lovebirds. It's time to eat our delicious feast before the food gets cold. I would, of course, still eat it no matter how cold it got, but Samira wants us to come to the table. So send your little kisses and tell each other good-bye."

He disappeared again, leaving a melancholy silence in his wake.

"I'll let you go, then, darling." Anthony said, determined to remain upbeat. He would not allow his self-pity to cast a pall on their dinner. He and Melody had a delightful vacation coming up very soon. The fact that he had to wait a few more days for it did not constitute a tragedy. "Have a wonderful dinner."

She nodded, eyes lowered and game smile firmly in place. "Will do."

"Call me later? Before you go to bed?"

Another nod.

"Right, then. Bye, darling."

More nodding. Her chin quivered.

"Bye," she said, hastily ending the call.

But not before he caught the shimmer of tears in her eyes.

The sight of them caused that ache in his chest to progress into a throb.

Then a stab.

Put it aside for now, chap, he told himself, but some feelings demanded attention and refused to be ignored. Loneliness was one of them.

He slammed the phone down on the desk. The loud noise made him feel a bit better, so he slammed his hands. *That* made the photos on the end of the desk jump and the one of his mother, the one he'd been pretending he didn't see, wobbled.

He slammed his palms again, punctuating it with a particularly heartfelt *"Shit!"*

"What a nasty word." His grandmother's clipped voice, materializing out of nowhere, damn near sent him into cardiac arrest. When she stepped in from the hallway carrying a tumbler of gin and tonic, with her little black handbag hooked over her arm and resplendent in her beaded green dress and enough blazing diamonds around her neck and on her ears to give her face sunburn, he almost wet his pants. "But *fuck* works much better when one is upset, don't you think? *Fuck.* Very satisfying."

Anthony goggled at her. *"Granny."*

"Right, then, AJ. You and I need to have a talk."

10

Anthony hastily stood and watched his grandmother perch on the edge of the nearest armchair in front of the desk, set her handbag at her feet and sip her drink.

"I'm, ah ... sorry?"

"For which?" She stared up at him, implacable as ever. "Sitting in my chair, abusing my father's desk or cursing like a sailor?"

"Whichever offends you the most."

A long moment passed during which she studied him with wizened eyes and he tried to dial back some of his agitation.

No dice.

"You didn't, ah, hear any of that, did you?" he asked warily. "My phone call?"

"What?" She looked surprised. "Oh, no, just a word or two at the end there."

Anthony exhaled a huge sigh of relief.

"Just something about your not being keen on Sandringham this time of year on account of your memories."

Anthony stiffened.

"Then there was something about you missing your Dr.

Melody dreadfully, the long-distance situation being excruciating and your wanting her to call you before she goes to bed." A delicate pause. "I assume that's when you young people do all your sexting."

"Granny! You'd better put down your drink. It's loosened your tongue. What do *you* know about sexting?"

"One knows everything with a smart phone, dear." She reached for her purse and pulled out one of the larger models, regarding it fondly. She held it up for him to see, flashing a bejeweled case with her insignia on it. "These things *really* are amazing, aren't they?"

"Granny! You can't slink about the place listening to people's private conversations! It's beneath you!"

Her eyes sparkled with amusement. "Who's going to stop me?"

That caught him up short as he thought it over. "Fair point."

She pursed her lips. "Do sit down, Anthony. Stop making an old woman crane her neck."

"Sorry." He started to sit behind her desk again, caught himself and looked around for another convenient seat. But the next available chair was a bit too far away for a conversation. "I'll just, ah…"

She heaved a long-suffering sigh. "You're welcome to sit behind the desk where you were. Perhaps you can help with my papers while you're at it. I'd be grateful if anyone could tell me what the bloody hell the prime minister is talking about in his latest dispatch on economic policy."

Anthony repressed a snort, sat and waited.

She crossed her ankles, set her drink on the side table and laced her fingers in her lap.

"Yes, well, first things first. I suppose I'll need to fire Mrs. Brompton. I'd told her to find you so I could have a word, but evidently that never happened because you never appeared and I had to come looking for you. So she's *out*."

She watched him, brows raised.

There was a pause.

"I hate to throw her under the bus, but it's probably for the best," Anthony said with a straight face. "She's never been very good at her job. And she eats all your little salmon sandwiches when you aren't looking. Being the gentleman that I am, I've taken the blame for it, but it's really been *her*."

"Just as I'd suspected," his grandmother said with a gleam of amusement in her blue eyes. "Did you have enough to eat at dinner tonight? How did you enjoy the haggis?"

"It was ghastly."

"Yes, it was, wasn't it? I wish they'd stop serving it."

"Someone with your clout could probably arrange that, Granny."

"Maybe, but I haven't the heart to tell anyone that I despise it. They've been making it since before Stonehenge was built."

"Ah."

They dimpled at each other in companionable silence for a moment. Then she went and ruined everything.

"How is your wretched father spending the holidays? Has he got any prospects for a child bride to marry and divorce in the new year?"

Anthony grimaced. "Don't know when he would manage the time. He's been far too busy meddling in *my* affairs."

"Oh?"

Anthony smoothed the leg of his trousers and seethed in silence for a moment or two, his desire not to whine in a death match with his desire to bash his father with someone who disliked him as much as he did.

Spite won in the end.

"He's hanging on to my trust for another five years."

"Oh." Granny frowned. "And what's put a bee in *his* bonnet?"

"Some nonsense about him wanting me to find my own purpose and goals."

"Ah," she said icily. "And those purposes and goals would be entirely separate from *us,* I suppose."

"Naturally."

"You haven't done so badly by me. You're to be ennobled next year. Finally come into your title and lands."

Anthony focused on adjusting his cuffs and said nothing.

"You gave your word, Anthony," she said, and there was a lot less kindly grandmother in her voice and a lot more queen. "Don't think you're going to weasel out of it."

The three whiskies he'd drunk had, in fact, set off a wave of magical thinking inside his brain, making him wonder if he could, for example, suggest that the earldom be postponed until his fortieth birthday as well, or if he could perhaps talk her out of it altogether. But no.

Scowling, he leaned back and propped his legs on her desk.

"Feet."

"Sorry," Anthony said, hastily swinging them down again.

Granny reached for her drink and sipped thoughtfully. "And what does your wretched father want you to do with yourself, pray?"

"God knows. He wouldn't cry if I showed up in Houston and demanded the corner office next to his, but I told him that's not going to happen."

"Hmm. And what does your Dr. Harrison say about it?"

Anthony stifled a laugh and ducked his head, feeling sheepish.

"She basically gave me a swift kick in the arse and told me to stop feeling sorry for myself because most people don't have the advantages I have and they're not marching about whining about not coming into their money." He shook his head, the memory making him grin. "We should probably run a genetic test on her. I'm convinced she's got some British blood in her, if you look hard enough."

Granny had been watching him closely, a speculative gleam in her eyes, but now she frowned thoughtfully and stared off in the distance to some point over his shoulder. His attention drifted to his mother's smiling face in her frame on the corner of the desk, and the pang in his chest would have knocked him down if he hadn't already been sitting.

Don't think about it, he sternly told himself, but it was already way past too late.

Impossible to keep his turmoil off his face.

"What's wrong, Bubba?" she asked, employing the childhood nickname she'd bestowed when teasing him about his Texan side. "Tell your old granny."

The soothing note in her voice proved irresistible, as it always did. As a Brit and a former military man, he vastly preferred to pretend he didn't have any inconvenient feelings and to cold-shoulder them when they insisted on showing up. Expressing his deepest hurts and fears put a chink in the invisible masculine armor he'd spent his life buffing and polishing.

But there was something about talking to Granny that felt okay. She'd seen him at his devastated worst after his mother's death when he was thirteen, after all. Plus, he could always later tell himself that he hadn't voluntarily demonstrated a moment of weakness but had been compelled by his sovereign.

Who could tell Granny *no*?

He opened his mouth. Met the steady warmth of her gaze. Gave himself permission.

"I can't stand the loneliness sometimes," he said, finally succumbing to the urge to rub his chest and soothe that unreachable ache. "It's like it's trying to choke me. When Mum died, I tried to remember that I wasn't the only one who missed her. That we were all in it together. And when I was overseas, I tried to remember that the boys were with me. That we were all equally afraid of dying. And now with Melody—"

Granny's gaze sharpened.

He floundered, trying to get his words to match his turbulent feelings.

"I don't feel alone when I'm with her. But I'm always saying good-bye to her. And now it's Christmas and I'm here and she's there and I just…"

He trailed off and shook his head, exhausted by the effort.

There was a pause.

"You told her who you are, I trust?" Granny asked.

He thought back to that difficult conversation and winced.

"Yes."

"And how does she feel about that?"

Anthony shot her a wry smile.

"It's daunting, but she's stuck around. Much to my astonishment."

Crisp nod from Granny. "Good."

He paused, then decided there was no time like the present.

"She's, ah, …Well, she's black, Granny. African-American."

"I know. And…?" she said blankly.

Anthony's lower jaw hit the desk. "You know? *How?*"

She frowned. "I looked her up on my smart phone, didn't I?"

It took everything Anthony had not to keel over in a dead faint.

"White mother. Black father," Granny continued. "Both physicians. She's about thirty-five, I believe? Beautiful girl. Unfortunate scar on her lower jaw and neck, but stunning eyes. Very bright. Promising future as a surgeon. Older sister who's also a doctor, as I recall. Am I missing anything?"

Stunned, Anthony could only shake his head.

"What's your point in mentioning her race to me?" Granny's tone acquired a sharp edge or two. A veiled note of suspicion. "You don't mean to imply anything about how I treat people, do you?"

"Absolutely not," he said, restraining a disbelieving snort.

Granny watched him, her sternest expression tempered with a hint of repressed laughter.

"Any other details you'd care to share about her?"

"Yes." Anthony's lips twitched. "You'd better know the worst. She was talking about getting herself a rescue cat for Christmas."

"A *cat*?" Unmistakable horror rippled through her body. "What kind of person wants a *cat* sneaking about the place? It's not a *black* cat, is it?"

"It might well be," Anthony said gently.

Harsh sigh from Granny. *"Bollocks."*

"Before you write her off completely, please know that she likes dogs. It's just that with her work schedule, she doesn't have time for one."

"Pity," Granny muttered.

"I know."

It took her a beat or two to absorb this disheartening news, but then she rallied.

"It's important for one to think things through very carefully. Know what one is getting into. What one can handle and not handle. Our life is not for everyone. There are tremendous sacrifices to go along with the tremendous privileges."

"I know," Anthony said, troubled by the implication that his relationship with Melody might have a shelf life. "That's why this *getting to know you* phase is so crucial. She needs time to adjust. Before the press gets wind of anything."

"Which they will. Probably sooner rather than later, if history is any guide."

"I know. Any advice for me?"

"Yes. Don't screw it up."

He barked out a laugh. "Noted."

She nodded with crisp satisfaction. "Now I have something for you."

He sat up a little straighter. "Oh? Will I like it?"

"I should think so. Hold out your hand."

He did, watching as she tugged one of the rings off her pinky and placed it on his palm.

He gasped as a faint bell of remembrance rang in the back of his mind.

It wasn't one of the glittering diamonds that threatened to blind bystanders every time the light hit her. It was a little silver ring.

He studied it, turning it from side to side.

"This seems so familiar. It almost looks as though someone's cut the end off a silver teaspoon and made a little ring out of it," he said.

"That's exactly what it is. Your mother made it—"

That was it. He quickly looked up, his heart a heavy lump in his chest.

"Mum?"

"Yes. When she was about thirteen, she insisted on going to a summer camp at a ranch in Texas when we wanted her to go to a little finishing school in Switzerland. Rode horses and took a class in metal shop. Whatever *that* is. Made this ring for herself and an identical one for me. We both wore them all the time."

"I remember now."

"They were very much loved. I haven't wanted to see them for a while. But maybe it's time to bring them out again."

He pressed the ring to his lips, his throat tightening.

After his mother's death, her jewels, of which there were many, had been whisked off somewhere for safekeeping. He hadn't thought about them since. But now there was something incredibly poignant about holding an item she'd worn. Something she'd made.

He looked at his mother's photo again. It was a black-and-white one of her wearing a white shirt and sitting on a sofa, laughing on some unremarkable day. His heart contracted almost to the point of pain.

Don't think about it, he told himself.

"Your mother always answered to her own conscience," Granny said. "Made her own path. Even when her path didn't make sense to anyone but her. She was strong that way. Very determined. For good or bad. You're very much like her."

"I'm not sure I am," he said glumly. "If I'm on a path, it's muddy and overgrown. Probably disappears into the woods up ahead. You may need to send a rescue party."

Exasperated sigh from his grandmother. "You're also very much like your father, Young Hamlet."

"Don't call me Hamlet. And don't you mean my *wretched* father?" he asked, idly rolling the ring between his palms.

"Probably. Thank you for the correction. Like you, he's far too sensitive about things."

"That old man is not *sensitive*," Anthony said, revolted by the idea. "When did he ever feel anything other than the desire to knock me down or to fuck inappropriate women? Sorry."

"He hides it behind all his bluster, dear. It's an act. You should know that by now."

Anthony gaped at her. "Put down the gin and tonic. I beg you. It's causing delusions."

Granny shot him a quelling look. "Your mother hurt him very badly when she asked for the divorce. I hate to say it, or to speak ill of the dead, but I'm not sure she ever gave him a fair shot."

"What are you saying?"

Granny hesitated, downed the last of her drink and set it down.

"I'm saying that one never knows what goes on in a marriage, but I believe that your mother shut him out. Washed her hands of him when he would probably have been willing to walk to China and back for the chance to work things out." Long pause. "I'm saying…She was no angel, Anthony. It's time you realized that."

Anthony had no idea where all this was coming from, but he didn't like it. At all.

"Maybe not, but she was *my* angel," he snapped, gripping the ring so tightly that it began to cut into his palm.

Granny remained placid. As ever.

"Maybe so. But your father was your father. Only it was hard for him to do much fathering when your mother was determined to shut him out. By bringing you back to London for boarding school, for example."

"I don't want to talk about my father," he said coldly.

"Fair enough. But perhaps you should think about him a bit more. He's the only father you've got and none of us are getting any younger. Don't look at me like that, Bubba. People have gone to the block for much less than glaring at their monarch."

Anthony would have smiled, but shock seemed to have knocked most of his senses and muscle memory out of his head.

"Since when do you stick up for my wretched father?"

"Every now and then, I like to step back and look at the big picture. Your wretched father may let his nether regions do far too much of his thinking for him, but in the big picture, both he and I want the very best for you. Which makes us allies. Uneasy allies, but still allies."

Anthony shrugged. Nodded. Wiped a fingerprint off the ring's band.

"Do you like the ring?" she asked.

He nodded and, with a heavy heart, started to give it back.

"Thank you for showing me," he said gruffly.

"Oh, no, dear," she said, holding her hands up. He saw the mate to his ring on her pinky. "I'm wearing my ring. That ring is yours now. To do with as you will."

Her gaze was a bit more pointed than usual, kicking off a wave of something that felt suspiciously like joy inside him. The feeling was so unexpected that he lost his head a bit.

He kissed the ring again. Pocketed it. "Love you, Granny."

Aggrieved sigh as she reached for her bag, stood and smoothed her skirt.

"Do stop indulging that American sentimentality, dear. On this side of the pond, one prefers to wonder whether one is loved or not."

He burst into laughter, the most heartfelt of the night. "I'll try to remember that in future."

"Good. Let's get back to the party. Uncle Dicky swore he wouldn't sing his 'Bell' trilogy until we came back. We might as well get it over with."

11

Anthony: What're you wearing?
Melody: Not much.
Anthony: A picture is worth a thousand words.

Melody read his text and stood there for a moment, stuck firmly on the horns of a dilemma.

On the one hand, everyone knew that phones and clouds could be hacked and no one's pictures were truly safe. Ever.

On the other hand, she really wanted to drive Anthony out of his freaking mind. For several reasons. First, because he'd shown up and showered her with such loving care when she was sick the other week. Second, because it'd been three weeks since they'd had sex.

Third and most importantly, because she lived to drive him wild.

Thinking fast, she stood in front of the open balcony doors, where sunlight shone through, posed with her back arched and her hip out, angled the phone so her face didn't show and hoped for the best as she took a few pics.

When it was all said and done, she had a workable shot of

the front of her body silhouetted through her sheer floral caftan. As she'd hoped, she made a curvy figure eight with her breasts and hips, her skimpy white panties were clearly visible against her skin and a couple of well-placed flowers covered her nipples.

Actually, it was pretty sexy, if she did say so herself.

Suppressing a laugh as she thought about what Samira would say if she could see her now, she hit SEND and waited.

Her phone buzzed. She eagerly checked and saw...

A scowling emoji.

Oh, no.

She frowned down at it, her heart sinking. *Stupid, stupid, stupid. Why* had she sent it? A person in Anthony's position always had to worry about being hacked, and here she'd—

Her phone buzzed with another text.

Anthony (with a heart-eyes emoji): Sorry! Cardiac arrest made my hands fumble! Meant to send a million of these.

"Whew!" she said, laughing as a wild swoop of relief zoomed through her. And that was *before* he sent her a final text:

Anthony: You never stop exceeding my expectations, do you?

Grinning and unexpectedly teary, she swept aside the fluttering white panels and went through the doors to the balcony, where glowing orange lanterns and fairy lights were strung overhead and through the nearby trees. She leaned against the railing. Enjoyed the cooling breeze. Breathed deep. Tried to recognize all the scents (verdant grasses; mysterious flowers; rain; soil; diesel exhaust; wood smoke;

grilled meat; cumin; cinnamon) and wondered how and when on earth her life had become this magical.

They were in *Tanzania*.

Africa, God. She was in *Africa*.

She stared out at the scenery, trying to process it all and wondering if everything she saw was a hallucinogenic by-product of her twenty-four-plus hours of traveling.

On the far side of the savannah horizon? A shimmering blood-red sunset straight out of *The Lion King*. In the near distance in front of the horizon? A watering hole. At the edges of the watering hole? A herd of zebra, a herd of elephants, including a crew of raucous teenagers who'd only managed to grow starter tusks, and giraffes who spread their legs into wide triangles in order to sink close enough to the water for a drink. Up in the sky flying off to parts unknown? A flock of gangly white birds with long legs stretched out horizontally behind them.

And the lodge!

It was a fantasia of luxury that made her wonder if she'd mistakenly been shown to Mariah Carey's suite. If so, that was just too damn bad. The only way anyone was getting her out of here at this point was if they shot her with an elephant tranquilizer dart.

Airy and light, with polished hardwood floors and trim, it had a massive poster bed piled high with pillows and draped with mosquito netting, potted plants, gorgeous rugs in indigenous prints, a drink cart featuring a bucket of champagne on ice and the biggest fruit basket she'd ever seen.

All but giddy with delight, she sat on one of the chairs on the deck and settled in to wait for Anthony, her thoughts reverting to when she'd seen him earlier at the hospital.

She and the other visiting surgeons, a group of about fifteen, had finished their tour of the small facility, which was in a decommissioned church. Austere with a ward full of wrought iron beds, it was scrupulously clean and run by a collection of some of the most caring and committed professionals she'd ever met. The sight of the operating room had gotten all her doctor's juices flowing.

The head of surgery, a stately dark-skinned gentleman with cotton fluff hair named Dr. Abdul Katika, had leaned in with a conspiratorial smile as they filed out and started down the hallway.

"You look as though you want to scrub in, Dr. Harrison," he'd said in his wonderfully cultured accent.

Melody glanced down at her linen shirt and khaki pants with a wry smile, doing her best to rein in her enthusiasm before she began bouncing on the balls of her feet.

"That obvious, eh?"

"That obvious. We will try to generate some hernias and fistulas for you to correct. That will make you deliriously happy—"

A ripple of excitement surged through the crowd as one of the nurses poked her head in the door and said something in Swahili. Melody didn't need a translator to know what that meant.

"Anthony's here," Dr. Katika announced, clapping his hands and beaming at them in turn. "We'd better go. Hurry. Hurry."

They left the relative cool of the hospital and stepped out into the shade-dappled late morning heat, which was pleasant summer day-ish and nowhere near the roasting alive she'd feared. Evidently they'd been through this drill before, because the hospital staff lined up by group. Staff doctors, with Dr. Katika at the head...visiting doctors...nurses...

support staff. A teacher organized her gaggle of chattering local children. The little ones wore green and white school uniforms, shushed each other and launched into an upbeat call and repeat song of greeting (one of the boys thumped out a rhythm on his drum) just as a caravan of rugged Land Rovers appeared at the end of the road, kicking up a cloud of dust as they approached.

Melody, who found herself at the end of the row of visiting doctors, gave herself a stern mental warning. Now was not the time to act like a giddy eighth-grader meeting her boyfriend by the lockers after drill team practice. She was a professional in a professional setting. As such, squealing was out. Jumping up and down was out. Kissing and hugging were out. Blushing and grinning were probably also out, but probably also unavoidable.

A polite smile and handshake. She could manage that.

And she meant to. She really did. She kept all her enthusiasm on lockdown as the SUVs rolled up and stopped about fifty feet away, as doors opened and security swarmed. She even kept it dialed back as Anthony's door opened and his foot, clad in a hiking boot, emerged.

But then the rest of his tall frame appeared, forcing her to stifle a gasp of feminine appreciation.

He wore baggy olive pants with a linen shirt like hers. Dark aviator glasses that made him seem sexy and mysterious. That golden hair, catching the sun from every angle and glinting like a halo. His ruddy skin, already beginning to deepen with a tan.

She knew him well enough now to detect nervousness in his tight jaw and squared shoulders. She'd thought, back home when she first looked him up online, that he must be used to this sort of thing by this point in his life, but now she had a whole new perspective on what he must go through.

The music. The throngs of grinning and cheering people and their palpable excitement. The clump of photographers and the relentless clicking of the shutters from their long-lensed cameras. The videographers. The security personnel.

This may be the life he led, but it wasn't normal.

This could never be normal.

Funny, wasn't it? Strangers stared at *her* because of her scar. Strangers stared at *him* because of his looks and status. Two entirely different reasons, yet staring was staring. It made her pretty freaking uncomfortable. Him, too.

She felt a stab of empathy for him. She also felt the thrill of understanding a bit more about him and his world. The excitement of knowing they had something else in common.

But mostly she felt breathless anticipation.

Especially when he took off his sunglasses, hooked them into his breast pocket, quickly scanned the scene and settled on her. Their gazes locked for a quick beat or two. She gave herself another stern reminder—*don't act a fool in front of all these people, girl!*—but she couldn't regulate her exploding grin any more than he could. When the joy of seeing him again threatened to topple her over backward and the rising heat in her cheeks became unbearable, she ducked her head and tucked her windswept curls behind her ear.

"Hello, everyone," he called, playing it off like a champ by quickly looking around and including everyone in his smile. "*Hujambo! Habari za asubuhi!* I'm so glad you decided not to make that fuss for my visit. Wouldn't want you to go to any trouble."

The crowd loved this and launched into a round of laughter and return greetings. Evidently the only thing better than a handsome prince was a handsome and charming prince who also spoke a little Swahili.

Melody decided to be grateful for the camouflage. Her

unstoppable grin wasn't so glaring if it matched everyone else's, right? She was grinning, clapping and swaying to the music, watching as Dr. Katika led Anthony to the beginning of the receiving line and began the introductions, when she saw them.

A group of five or six small kids, too young for the school uniforms just yet, standing off to her left.

They stared at her. Pointed. One of the kids said something to the others and gestured at her own throat and cheek. The kids nodded, then looked back at Melody, their eyes wide.

Melody's heart sank.

They can't hurt you, Mel, she reminded herself. *Nothing can hurt you if you don't let it.*

But she sure felt hurt.

Funny how her scar couldn't let her have a fun moment without crashing the party.

Funny how these little moments always popped up to remind her that she was an oddity.

She hesitated and sighed, wishing that she was the type of person who could let it go, just this once, and knowing that she wasn't.

Sparing a quick glance at Anthony, who was now about halfway done meeting the staff doctors, she edged out of her own line and over to the little kids, plastering a bright smile on her face as she went.

The kids all started and exchanged guilty looks.

"Hujambo!" She bent at the waist and held out a hand to the pointing boy, who seemed to be the little ringleader. "I'm Dr. Melody. Who are you?"

To his credit, he stood a little straighter, stuck out his chest and had a firm grip and good eye contact. "Darweshi."

"*Jambo*, Darweshi. Did you notice my scar?" She pulled

her hair aside so he could see it better. "It's okay to be curious. I got burned when I was younger. That's why you shouldn't run and play in the kitchen."

He nodded solemnly. "You shouldn't run by the fire, either. That's how my sister got burned."

With that, he gestured to a little girl in the back who wore her bandaged arm in a sling and had a bouquet of wildflowers in her free hand. Melody smiled encouragingly at her, but the girl just stared at her with her liquid brown eyes, the apparent victim of stage fright. Until one of her cronies whispered something in her ear and nudged her forward a couple of reluctant steps.

"Jambo," Melody said. "What's your name?"

"Bupe," the girl said, her attention riveted on Melody's scar. "Does it hurt?"

"Not anymore," Melody said, her heart melting at the sight of this worried little cutie with her braids, pink dress and dusty feet in her sandals. "And yours won't always hurt, either. Not once it heals."

"Will it be ugly?" Bupe asked.

Melody kept her smile firmly in place. She decided not to focus on the unspoken rest of Bupe's sentence (*Will it be ugly like yours?*) and instead drill down on the lesson she'd walked over here to teach.

"How could anything be ugly on a smart and beautiful girl like *you*?" she asked.

Bupe gasped. Exchanged a shy smile and sidelong looks with her friends and brother, who laughed and thumped her on the back. Then, with no further warning, she launched herself at Melody for a hug.

"Thank you!" Melody cried, squeezing her around the shoulders and taking great care not to touch her wounded arm or smash the flowers. "I *love* hugs!"

"These are for you," Bupe said, flashing a gap-toothed and dimpled smile as she thrust the flowers at Melody. "In case your scar starts hurting again."

Melody pressed a hand to her heart and tried not to get teary. Moments like this reminded her why she'd happily dedicated her life to helping children.

"Thank you, sweetheart," she said, turning Bupe loose after a final squeeze. "They're beautiful."

Which was right about the time a pair of dark hiking boots and olive cargo pants came into Melody's field of vision. Her heart skittered to a stop.

"What's all this?" Anthony asked in that thrilling voice of his. "Where are *my* flowers? *I'm* the special guest today."

"You don't get any flowers, silly," Bupe said with childish delight at putting him in his place. "You're a *boy*!"

There was a round of shrieking laughter as the kids raced off, leaving Melody to straighten and work on her acting skills as she greeted Anthony in front of Dr. Katika.

Anthony didn't make it easy. His face flushed and his eyes seemed especially luminous at the sight of her, a blazing indigo that was the most beautiful color she'd ever seen.

"Hello," he said with a glimmer of wicked amusement as he shook her hand. "Dr. Harrison, isn't it? Thank you for that warm welcome. What a graceful curtsy."

She raised a brow and felt her internal temperature rise another ten degrees or so as the electrical current from that point of contact zinged through her body. Somehow she lassoed her smile and tugged it down into rueful territory.

"Oh, no. I hate to tell you, but that was *not* a curtsy. I bent over to speak to the little kids."

"I see." He made a show of frowning after the kids, then back at her. His lips twitched with poorly repressed laughter.

"But you would have, surely. Once you saw my regal approach. In fact, there's still time, if you hurry."

Not bursting into laughter damn near killed her. But if he wasn't going to break character, neither was she.

She made a pained face and sucked in a breath.

"Ooops. Sorry again. This is awkward but, as an American, I'm not in the habit of curtsying. And I may be mistaken, but I thought you were sort of a junior royal who didn't require all the formalities. Almost like a civilian. Am I wrong?"

That almost broke Anthony up. He pressed his lips together, crossed his arms and tapped an index finger against his lips in a valiant effort to maintain a stern expression. But there was no hiding his dimples.

"Sir?" One of his security people materialized at his elbow and spoke in his ear, probably to hurry him along because he still had several people to meet. "We need to—"

"One second," Anthony said, holding up that index finger and sparing his security guy a quick glance before returning his attention to Melody. "You Americans are quite seditious, aren't you?"

"It's a bad habit, I admit," she said.

"And how are you enjoying Africa, Dr. Harrison? Your first time, I believe?"

She sighed helplessly. "Africa is spectacular. I think it might even be life-changing."

"Indeed." His gaze lingered on her face, a loving touch almost as tangible as the stroke of his fingers across her cheek. "I'm sure you're right. Will you be staying here long?"

"No. I'm heading to a lodge about an hour from here for some animal watching. Skytops. Have you heard of it?"

"I *have* heard of it. I've always wanted to go." His voice

turned husky. "I'm certain it would be the adventure of a lifetime."

"Sir..." the security person said, edging closer again.

Anthony blinked. Shuttered all of his smoldering intensity and nodded crisply, recapturing his aura of professionalism. "Well. I hope you have a wonderful vacation, Dr. Harrison. And thank you in advance for all the brilliant work you'll do at the hospital."

She nodded and did her best to swallow the gathering lump in her throat. It didn't do any good to remind herself that she'd see him again tonight at the lodge. They spent far too much of their time telling each other good-bye.

"Thank you," she said, trying to match his briskness. "It's a pleasure meeting you."

Anthony nodded, turned to Dr. Katika and gestured for him to lead the way to the next group for the meet and greet. "Shall we?"

With some difficulty, Dr. Katika, who had witnessed the entire exchange, dragged his gaping lower jaw up off the ground, blinked, shot Melody a speculative look and headed off.

"This way, sir. Over here, we have the..."

Anthony looked back over his shoulder at Melody.

"I'll see you later, darling," he murmured in his silkiest voice, for her ears alone.

She almost swooned.

He really had the most remarkable eyes she'd ever seen. The fact that they'd looked twice at her was a mystery she'd have to ponder another day.

"Later, Blue Eyes."

Anthony went very still. His gaze, hard and searching, held on tight and refused to let her go. He hesitated. Opened his mouth—

"A-hem." Dr. Katika said loudly from several feet away, where he'd evidently just realized that Anthony wasn't right on his heels. "Anthony? Are you with me?"

"Of course," Anthony said, walking off without a backward glance at Melody.

Now here she was, waiting for him.

She checked her watch, wishing she'd thought to ask him how far away he was and how long he'd be. It was about an hour to the lodge from the hospital, so it probably wasn't—

Hang on. Were those footsteps outside her door? And muffled male voices?

Sure enough.

"You're going to love your room, sir," said a local man.

"I'm sure I will." Anthony's voice carried more than a touch of impatience. "But I'm happy to take it from here—"

"It's no trouble at all, sir."

She had just enough time to duck out of sight on the balcony (she wasn't exactly dressed to greet anyone but Anthony at the moment and they were trying to keep a low profile) before the front door swung open and a bellman strode in carrying Anthony's bags.

Anthony was hot on his heels. While the bellman busied himself placing the luggage just so, Anthony quickly scanned the room, spotted her making a valiant attempt to blend in with the fluttery drapes and positioned himself to block her from the bellman's view as he turned back to Anthony and handed him the key.

"Dinner is at eight."

"Appreciate that." Anthony clapped a hand on the man's shoulders and steered him back to the door. "I'll call the front desk if I need anything else."

The man looked a little startled. "I'm supposed to open the champagne for you."

"Don't trouble yourself." Anthony slapped a tip into the man's hand, ushered him back to the door and opened it for him. "Thank you so much. Have a lovely evening."

"But—"

Anthony gently but firmly shut the door in the man's face. Locked it.

Grinning at Anthony's delightful display of impatience, she edged out from her hiding place and stood where she was, knowing full well that the setting sun backlit every inch of her barely dressed body.

"Hi," she said.

"Hi," he said on a shaky exhale.

They stared at each other.

She greedily noted everything about him.

The gleaming hair. The sun-kissed color in his cheeks. His avid gaze as it skimmed her from head to toe, lingering on a few key points (her aroused nipples; her belly; her pussy; her bare legs) in between.

"You're looking very serious," she noted quietly, her heart pounding.

"I, ah…" He hesitated. Took a deep breath. "The thing is…I thought I was doing pretty well in life. But I can't figure out how I got lucky enough to have you here with me."

This was not the ideal moment for ghosts from her past to show up to the party, but they crept in like a group of underaged teens trying to sneak past the bouncer and into some hot club.

She thought of the guy in college who'd seemed to like her, but had never wanted to introduce her to his buddies. The blind dates who'd done their poor best to keep their game faces on when she showed up, then stared uncomfortably at her scar for the rest of the night, too distracted to carry their half of the getting-to-know-you chitchat. The people who stared at her on the street, the murmuring commenters who thought she couldn't hear them when they said, as they always said, *she'd be so pretty if she didn't have that scar*.

And now *this*.

Him.

"There's a lot of luck going around today," she said, unexpected tears making her voice husky. "Are you going to kiss me?"

Long hesitation.

"In a minute." He gestured vaguely over his shoulder at the bathroom. "I need to shower first. You look amazing, yet I probably smell like one of the elephants out by the watering hole at this point."

She laughed, incredulous, as she came closer.

"You think I care about whether you showered or not? When you came and took care of me when I had the *flu*? I am so hot for you right now." Just in case he wasn't getting the message, she let her head fall back and sifted her fingers through her hair and down either side of her neck. Palmed her breasts, squeezing them together. Ran her hands over her sex, making herself gasp and her flesh leap as frissons of sensation sparked between her thighs. "Don't make me wait. I can't wait."

"Christ," he said, looking to the ceiling fan hanging from the rafters. "You don't make things easy for a fellow, do you?"

She laughed. "I don't know how much clearer I can make this: I don't want easy."

Her challenge thus issued, she tipped up her chin and started to wrap her hands around his neck.

He tensed with a muttered curse, caught her wrists in a

hard grip and lowered her hands between them. She had him tiptoeing along the edge of his limit, which was right where she wanted him. It was all there in the rigid planes of his face, shallow breathing and glittering, speculative eyes.

"Perhaps I need to cool you down a bit first." His voice, so throaty and resonant now, made nerve endings tingle to life as though he'd trailed a feather down her inner arm. "Hmm? Would you like that?"

"I need that," she said helplessly. "I *need* that."

He laughed, a hoarse sound of triumph and anticipation, and freed her hands.

Then he reached for her.

12

Anthony kissed her with all the pent-up urgency she felt. Hot. hard. Deep. His insistent mouth made its way across her lips, claiming and demanding until she felt raw and breathless, coaxing until he'd wrought every helpless mewl out of her and left her with nothing but dazed amazement.

No one else kissed like this, alternately nipping and sucking with such relentless skill that it was hard to keep up. She clung to him, locking her arms around his neck and sifting her fingers through his hair as she delved for the warmth of his scalp beneath.

She was so enthralled with everything about him, so delirious with the thrill of his unyielding arms sliding down to hold her around the waist and the hard slabs of his chest against her throbbing nipples, that she barely registered that they were moving.

Until he backed her into the bed, caught her wrists again, broke the endless kiss and pulled free of her grasping hands.

They stared at each other for one stunned moment, trying to catch their breath. His glittering gaze dipped to her lips. She involuntarily licked them. With a rough groan, he lowered his head and let his tongue glide into her mouth, slow and easy this time.

Her inner muscles clenched, damn near making her come on the spot.

And that was before his talented hands stroked their way up her torso and hovered, feather-light, on the sides of her breasts.

She could take a lot of things, but she couldn't take *that*.

Breaking the kiss, she covered his hands with hers and tried to move them over a few inches, to her achy nipples.

But he let her go and eased back enough to stare her in the face.

"Lie down," he said.

She didn't need telling twice. She reached for the bottom of her caftan first, starting to sweep it off—

"Leave it."

Startled, she hesitated with the hem bunched up around her waist.

He watched her in utter stillness, his color high and his jaw set.

She left it.

Never breaking his gaze, she eased back against the pillows and started to stretch out—

Looming over her, he made a rough sound of impatience as he grabbed her hips and deftly dragged her to the edge of the bed so that her toes grazed the floor.

Most of the air whooshed out of Melody's lungs.

The remaining little bit also disappeared once he knelt on the floor, eased between her thighs and ran his hands down the front of her body.

There was something wonderfully illicit about being dressed in clothes that covered her up and yet were thin enough to allow her to truly feel and enjoy his touch. Something deliciously erotic about the way his hands and the fabric slid over her skin, making her belly quiver and her nipples pucker. Something thrillingly X-rated about the way he looked up the length of her body at her face, his eyes an unblinking blaze of blue as he reached *under* the caftan, hooked his thumbs under the sides of her lacy white bikinis and slid them down her legs and off while she wriggled to help him.

"How are you feeling *now,* Dr. Harrison?" he murmured, skimming a thumb over her manicured patch of hair. "Any cooler?"

Shaky laugh. "Not exactly."

"Hmm," he said, lowering his head as he used thumb and forefinger to open her up and expose her clit to his skilled lips. "I'll have to see what I can do about that."

He could do a lot, as it turned out.

He anchored her hips in his firm grip and pressed his slick tongue to the exact perfect spot she needed. Worked her with his mouth, applying a steady and rhythmic pressure and doing the same thing over and over, into infinity. She cried out in a strangled attempt at his name. It was also a plea for him to let her go and leave her alone because she couldn't take it. Oh, and also for him to never ever stop, no matter what she said or did.

She tensed and gripped his head, holding him in place until her spiraling need caught up with her growing languor. Her breath caught. She teetered on the edge of that cliff for one endless second of anticipation until the balance tipped and she hurtled through space.

She stiffened and then slackened into ecstasy, his name pouring out of her mouth.

He made his way up her body with nuzzles and kisses, paying special attention to her belly button, each nipple and her scar. She cooed for him, her eyes rolling closed as she melted into the sensations. He loved the damaged side of her throat the hardest, wringing even more pleasure from her body via the sensitive tendons in her neck.

When he finally made it to her mouth, helpless tears burned the backs of her eyes. It took a lifetime's supply of courage to open her lids, look him in the face and let him see what he did to her.

He met her gaze with heat. Quiet male satisfaction. Open adoration.

"Was that good, darling?" he asked, kissing away a tear as it fell and trailed down her temple.

"So good."

"Am I allowed to shower now?"

She snorted back a laugh. "Just be quick about it. And you owe me an apology for ruining everything with your funky smell."

He burst into laughter as he toed off his shoes and worked on his belt.

"My *funky smell*?"

"Hurry," she said, pointing to her watch. "Tick-tock."

He disappeared into the bathroom with his overnight bag, still chuckling, and returned just as she'd caught her second wind. The instant she heard the rattle of the bathroom doorknob, she rolled onto her side and propped her head on her hand, determined not to miss a single detail about his entrance.

She was not disappointed.

He appeared amid a cloud of earthy and sophisticated-smelling steam, tall and lean with muscles rippling in his arms and across his torso as he wrapped a towel around his waist. His hair was wet. Actually, all of him was wet. Water droplets dotted his broad shoulders and trailed through his cornsilk-dusted chest, grooved abs and notched hips, disappearing beneath the towel to intriguing parts below. He had the shapely calves of a lifelong soccer player and good feet in flip flops.

A promising erection tented the front of the towel.

They stared at each other.

She wasn't shy about checking him out.

He wasn't bashful about letting her look.

He seemed relaxed but alert, ready and willing to return any volley she cared to send his way.

"You're very sexy," she told him in a husky voice that sounded, to her ears at least, as though she'd stolen it from some other woman.

"You think so?" he asked quietly, unsmiling as he turned out the bathroom light and came closer. "I believe you called me Blue Eyes earlier. Is that my new nickname?"

"Or just *Blue*. I thought I'd try it out."

"Hmm. I thought Sinatra had had Blue Eyes copyrighted."

She shrugged, levered herself up and settled on her knees. "Maybe, but he's *Ol'* Blue Eyes."

"And I am…?"

"*Sexy* Blue Eyes." She cocked her head and thought it over. "Although, to be fair, Sinatra was also very sexy."

His attempted glare only deepened his dimples as he reached the bed.

"Not as sexy as *me,* surely."

She somehow managed not to look away as the blush streaked across her face.

"No one's as sexy as you."

His breath hissed.

Time to make her move.

"Oh, no. You're wet," she said, trailing her fingertips

down his chest and across his belly. "I can't let you in the bed like that."

"My current state is *your* fault." He shivered, goose bumps erupting all over his skin. "You barely let me out of your sight to shower. I didn't dare test your mood by taking the time to dry off, did I?"

She reached for his towel. Slowly unwrapped it.

"You don't mind if I borrow this, do you?"

He swallowed hard.

"Not at all," he said softly.

Never breaking eye contact, she rubbed one arm dry. The other arm. His chest. His belly, taking great care not to go any lower.

She had his rapt attention.

"Turn around," she told him.

The soul of compliance, he turned and presented her with a delightful view of those wide shoulders and a toned back tapering to narrow hips on the sides and flaring to an ass that was high and tight.

She *loved* that ass. Thank God for soccer.

She rubbed him with the towel again, running it down the perfect curve of his spine and over the dimples right above where back gave way to ass. And then, because she couldn't resist, she let her lips and tongue follow the same trail.

But she couldn't do what she wanted to do while kneeling on the bed. So she gently pushed him forward a step or two, stood and ran the towel around front, to his groin. If she was a bit rougher about a few lingering strokes while she dried him there, he didn't seem to mind. Not judging from the sudden catch in his breath or the way his lungs began to heave.

Nor did he raise a protest when she squatted, squeezed his balls and bit his ass.

In fact, his earthy and unabashed groan and the way he shuddered seemed to suggest that he *loved* it.

But of course the only way to test her theory was to do it again, on the other side.

A shocked cry this time. The strangled sound of her name on his lips. Which made her wonder what other reactions she could incite and how best to incite them.

One thing in particular quickly came to mind.

"I *think* I want to taste you," she said, standing and hugging him from behind, grateful for the chance to rub her face and nipples, which were starting to ache again, against his warm golden skin. "How does that sound?"

Shaky laugh from Anthony. "I think it sounds like you're trying to finish me off."

That made *her* laugh. "I *am* trying to finish you off. Duh."

"Yes, but you're also trying to do me in," he said grimly.

"Poor thing." She propelled him toward the nearest wicker chair, trying to smother her laugh. "You're just a victim, aren't you?"

"You don't seem very sympathetic."

"I'm not." She spread the towel on the chair's seat and pointed. "Sit."

"I'm dying to get inside you." Unsmiling, he turned to face her with his gleaming eyes and ran his thumb across her lower lip. She sucked it deep into her mouth, making him gasp before she slowly let it slide out again. "On the other hand, I *do* love what this beautiful mouth can do. What should I do?"

"Up to you." Taking all the time in the world, she slowly gathered the bottom of her caftan, swept it up her torso and off, tossing her hair and exposing her breasts with a bounce. He made a choked sound. And that was before she nimbly dropped to her knees, rubbing her face against his crotch on the way down, and stared up the length of his body to maintain eye contact. "But I'd sit if I were you."

He sat with a glimmer of wary amusement. "But you *will* take it easy on me?"

"Oh, absolutely." She gave him her gravest look. "As easy as you just took it on me."

"Fuck," he said, gripping the chair's arms to brace himself.

She scooted forward, eager to get his ripe head in her mouth. She sucked and licked, swirling her tongue around and around and ignoring the rest of his dick until, with a hoarse attempt at her name, he clamped his hands on her head and thrust his hips.

She laughed with triumph. Sucked hard. Took him as deep as possible. Bobbed her head up and down, letting him slide in and out. Let him go entirely, then ran her lips and tongue up and down his length, licking him all over. Cupped his balls. Squeezed them until his lungs heaved and his groans became particularly raw.

If she thought of it, she did it, determined to be as generous with him as he always was with her.

There was a distinct possibility that she'd been with the wrong sorts of men in the past, but they always acted as though just because they showed up with a dick when they swaggered into the room, any available woman should be happy to suck it.

But Anthony.

Anthony.

In addition to being a freaking selfless Einstein when it came to the erotic arts, he fascinated her. Delighted her. Cared for her. Showed up when he said he would. Called when he said he would. Exposed himself to the flu to make sure she was okay, and it wasn't as though they'd exchanged any *in sickness and in health* vows. He'd brought her *here,* to the earthiest and most beautiful place she'd ever seen, and he regarded *her* with wonder, as though *he* was the lucky one.

Half the time, she wasn't sure he even remembered that she had a scar.

A hundred percent of the time, she was positive that the scar didn't matter to him.

So for this one man, she was happy to give everything she had. Happy to suck and suck and suck until her tongue, cheeks, knees and thighs hurt. Happy to have him grab handfuls of her hair and pull her closer.

With Anthony?

She was *happy.*

"That's enough," he said in a choked voice, staring down at her with glazed eyes as she let him slide free. "I can't take it."

Surging to his feet, he reached down to help her up. She held his hand as she backed up to the bed, then turned down the covers and stretched out as he reached for one of the condoms she'd left on the nightstand earlier.

He watched her the whole time he sheathed himself, his eyes darker now. Stormy. Meanwhile, the lines of his jaw and chin tightened down into sharp angles, and she was pretty sure she caught the glimmer of a tear as he levered over her, settling on his elbows, and cupped her face.

"I *missed* you," he said, his gaze searching and urgent. Maybe even a little bewildered as he smoothed the hair at her temples. "You're all I can think about. Every second."

Truer words were never spoken.

"I missed you," she said, staring him in the face and losing herself in the moment's intensity even though it was like staring at a solar eclipse without the special glasses. "I missed *you.*"

He shifted his weight and reached between them. She angled her hips. He thrust home, stretching her. Filling her. Leaving her breathless and shocked that, on this perfect day of perfect days, nothing else came close to the exquisite sensation of having Anthony inside her.

The stunned look on his face reflected it all back at her.

Maybe being in Africa did something primitive to her. Maybe it was the fact that they'd been apart for a couple of weeks this time. Maybe it was just that she was beginning to realize how much this man meant to her.

Whatever it was, she was categorically incapable of holding anything back.

"Anthony," she said, letting her eyes roll closed and her back arch as she rose up to meet him.

Their mating was frantic from the beginning. There was no other word to describe it. They'd spent too much time apart and she'd wanted him too desperately during all those lonely nights. She'd ached for *this*. Counted the days for it. Lived for it.

No detail escaped her notice.

The unrelenting hardness of every part of his body as he pressed her deep into the mattress and thrust for all he was worth. The way she dug her fingers into his back and reveled in his groans and his sweat and his flexing muscles. The surge and retreat of his tongue and the minty flavor of his insistent mouth. The saltiness of his skin when they finally broke the kiss and she ran her lips down the strong column of his neck. The clenching halves of his ass, which formed perfect globes for her hands to grip and to smack, urging him faster…harder…deeper.

The way his big dick stretched her to the exquisite edge of pain, unerringly rubbing her sweet spot with every powerful surge. The way all of her sensations intensified if she drew her legs in so she could cross her ankles behind his back and open herself wider. The way doing so wrung strangled noises from him and made his rhythm falter.

The way he watched her the whole time, his eyes bright in the fading sunset. The way her name poured out of his mouth on an endless wave of astonished whispers and groans.

He kissed her again, nipping nuzzles and tastes that made her lips feel deliciously swollen and never gave her the chance to keep up with him, much less catch her breath or say anything other than gasping attempts at his name.

And all the while, need spiraled lower and coiled tighter inside her, collecting at that one perfect spot between her legs. It didn't take long for the clenching to begin, little rippling spasms of her inner muscles announcing that while she may have had the orgasm of her life a few minutes ago, that record was about to be broken.

"Anthony," she said helplessly, her voice shaky because this wasn't normal. Nothing that happened between them was normal, in bed or out, and surely she wasn't the only one who'd noticed how phenomenal they were together.

He levered himself up on his elbows and stared at her with those amazing eyes. His expression seemed bewildered but also exultant.

"It's not too much, is it?" he said hoarsely. "The way I already feel for you?"

She hesitated, knowing what he was asking.

These things took time.

You didn't just meet someone and cede them a big chunk of your heart on a silver platter.

You weren't supposed to give everything you had to a person who didn't even live on the same continent as you.

The potential for heartbreak was far too great.

Right? *Right?*

But as she looked up at him, this man who'd become every noncareer thought in her head, she didn't want to slam any doors on him any more than she wanted to strap a raw steak to her chest and step outside to see if she could find a lion.

This was right.

They were right.

"No," she said, reaching up to cup his beloved face in her hands and bring him in for another kiss. "It's not too much."

There was the glimmer of his smile as his mouth found hers again. With that, she bore down on her inner muscles, gripping him tightly inside her body.

He tensed. Thrust once more…twice…

He stiffened and came with an unabashed groan and a final thrust that made the pulses of electrical sensation between her thighs crescendo into waves of spasming pleasure that she had to vent from her body on an astonished cry.

They rode it out together, their breathing harsh in the relative silence as his head dropped down into the hollow between her head and shoulder and they held each other tight.

13

After a few minutes, he rolled to one side, taking her with him. They slid into that euphoric post-coital zone that wasn't quite waking, wasn't quite sleeping and always required drowsy half-smiles.

Then his wry voice rumbled through the growing darkness.

"I meant to ask if you were back to a hundred percent after your bout with the flu, but I'm going to hazard a guess that you *are*."

She laughed, smacking him on his washboard abs.

Unsmiling, he caught her hand and kissed it.

"Do you know how hard that was earlier? Not touching you when I hadn't seen you in weeks? Pretending I didn't know you?"

"You didn't do much pretending in front of Dr. Katika," she noted quietly, running the backs of her fingers over his lips.

"Don't worry. He's an old friend. Very discreet."

"I liked him a lot."

"Good."

They stared at each other for a long moment of mutual satisfaction and sensual knowledge. Anthony's avid gaze covered her from head-to-toe, touching on everything from the wild tumble of her hair to her puckered nipples, cooling in the night air, and the cleft between her legs.

"Much as I'd like to lie here forever," he murmured, trailing his fingers over her belly and making her flesh leap, "they're expecting us for dinner. They've made a big fuss."

"Well, I *did* work up an appetite."

He grinned with unmistakable male smugness.

"But aren't you concerned about so many people seeing us together here? Where everyone knows who you are?"

"Don't worry about them, darling. They're very discreet, I'm told. But before we get dressed, I want to give you your Christmas presents."

"My Christmas presents?" She gaped at him, stunned, as always, by his generosity. "I thought this trip was my Christmas present."

"Don't be silly. Your coming to Tanzania with me was *my* Christmas present."

"Wow," she said, laughing. "Win-win."

They both laughed as he got out of bed and leaned in for a quick kiss before heading to the bathroom.

"I'll be right back."

"Hmm," she said, temporarily distracted by the sight of his tight ass, sculpted torso and long legs as he left. Then she leapt up and reached for her overnight bag.

By the time he returned wearing a pair of silky boxers, she'd slid back into her kaftan and had her brightly wrapped flat presents for him sitting on the coffee table. He grabbed his own bag before he joined her on the sofa, then froze at the sight of his gifts.

"What's all this?" he asked with an incredulous delight

level that suggested she'd gifted him with the deed to a nearby conflict-free diamond mine.

"They're for you," she said, beaming and trying not to bounce up and down with the thrill of surprising him. "I hope you like them. You're really hard to shop for."

He stared at her, his big heart shining in his eyes.

"You didn't have to do this for me. I didn't expect anything."

God, this man touched her.

"It's my pleasure," she said, cupping his cheek as she leaned in for a kiss. "Open the small one on top first."

He hastily cleared his throat and, grinning widely, untied the ribbon.

"This had better not be a book," he said, now tearing the paper and sliding it aside. "If there's one thing I hate, it's reading *books—oh, my God*."

It was a copy of Nelson Mandela's autobiography, *Long Walk to Freedom*.

"Open it," she said.

But he'd gone into a semiparalytic state, staring at it amazement, then blinking up at her.

It took him forever to speak.

"Melody, you didn't."

"There's one way to find out."

He checked the copyright page, then the title page.

"This is a signed first edition," he said, gaping at her.

"I know! Do you like it?"

"*Like* it?" He shook his head helplessly, then gave her cheek a lingering kiss. "Thank you. I'm not sure I've ever had such a meaningful gift."

"Good." She reached for the larger package and gave it to him. "Because I'm not sure how you're going to feel about this one."

"There's more?" he asked, aghast.

"There's more. So you'd better brace yourself."

Recovering slowly, he ran his fingers over Mandela's signature, shut that book and set it down before setting to work on the other one.

"I'm afraid to look," he said on a shaky laugh. "Not sure what could top the other one."

But the disbelieving look on his face as he saw what it was told her she *had* topped the first gift.

"This is…" He flipped the large workbook over, possibly to make sure he wasn't seeing things. "This is a study guide for the bar exam. In New York."

"Yep! And there's more. Look inside."

He did, discovering a sheaf of papers, which he quickly flipped through.

"This is…" He had to stop and clear his hoarse throat. "This is an application to complete the coursework so I can become a barrister back home."

"It is," she said, laughing at his absolute stupefaction. It was better than anything she'd envisioned in her wildest dreams. "I wasn't sure whether you'd want to become licensed in the US or the UK, so I got you both."

Long pause, during which some of her giddiness slipped away.

And that was *before* he looked up at her, his expression stricken.

Her heart sank all the way to her toes.

Oh, God.

She'd somehow gone and screwed everything up. What a way to end an otherwise perfect day. Was she a regular genius, or what?

"Only if you want to," she said quickly. "I can take them

back. I just thought that you seemed like you kind of wanted to pursue your legal career when we—"

"That's just it," he said, eyes flashing. "I don't *have* a legal career."

Melody met his turbulence head-on, absolutely determined to do what was right for this man, even if he wasn't yet ready to confront his choices.

Even if he didn't yet realize that he *had* choices.

"You could, though." She shrugged. "Maybe it's time for you to think about whether you want one. And if you do, how much you want it. But, hey. None of my business."

She stared at him, trying not to smile.

He stared back at her, his gaze ambivalent.

Whether he was trying to decide what planet she came from and where she got off making suggestions like this to him, or whether to take her back to bed and worship her for the rest of the night, she couldn't quite tell. But she really hoped it was the latter.

He was still stunned speechless when she snapped her fingers and remembered the other thing she'd brought for him.

"Oh, and I almost forgot," she said, reaching into her bag again. "This one just arrived before I left to come here, so I didn't have time to wrap it. I hope you don't mind."

She unfurled it with a flourish and held it up for him to see:

It was a Mandela quote on a black T-shirt with white lettering:

It always seems impossible until it's done.

This seemed to be too much for Anthony.

He took the T-shirt from her and, looking dazed, pressed it to his mouth.

She waited, half afraid she'd made him cry, but when he

dropped his hands, he merely shook his head and regarded her with the sort of fascinated disbelief with which he might view a flying elephant.

"Are you an illusion? A figment of my imagination?"

"What?" She snorted back a laugh. "Of course not. Why would you ask that?"

"Because," he said, his voice and expression softening and his attention dipping to her lips. "You go so far beyond my expectations every single time I'm with you that I can't believe you're real. Either way, I'm fairly certain that it's too late for me to stop myself from..."

Falling in love with you.

The words lingered in the air, terrifying, thrilling and tantalizingly out of reach as the color rose in his cheeks.

Melody froze, afraid he meant it and equally afraid he didn't.

The silence mushroomed, eventually becoming excruciating.

Words crowded onto her tongue, demanding to be said. Things about how she might also be falling for him, but the woman who took him on had to be extraordinarily strong and that clearly wasn't her. Things about how much better her life was with him in it, but how she couldn't quite see how either one of them could fit in the other's world permanently.

He needed to know all of this, but none of it came out when she opened her mouth.

She faltered.

He nodded and quickly turned away, rubbing his nape.

"I'd ah...I'd better give you *your* gifts if we want to make dinner in time, hadn't I?"

"Anthony..."

"Number one," he said, giving her a beautifully wrapped box about the size of a—

"Oh, it's a *mug*," she said, laughing with delight when she got it open. "I *love* mugs. And it says...*Best Fucking Doctor Ever*. Oh, my God."

"You like it?"

"It's perfect. Thank you!"

"Well, I saw it when I ordered the queen one for Granny, so I had to get it for you. And of course a perfect doctor needs..."

He reached into his bag and pulled out another gorgeous box with satin bow, this one about the size of a trade paperback.

"Did you wrap these yourself?"

"I did," he said modestly.

"They're gorgeous. Your mother was a good teacher, wasn't she?"

"The best."

She shook the latest package. "What is it? Tell me."

"Or you could just open it."

"I think I will."

She ripped into it, her nerdy doctor's heart breaking into a happy dance when she saw that it was—

"Oh, my God! This is like the Rolls Royce of stethoscopes! This is amazing! Thank you! I'll be able to hear almost all the little kids' hearts with this baby!"

He laughed indulgently. "I'm all for that."

"How did you know?"

"I did a little research. *Great gifts for doctors*. And I have one more thing for you."

He handed her a small flat box, about the size for a bracelet, but she wasn't done with her new toy just yet.

"Hang on," she said, putting the eartips in. "You can be my patient for a minute so I can test this thing out. Let's see if you have a heart in there—"

"You know I have a heart," he said huskily, catching her wrist just as she reached out with the chestpiece. Bright patches of color resolved over his cheekbones. "It beats for you."

Overcome, she scrambled onto his lap, the better to wrap her arms around his neck and rain kisses on his face and lips. The heat rose between them, as it always did, and it wasn't long before they were breathless again and the unmistakable length of his erection pressed against her thigh.

Just as she began to wonder whether they had time for a quickie *and* a shower before dinner, he broke away and lowered her hands from either side of his head when she would have pulled him back in.

"*When* can you come to London? We have to see how you like it there."

Passion and urgency turned his eyes to indigo, two vivid flames that seemed likely to consume her whole. And suddenly it all became too much. Losing herself to this man in the privacy of their vacation lodge or in the familiar comfort of her apartment back home was one thing. Entering into discussions that could ultimately lead her to moving to London—*London!*—to be with him was something else altogether.

She stiffened involuntarily. "Anthony…"

Just like that, the flame inside him went out, dimming the light in his face by a good fifty percent.

"You don't want to come," he said dully.

"*No*. That's not it. It's just that this is a lot. And we're just starting out."

His expression cleared. "If this is about my grandmother, I told her about you."

His grandmother had been one of the last things on her mind at this particular moment, but now she paused, arrested.

She already knew that Anthony kept his word, but there was a world of difference between keeping your word about calling at a certain time or remembering to grab a gallon of milk on your way home and keeping your word about initiating what could well be a difficult conversation with your grandmother and sovereign.

"You did?"

"Yes. She doesn't care about anyone's demographics."

Whoa.

Melody blinked, shocked.

It wasn't that she'd suspected that the Queen of England was a closet racist or would object to her beloved grandson becoming seriously involved with a black woman. It was that Melody's understanding of the British aristocracy led her to believe that there were classes and expectations. People like them, and people like us. Did Melody come from a lovely upper middle-class American family that could afford a weekly gardener and housekeeper? Sure. But that had no more connection to the type of wealth Anthony was used to than a kangaroo had to a sea horse. And it hadn't escaped her notice that, unless she was visiting with some African dignitary or President Obama, the Queen didn't exactly spend a lot of one-on-one time with black folks. Or middle-class folks.

She nodded, equally shaken and excited about this removal of what would have been a huge obstacle to their deepening relationship.

"You're scaring me," he said, and he *was* beginning to look a little green around the edges. "Is it that you see this relationship only going so far?"

Now *there* was a ridiculous question, one that buffed some of the rough edges off the sudden flare of fear she'd experienced. As if she could control the way her heart pounded when he looked at her or regulate her growing determination to spend as much time as possible learning everything she could about this intriguing man.

"No," she said. "That's not it at all."

Heartfelt sigh of relief from Anthony, who gripped the hair at her nape and pulled her in for a fervent forehead kiss.

"What is it, then?"

She took a minute, determined to get her words just right.

"It's that…my life and career are in Journey's End. My friends. My family is nearby. The issue isn't whether things are good between you and me. They're *amazing*."

He grinned and brought her in for another forehead kiss.

"But this is all too much to absorb right now. We need to spend way more time together before we start talking about changing anyone's geography. Plus…"

She trailed off and shook her head, not wanting to go too far and hurt him.

But his eyes already glinted with sharpening interest.

"Plus?"

She paused. Took a deep breath and decided that their relationship deserved her complete honesty.

"Plus, I saw so much more about your life today."

He tensed.

"My…*life?*"

"The crowds. The security. The cameras. It's insane. I don't know how a person gets used to that. I know it's a tremendous privilege to be able to live the life you live and travel and meet people, but I see the sacrifice that goes with it. I saw the look on your face. I know you well enough to know when you're nervous and uncomfortable. I mean, how do you get used to *that*?"

His jaw hardened.

"I'm not sure one ever gets used to it. But it's always been like this for me back home and during engagements. It's what I know."

"But...when you went to NYU?"

"That was a brief period of anonymity that I never expected to last. I've made my peace with it."

"Right. And the woman who winds up with you is going to have to make her peace with it, too."

It was hard not to see the hurt in his face. The bewilderment.

"The woman who winds up with me?" he asked faintly.

She nodded, sudden misery making her throat tight.

"Don't look at me like that. I can't take it."

"So..." He shuttered all that emotion away and cleared his throat. "So what are you saying?"

As if she knew.

She thought it over. Weighed her words.

"I'm saying that since you're putting a lot of emphasis on London, maybe it would be best if we hold off on that for a while. Maybe I could plan to go over for your investiture in September."

"September?"

"I know I can't attend the ceremony as a girlfriend, but I'd love to support you behind the scenes. In the meantime, we can, I don't know, meet in other places. Paris, maybe. Bermuda. Toronto. I don't expect you to come to me all the time."

"What about Journey's End?" he asked, looking stricken. "I love it there. It's a lovely little town. Don't you want me back?"

"Of *course* I want you back. I love it when you come. And things are easier in Journey's End, anyway, aren't they? We don't have to be as discreet there because no one knows who you are. So we're free to go where we want to go and do what we want to do without having to be undercover all the time. And it's not forever. Just until we have a stronger foundation and we're both sure what we want."

"'Until we're *both* sure what we want,'" he echoed dully, and maybe it was her imagination, but she was pretty sure she heard a trace of bitterness in his voice.

And she, once again, couldn't take it.

"Anthony." She palmed his face and kissed his forehead...his eyes... his nose...his mouth...anything she could do to wipe away the disappointment. "Don't be upset. Please don't be upset. You know I'm talking good sense. I don't see how we can fly under the radar in London like we can in other places."

Harsh sigh from Anthony, who gave her a final kiss, then pressed his lips to her neck and pulled her in for a tight squeeze.

"You know I can't be upset with you."

She eased back enough to check him out and see whether he was serious or not. His face still held shadows that hadn't been there a few minutes ago, but he seemed resigned, and that was good enough for right now.

"Are we good?"

"We're good," he said.

"Thank God. I guess we should get ready for dinner, huh?"

"I guess we should."

She stood, sending something tumbling to the floor with a quiet *thump*.

It was the last gift in that small flat box, she saw.

"I never opened my final present," she said, stooping to pick it up.

He looked uncomfortable.

"It's okay. Now is probably not the time."

Her heart sank. Despite what he'd just said, he really *was* upset, wasn't he? Maybe he didn't want her to have the gift now that she'd hurt his feelings.

She offered it back to him, her heart aching.

"I can open it later, if you want. And I'll understand if you don't feel like giving it to me now."

They watched each other for a beat or two, then he blinked away the lingering traces of hurt and dimpled at her.

"I want you to have it."

"You sure?"

"I'm positive."

Grinning and thrilled that her introduction of a note of caution into the proceedings hadn't ruined the whole trip, she sat on the coffee table in front of him and tore into the package. Inside the box was a tiny velvet drawstring pouch. Inside the pouch was—

"Oh, my God. It's a spoon ring!"

He looked startled. "You know them?"

"Of course I know them. Kids make them in metalworking classes. But I've never seen one like *this* before."

It was gorgeous. Highly polished sterling silver with ornate shellwork that fit perfectly on her right pinky.

"I love it!" she cried, pressing her hands to her heart. "Thank you."

"You're welcome, darling."

"It looks like an antique. Where did you find it?" she asked, basking in the renewed warmth of his steady gaze.

He started to speak. Hesitated.

"I knew you had to have it when I saw it," he said finally.

"I really love it," she said, admiring it on her finger.

He stood, pausing to press a kiss to the top of her head before getting up and heading to the bathroom. "I'm glad. I'll just be a moment."

"Okay."

But he turned back on the threshold, his expression troubled once again.

"You're not gearing up to break my heart, are you, Dr. Harrison?"

A fervent denial rose up her throat but never made the border crossing into her mouth.

Was she gearing up to break his heart? Absolutely not. Not when he was such a wonderful person with whom she had many important things in common. Not when their blossoming relationship seemed so bright and promising. Not when she was pretty sure that breaking his heart would also break hers.

But...

Was she ready to discuss London and think about the possibility of leaving everything she knew and loved behind in Journey's End?

No, she was not.

She turned away, the words stuck in her throat.

He turned away, his expression shadowed as he returned to the bathroom and shut the door on her uncertainty.

14

NINE MONTHS LATER

"Sorry I'm late."

Melody put down her cup of tea and glanced up from her phone in time to track Samira's stroller-pushing approach to their table at Java Nectar, Journey's End's local coffeehouse and bustling activity hub on this bright Saturday morning in September. The new mom and bride-to-be looked harried as she parked the stroller, gave Melody a quick peck and dropped into her chair, but Melody only had eyes for the baby.

Who was *awake*!

"Hi, handsome," she cooed, reaching out to unlatch him from all his restraints. He wore the cutest little mossy green romper that matched his eyes and had white booties on his feet. "How are you? Come to Auntie Melody."

"We had to swing by the florist, which took forever," Samira continued. "And I had my final fitting before that. So it's been a busy morning. But your little friend here slept most of the time, so he's doing his part."

Melody, who now had nearly two-month-old Jean-Luc

settled in her lap, made a show of scanning the room, looking everywhere but at Samira.

"I'm sorry. Did someone somewhere say something?" she said in her most soothing voice. "I thought I heard a noise, but I was too busy admiring all these little fingers and these chubby cheeks to notice who was talking. Yes, I was. Yes, I wa-as!"

Samira rolled her eyes but gave the pair of them a resigned *why fight city hall?* smile.

"I'm getting used to being invisible when the baby's in the room. Although I *do* hope a couple of people notice me on Saturday. At my *wedding*."

"Stop whining." Melody snapped over the top of Jean-Luc's curly dark head. "Your wedding is not all about *you*."

They both laughed.

"You can't blame people," Melody said, caressing the baby's silky little arm and categorically unable to look away from his soulful green eyes, so much like Baptiste's. With his honeyed skin and Samira's lush mouth, this one was going to break a lot of hearts when he grew up. "This is a gorgeous baby."

Samira's radiant glow threatened to subsume everyone within a three-mile radius.

"He *is* pretty special, isn't he?"

Melody slung him over her shoulder and patted his back, reveling in his solid weight and powdery fresh scent, which was catnip to her aging ovaries. Sudden longing actually made her breasts and belly ache.

"He's *amazing*. I think I'm going to keep him."

Samira snorted. "Good luck with that. You know Baptiste threw a fit when I told him I was bringing him with me today, right?"

"Too many germs?"

"Too many germs. Too loud in here with all the chattering and the music. You name it."

"You need to lock that down before Baptiste turns into a full-blown helicopter dad."

"I'm working on it, but it may already be too late," Samira said grimly. "It's not that easy to—oh, hello, guys! How are you?"

Melody looked around in time to see the final approach of eight- or nine-year-old identical twins Noah (with the glasses) and Jonah Lowe, who were the sons of Miranda, owner of Java Nectar. They were evidently on duty again this morning. They both wore small white aprons tied around their narrow, jeans-clad hips, and Jonah set a handful of napkins and cutlery on the table, while Noah presented them with menus.

"Hey, fellas," Melody said, turning the baby around so the twins could see him.

"Is that your baby, Ms. Samira?" Noah asked, peering down at Jean-Luc, who stared back with avid interest.

"It is," Samira said proudly.

"Glad you finally had him," Jonah said. "You were pregnant for, like, two years."

"Yeah. You were huge," Noah added.

"Anyway," Samira said loudly, shooting quick death glares at the boys, "His name is Jean-Luc."

The twins broke into ecstatic grins.

"Like Jean-Luc Picard from *Star Trek: The Next Generation*?" Jonah cried. "Cool!"

"Did you give him a cool middle name, too?" Noah asked eagerly. "Like McCoy or Chekov?"

"Actually, I hate to tell you this, but he's named after Baptiste," Samira said gently, managing to repress most of her amusement. "Baptiste's full name is Jean-Baptiste. And the baby's middle name is Joseph, after my father."

The boys blinked, looking crestfallen.

Then Jonah brightened. "Well, at least he's got hair."

"Yeah." Noah took a closer look at the baby. "And he doesn't look as much like a shar-pei as that baby that was here last week, so that's good."

"You don't tell someone their baby looks like a shar-pei, dummy!" Jonah said, thumping his brother in the belly with the back of his hand. "It's rude!"

"I said he looks *less* like a shar-pei!" Noah cried. "What's wrong with that? It's a compliment."

Jonah turned to Melody and opened his mouth, darting a look at her scar. But then he seemed to think better of it and stopped himself.

Melody shot Samira a discreet *here we go again* eye roll and plastered a pleasant smile on her face.

"Did you want to ask me something about my scar, Jonah? You can go ahead. I don't mind."

Jonah hesitated.

"If *you* have a baby, will it have the same kind of scar?" he asked with bright innocence. "On his neck and cheek and all?"

"Nope." Melody kept her voice upbeat even when she saw the wave of relief sweep across the boys' faces. "I wasn't born with the scar, so I can't pass it on."

"Not that there's anything wrong with your scar," Noah added hurriedly. "I think it's cool. Like a pirate. Pirates have cool scars. Or maybe you were in a knife fight or something."

"It doesn't look like a knife-fight scar, stupid!" Jonah cried. "That would be like a slice! Not—"

"Ah, guys?" Melody asked, smothering almost all of her laugh and trying to divert the conversation before it devolved into fisticuffs. "How's school going?"

"Great!" Jonah said, nicely distracted. "We get to start band this year."

"Band?" Samira said. "Awesome! What instruments are you playing?"

"Alto sax," Noah said.

"Tuba," Jonah said.

Samira and Melody blinked at each other. Melody decided to dive in and just ask.

"Ah, Jonah? Isn't the tuba about as big as you are?"

"It is. But I'm committed," Jonah said gravely.

"And how do your folks feel about you playing the tuba?" Samira asked, lips twitching.

"Not that excited, now that you mention it," Jonah said, frowning thoughtfully. "I wonder why?"

Disbelieving snort from Noah.

"It's because you sound like a constipated elephant when you play!" For dramatic effect, he balled up both fists, lined them up in front of his mouth and blew, producing a hair-raising sound that attracted the attention of people at nearby tables and did, in fact, remind Melody of an elephant suffering from gastric difficulties.

But the teasing did not go over well with Jonah, who went beet red and turned on his brother.

"Like *you* sound any better, idiot! And Mom told you to stop making fun of me!" He pivoted and took off toward the kitchen, propelled by righteous indignation. "Mom? Mom!"

"Stop being such a snitch," Noah called after him, hot on his heels.

They banged into the kitchen, the door swinging furiously behind them.

The women burst into laughter.

"That's what you have to look forward to in a few years, Sami," Melody said.

"I know, I know."

Melody handed the baby a teaspoon. He examined it carefully before placing it in his mouth and gnawing on it.

"So is everything all set for the big day? Need me to do anything?"

"We're in good shape," Samira said happily. "The wedding planner has everything under control."

"Good. I keep thinking about your almost wedding with Terrance last year. Remember that?"

Samira's ex-fiancé, Terrance, had canceled their wedding the night before, when he came out as gay. All that had happened a scant month or so before she met Baptiste, the love of her life.

"I *do* remember. I know hindsight is twenty-twenty, but I can't figure out what I was doing back then. It wasn't like I had a good feeling about the wedding. I had the biggest knot in my stomach that whole week. Think that was a clue?"

"You did?" Melody gaped at her. "Why didn't you say anything?"

Rueful shrug. "I didn't want to admit anything was wrong. The wedding train was already roaring down the tracks. I couldn't figure out how to jump off."

"Well, thank God Terrance pulled the cord, otherwise you wouldn't have *this* precious little guy." Melody kissed the baby on top of his head. He popped the spoon out of his mouth, looked up at her, then popped it back in again. "*And* a sexy billionaire fiancée who worships the ground you walk on and always has. I don't see Baptiste walking out on you the night before the wedding. At all."

"Yeah," Samira said, beaming and blushing to the roots of her hair. "He's not walking out on me."

Melody reached across the table and gave her hand a squeeze.

"I'm so happy for you, Sami. You deserve all this and more."

"Thanks," Samira said, returning the squeeze. "And *you*! I don't know how you think you're going to help me out this week when you're taking off for Anthony's investiture in London. What kind of maid of honor are *you*?"

"I know, I know. Sorry about that."

"Are you kidding?" Samira asked. "It's way past time you went over there."

"Don't start on me again. I wanted to be cautious. And I seem to recall that *you* were cautious when you and Baptiste first got together. If he'd suggested you start spending time in Paris to see if you wanted to move there, it would have freaked you out a little, too."

"Oh, whatever," Samira said. A sudden shadow dimmed some of the light in her eyes. "So…you're open to moving to London with him? I need to prepare myself if I'm about to lose my best friend."

A fair question, but one that still made Melody's chest tighten with uncertainty.

"I don't know. I can't imagine leaving Journey's End. I was born here. I grew up here. All my friends are here. I love the hospital and all my colleagues. My department just got that research grant…"

She shrugged helplessly, not really sure where she was going with this.

"But…?" Samira prompted.

"I'll be thirty-six soon. I want a couple babies like this one." She smoothed Jean-Luc's sweet-smelling hair. "Time is not on my side."

Samira nodded thoughtfully.

"In more ways than one. You're lucky the press hasn't found out about you yet. You know that, right? Especially with his investiture coming up. I stumbled onto one of those *Most Eligible Bachelor* stories about Anthony last week in the *Daily Universe*."

"The *Daily Universe*? You read that tabloid rag?"

"For the recipes and crossword puzzles, yeah," Samira said, trying not to laugh at herself. "Okay, yeah, I read it. Don't judge me."

"You make it hard," Melody said, rolling her eyes. "And that's one of the reasons I haven't gone to London before now. We can do whatever we want over here. You think we'd get away with that in London?"

"You're lucky he's willing to do that much flying all the time."

"I know. But we *did* spend that weekend in Paris with you and Baptiste. And we've met in Toronto and Bermuda, remember? So I've done *some* of the traveling. But Anthony loves Journey's End."

"The point is, it's time for you and Anthony to start discussing the future. And I'm betting he would have done that way before now if you hadn't shut him down."

"What's to discuss? Me giving up everything I've worked for and everything I know for a man who hasn't proposed and who's never even told me he loved me?"

"It's called *building a life together*. And if you think someone who didn't love you would take care of you when you have the flu, you're sadly mistaken. *I* love you to death, but I was happy to let you tough it out by your damn self and pray for your survival from afar."

"Thanks for that."

"You're welcome."

"It's just…It would be a huge sacrifice for either of us to move. I don't even know if he *can* move," Melody said. "But I can't picture my life without him. And only seeing him on the weekends? And only when we can make that happen with our schedules? We can't keep going like this. It's way too hard—"

Melody's phone chimed. The display showed that it was her sister Carmen wanting to video chat. She groaned and held it up for Samira to see.

"The Perfect Princess?" Samira asked, cringing. She and Carmen knew each other well and got along fine, but as Melody's best friend, Samira was well apprised of all the complicated sisterly dynamics.

"It's her birthday. She's returning my call."

"Oh, that's right. You want me to take the baby?"

"Nah. I got him." She hit the button and watched while the picture resolved and Carmen came into view. "Hey, girl! Happy Birthday! Look who I've got with me."

"Is that Jean-Luc?" Carmen beamed at him. Jean-Luc gurgled. "Hi, baby! Tell Samira I'm going to give him a big fat kiss when I see him at the wedding."

"Tell her yourself," Melody said, turning the phone around.

"Hey, Carmen," Samira said, waving. "Happy birthday! See you next Saturday!"

"See you next Saturday!"

Melody turned the phone back around. "So what're your big plans for your birthday?"

Carmen twiddled with an earring. "Ummm...not really sure."

This was a shocker, especially since Carmen was one of those folks who turned their birthday into a yearly weeklong extravaganza for her wide circle of snooty friends and never quite understood why the momentous occasion wasn't declared a national holiday. In the past, there'd been girl's trips to Vegas and Miami, spa weekends, cocktail parties, surprise parties, concerts and dinners. Last year, as documented by Carmen's minute-by-minute social media postings, Carmen's boyfriend, Leonard, had whisked her away to a surprise weekend in Cabo, the culmination of which was supposed to be an engagement ring. Yet Carmen remained stubbornly unengaged.

Melody, who had watched these Manhattanite proceedings from a safe distance here in Journey's End, found the whole thing exhausting, but to each his own.

Now this?

Squinting, she leaned in to take a closer look at her sister and didn't like what she saw. Carmen normally sported perfect hair, nails, clothes, shoes, bags, cars and pets, but not today.

Today, much to her surprise, Carmen looked drawn and tired, probably because her false eyelashes and accompanying makeup were not yet in place. Her hair was piled on top of her head in a messy ponytail and she seemed to still be wearing her workout clothes even though she'd normally be on her way to shopping and lunch with girlfriends this late on a Saturday morning.

"Everything okay, Carm?"

Carmen, naturally, got defensive.

"Of course I'm okay," she snapped. "Why wouldn't I be?"

"I don't know," Melody said, maintaining her pleasant attitude as best she could. "That's why I'm asking. Where's Leonard? How's he doing now that the campaign's in full swing?"

Carmen's boyfriend was running for the US Senate.

"He's great," Carmen said, but her smile looked more like a grimace, and Melody was almost sure she saw the glimmer of tears. "Hey, listen, I gotta go get ready. I'm sure he has something special planned for me. You good?"

"Yep." Melody, who'd been thinking she might finally mention Anthony to Carmen, decided that now was *not* the time. Carmen was never too keen on discussing other people's lives and Anthony's growing place in Melody's life deserved more attention than it seemed likely to get with Carmen's dwindling attention span. "I'll see you next weekend. Have a great night, okay?"

"Love you. Bye."

Carmen shot her an air kiss and hung up.

Melody sent Samira a raised-brow look across the table.

"What was all that about?" Samira asked.

"I don't know, but it was weird, right?"

"*Very* weird—"

"And here they are," said an amused male voice with a French accent. "The two most beautiful women in Journey's End."

They looked up in time to see Baptiste arrive at the table trailed by Anthony.

15

Having just finished their round of golf, they both had flushed faces and looked very sporty in their polo shirts and shorts. Anthony's avid gaze swept over Melody and the baby. He smiled, making her blood hum with pleasure. Once upon a time, she'd wondered if he would one day stop having this effect on her, but now she'd ruled that out as a possibility.

The groom-to-be, looking every bit as effervescent as his bride, leaned in to give Samira a kiss.

"*Êtes-vous contente, ma reine?*" he asked her.

Samira beamed up at him, happiness personified. "*Oui. Très contente.*"

Anthony, meanwhile, went straight to Melody for *his* kiss. It was unabashed and sweetly lingering as he cupped Jean-Luc's head for a little rub. Then he whispered in her ear.

"You look very good with a baby, darling."

"You think so, Blue?"

"Absolutely," he said as he withdrew, gave Samira a peck and sat.

Baptiste came around to give Melody her customary

double-cheeked kiss, then leaned in to plant several particularly wet raspberries on his son's fat cheek. The baby squirmed and waved his fists.

"He's going to smile very soon," Baptiste announced to the table at large. "I can feel it—*what's this*?"

He dodged as Jean-Luc nearly nailed him on the nose with a fist.

"A spoon?" He took the offending object and examined it in minute and slobbery detail. "Who gave him this? Was it washed first? I don't want any germs to—"

"Yes, yes, I know, you don't want any germs," said Melody, who was sick to death of this overprotective father routine, which was already wearing thin a few short weeks into the poor boy's life. "You *do* realize that I'm a highly trained medical professional who specializes in children, right? You think I had everyone in the room suck on the spoon before I gave it to the baby?"

Baptiste blinked.

"Honestly, you need to pace yourself," Melody told him. "What's left? Building a plastic bubble for the boy to live in?"

"Already ordered," Baptiste said with dignity. "It will be here in two days."

"Oh, my God," Melody said, smacking her forehead as they all laughed. "So how was golf?"

"Samira's father, Daniel and I did very well, obviously," Baptiste said, referencing Daniel Harper, one of his close friends here in Journey's End, as he squirted sanitizer from the little bottle he now kept dangling from one of his belt loops and cleaned his hands. Then he reached for the baby. Melody gave Jean-Luc a final kiss and sadly relinquished him to his doting father, grateful she'd been allowed any time with the boy at all. "Anthony was a tragic embarrassment. To no one's surprise."

"Are you going to let him talk about you like that?" Melody asked Anthony.

"It's true," Anthony said, sighing harshly and hanging his head in shame. "Stank up the place so badly the groundskeepers came out to see if there was a decaying whale carcass somewhere on the course."

More laughter all around as Baptiste sat next to Melody and settled the baby on his lap.

"But the course is spectacular," Anthony continued. "High up on the hill overlooking the river and the mountains on the other side. I don't think St. Andrews has much on it, to be honest."

"High praise," Samira said.

"Yes, well, there's a lot about Journey's End to love, isn't there?" Anthony said thoughtfully. "Lots of hidden gems."

"*I* have certainly fallen in love with it," Baptiste said with a loving glance at his fiancée.

"Just think," Melody said. "This time next week, we'll have a newly minted earl and a pair of newlyweds amongst us. Are you ready for your big day, lovebirds?"

Baptiste and Samira exchanged one of their customary smoldering looks.

"We're ready," Samira said, blushing.

"We would be long married by now, if I had my way about it," Baptiste said. "But what do *I* know about it? No one was listening to me."

"And no one wants to hear your tragic tale of woe, either," Samira said, laughing. "Anthony, I'm sorry we can't come to your investiture. If it had been any other week—"

"Yes, well, you're a bit busy at the moment," Anthony said. "I understand."

"And speaking of," Samira said, eyeballing Baptiste and tapping her watch. "We still need to run to Target."

"Target?" Anthony asked.

"We need diapers for Jean-Luc and toiletries for the honeymoon," Baptiste said, all but levitating with excitement. "I love the travel section. They have a whole wall of sample sizes. There's no place like Target. I've always said so."

"What can I say?" Samira asked Anthony and Melody with an indulgent smile. "I'm marrying a simple man with simple tastes."

"I am *very* simple," Baptiste deadpanned to more laughter. He stood and put the baby in the stroller. "All I need for a happy life is Samira, the baby and good friends, with maybe a nice bottle of wine and a cheese plate. *Voilà.* That's me."

"What about the Tesla?" Melody asked.

"Well, yes, obviously I also need the Tesla," Baptiste said.

"And the jet," Anthony said.

"The jet doesn't hurt," Baptiste admitted. He hesitated. "You know who is also a very simple man, Melody?"

Melody's cheeks flamed.

"Don't start," Anthony muttered before she could answer, shifting uncomfortably and tugging his ear. "Haven't I suffered enough embarrassment for one day?"

"You two just make sure you're back from London in time for the rehearsal dinner Friday night," Samira said with a stern look as she stood and slung her Chanel bag over her shoulder. "I don't want any delays or drama. Got it?"

"Got it," Melody said, raising her right hand in an oath.

"And I meant to tell you that Nick will be here Friday," Baptiste told Anthony. "We'll have to warn all the local women to guard against his Latin charm and stunning good looks."

"Noted," Anthony said.

"Travel safe," Samira told them as good-byes were exchanged all around. "See you Friday."

"See you Friday."

Anthony watched them go, then sank into the chair across the table from Melody, his color high. "Have I mentioned how excited I am about our London trip?"

"Oh, I know. You've been dying for me to try your authentic fish and chips with the skin still on, haven't you?"

He repressed a snort. "No. I've been dying to have you on *my* turf for a bit. See if I might persuade you to spend a great deal more time there, as you well know. I think we're ready to come out of the shadows now. Don't you?"

No. She didn't.

As someone who'd spent half her life in the shadows, hiding behind her hair, her surgical mask and her career, she felt quite comfortable with the shadows. The shadows were her friends.

What she wasn't ready for?

People staring at her for a whole new reason. Pointing. Whispering. Invading her privacy.

"And did I mention that Granny's set up tea with me and my father? She thought it was a good idea since he'll be at the investiture. The two of them hate each other's guts and they haven't seen each other in years. Granny's hoping to *smooth things over*"—he made air quotes —"before the ceremony. She'd sooner resurrect my mother and get *her* to the ceremony, but there's no reasoning with Granny when she gets something into her head. It'll be a nightmare," he concluded darkly. "You mark my words."

"I'd love to be a fly on the wall."

"And speaking of…I'm sorry you can't attend the ceremony, darling. It's protocol."

"It's okay," she reassured him for what felt like the

dozenth time. "Girlfriends don't go to things like this. Only fiancées, and only after they've met the Queen."

He didn't look at all convinced. "You're sure?"

She kept her game smile firmly in place, secretly relieved that she wouldn't meet the Queen just yet. This new phase of her relationship with Anthony seemed daunting enough without *that* additional complication right now.

"I'm positive."

"I'm sorry this first trip will be so short. And that we can't fly together. But I've got to get back early for preparations and whatnot."

"And I need to stay and help Samira with a few wedding duties. Strange that we have two huge events scheduled for the same week, isn't it?"

"Yes, well, I can't expect Baptiste to schedule his wedding around my investiture. But it'll all work out. I can't wait to show you everything. All the museums. Westminster Abbey. The Tower. St. Paul's. The bridges. The local pubs and markets. Not all on *this* trip, of course, but soon."

She laughed, wondering when she'd seen him this excited about anything.

"I don't hear you saying Harrods and Selfridge's. Is that an oversight, or…?"

"You don't want *me* showing you around department stores. I don't *shop*." He shuddered. "My head would explode and shower brain matter all over the lovely display cases. It would be disastrous for everyone."

She laughed.

"You won't need your own car this go round," he continued.

A *car*?

"But next time I'll have to start teaching you to drive on the other side of the street."

"Don't you mean the *wrong* side?" she said, trying to keep it light before her head began to spin with everything he'd just thrown at her. Was he seriously thinking of getting her a *car*?

"Funny. You can borrow my car for now. We can drive around the grounds at first. Make sure you don't kill too many unsuspecting members of the general public. And then we'll eventually look at getting you your own car. Oh, and I want you to see the hospitals. You'll love St. Mary's. It's not too far from KP. Very manageable."

As always when they tiptoed to the edge of this line, she felt the inevitable prickle of nerves up and down her arms and a growing tightness in her chest.

"I can't wait to see all of it," she said, which was true even if the thought of her pending introduction into his world —and the attendant expectations—overwhelmed her.

There was a pause while he eyed her a bit more closely than she would have liked.

"So why do you look so scared?" he asked gently. "And don't bother denying it."

Why did she—?

Did he seriously need to ask?

"Oh, I don't know. Maybe because I'm about to step way outside my comfort zone. Maybe because I'm about to become the world's biggest fish out of water, spending time on the grounds of *Kensington Palace,* which is where my boyfriend, the *prince,* lives."

"I'm not a prince."

She barked out an incredulous laugh. "Do you want me to smack you right now? Is that it?"

"Look," he said, leaning in and hunkering over the table as he lowered his voice. "This is about you and me and our relationship. Bottom line. And I am very clear about my feelings for you. I'm equally clear about my determination to protect you. I know my world can be daunting—"

"*Can be?*"

"But I will always do everything in my power to smooth the way for you. To make sure you have the best possible life."

She said nothing, frozen inside her ambivalence and her equally strong desire not to hurt his feelings.

He frowned. "What? Why are you looking at me like that? Don't you believe me?"

She ran a hand through her hair, struggling for the right words.

"I believe you mean it. But I've seen some of the coverage your cousins and their spouses have gone through. I saw some of the things the tabloids said about them. Slut-shaming and weight-shaming and fashion-shaming. You name it. The way their privacy got destroyed and everyone they ever knew and trusted, down to their kindergarten teachers, sold stories about them. Were *they* protected? Isn't it a pipe dream to think you can protect someone?"

"These are bridges we'll have to cross when we get there. Because the two of us are a great team. And we're very happy together." His gaze, hard and searching, held hers. "Aren't we?"

With that, he melted her heart. The way he always did.

"We're ecstatic together."

He smiled without smiling, an event that deepened his dimples and made the corners of his eyes crinkle, and reached across the table for her hand.

She gave it to him. They held on tight while he smoothed a thumb over her spoon ring, a long and delicious moment of complete understanding.

"Isn't that the most important thing?" he asked. "Aren't all the rest minor details to be worked out later?"

It would be so easy to swallow her trepidation, take a handful of antacids to mitigate the resulting stomachache and agree with him. She *wanted* to agree with him and bask in this glowing warmth forever. But she'd lived too long and knew too much about life to ignore her gut feelings. No matter how tempting it was to do so.

She thought about her hospital, which she loved.

Her colleagues and friends, including her mentor, Dr. Muhammed, who she loved.

Her apartment, which she loved.

Her town.

Her *life*.

Was she ready to let all this go, move thousands of miles away and engineer an entirely new existence solely around her relationship with a man, no matter how much she cared about him?

Could she do all of that?

Her doubts crowded into the front of her mind, demanding to be recognized and counted.

She withdrew her hand and put it in her lap with the other one, sorry to see his expression fall.

"That's easy for you to say," she said quietly. "Because all the *minor details* are on my side of the equation."

He blinked and turned away, his jaw hardening.

"Is that you, Melody Harrison?" said a cheery male voice to one side of their table. "Just the woman I need."

Startled but also eager to exit this increasingly difficult conversation with Anthony, she manufactured a pleasant smile and super-glued it to her face, hoping it looked authentic. Then she looked around to discover none other than Raymond Martin, Journey's End's real estate agent extraordinaire, accessorized with a bright smile and a to-go coffee cup. Today's dapper ensemble included a Panama hat, pumpkin colored Oxford shirt and dark pants creased to razor-edged perfection. His dog and omnipresent sidekick, a terror of a Jack Russell terrier named Bobsy, wore a bandana speckled with fall leaves in coordinating colors and carried...yes, that was a stuffed hedgehog... in his mouth.

"Hey, Raymond," Melody said, standing for a quick hug and kiss. "Hey, Bobsy. What've you got there?"

Raymond grimaced.

"The vet says this canine is too anxious. Probably because I'm always yelling at him when he gets into stuff. Like the neighbor's root garden the other day. Bobsy ate every turnip, carrot and beet in sight. He ignored the parsnips, but I can't really blame him for that. So the vet suggested he needed a support object to take with him everywhere and keep him occupied."

"Is that working?"

"Well, since he's chewed up the stuffed bunny, the stuffed cat and the stuffed bear so far this week, I'd say that's a big, fat, expensive *no*. Hello," he said, turning to Anthony and extending his hand. "Raymond Martin. Don't I know you?"

"I don't believe so," Anthony said, looking amused as they shook. "I'm—"

"Oh, my God, you're Anthony Scott, the Queen's grandson." Raymond gaped at him, covering his mouth with his free hand. "I just saw you in a documentary about the Queen a couple of weeks ago."

Oh, *shit*.

"Well...yes," Anthony said. He glanced around to make sure no one else was paying them any attention, shot Melody a *let me handle this* look and leaned closer to Raymond, acquiring a conspiratorial air. "Could you do me a favor and not mention it, though? I'm on a, ah, private visit here. I'd hate to have it ruined by the paparazzi."

"Of course," Raymond cried, now pressing Anthony's hand between both of his and shaking vigorously. His speculative gaze, meanwhile, swung between Anthony and Melody. Melody focused on keeping her polite smile in place and looking innocent of any romantic activities, but to no avail. She saw the exact moment the lightbulb went off over Raymond's head and the corresponding widening of his eyes. "Of *course*. I'm the soul of discretion. Well, not normally," he added with a rueful chuckle, "but I will be this time. I won't even tell my husband, Fletcher. Who would die if he knew. Tell me…what's she like?"

Anthony looked startled. "Who? My grandmother?"

"Yes! Who else?"

"Well, she's terrifying, obviously," Anthony said after a thoughtful pause.

"I knew it!"

"And also a huge teddy bear. But I will deny I ever said that."

Raymond laughed and finally turned Anthony's hand loose.

"I like him," Raymond told Melody.

"Glad to hear it," Melody said, pointing at Bobsy. "But your little friend is about to get himself into trouble."

Bobsy, true to form, had taken advantage of Raymond's distraction, dropped the hedgehog, put his paws up on a recently vacated but uncleared table and was happily helping himself to the remnants of a giant muffin and a bowl of fruit.

"Bobsy!" Raymond cried. "Bad dog! See what I have to deal with? *I* should be the one with the emotional support toy. Get down, Bobsy. *Get down!*"

Anthony and Melody grinned and did their best to

smother their laughter behind Raymond's back while Bobsy took his time about finishing his snack and lowering his front paws to the floor.

"Oh, for God's sake," Raymond said, now brushing crumbs off the dog's bandana. "We'd better get out of here before the health department shows up. I'm sure your British dogs are much better mannered, Anthony."

"Not at all," Anthony assured him. "My grandmother's beagles are just as bad."

"I knew it!" Raymond grabbed the hedgehog from the floor, handed it to Bobsy and focused on Melody. "Good news, Mel. The Jamesons have finally decided to make the move to the retirement community. I knew you'd want to be the first to know."

"The Jamesons?" Melody clapped her hands together while her excited heart thundered into high gear at this news that her dream house might finally be coming to market after she'd had her eye on it for over a year. It actually sat high on the hill overlooking the gazebo, down the street from Howard's Folly, the house Baptiste and Samira had recently renovated and now occupied. The Jameson house was about a third of the size of that house, but it would be perfect for Melody's needs with its four bedrooms, solarium, newly renovated gourmet kitchen and proximity to the hospital. "Are you serious? Don't toy with my emotions."

Raymond grinned and crossed his heart. "I'd never lie about something like that. They'll need about a month to declutter and get it listed, so now's the time for you to make sure you have your financing all set."

"What's all this?" Anthony's gaze, flinty now, swung between the two of them. "What's going on?"

Melody froze, her heart crashing through the floor as her two worlds collided.

Oh, shit.

Oh, *shit*.

She couldn't very well buy a house here in Journey's End while also exploring the possibility of moving to London with Anthony, now could she?

"My dream house is about to hit the market," she said, watching the color slowly leach away from Anthony's face.

16

London!

She was in. Freaking. *London!*

Melody hurried down the jetway, rolling her carry-on behind her and turning her phone back on with her free hand. Honestly, she didn't know why people complained about jet lag when they flew to Europe. You hopped an overnight flight, you popped a sleeping pill and—boom! There you were, refreshed and ready for your grand overseas adventure. Someone had even ordered up a sunny fall day for her. No rain in sight.

Grinning to herself, she sped up, dodging a slow-moving couple that evidently had nowhere to be today or possibly ever.

Okay, so...Think, Mel. Get yourself organized.

First thing? Let Anthony know she'd landed safely. And he'd sent a driver to meet her, so she should also send him a quick text to let him know she'd made it to the gate—

Her phone pinged.

And pinged and pinged and pinged. Like twenty times.

She frowned down at it, resisting the nightmare thought that someone had died.

The first message was from Samira:

OMG! I'm so sorry! Call and let me know when you land!

Next message? Anthony:

It'll be okay. Call me.

Dread crawled up her spine and tightened around her throat.

From her mother:

Call us, Sweetie. We love you!

After that? A bunch of messages from people at work that she didn't bother reading.

But what the hell had happened? She darted out of the flow of traffic and over to the nearest wall, where she frantically scrolled through her messages with rising frustration. Why didn't anyone say what was going on—

And there it was, finally, a British tabloid article's image and headline popping up in a message (*WTF??? Why didn't you tell me???*) from one of her med school besties:

The Earl and His Girl?

And it included a picture of Anthony smiling down at her in the receiving line back in Tanzania all those months ago. With the veiled heat on their faces as they looked at each other, they might as well have been caught doing the morning-after walk of shame outside the presidential suite at the Waldorf. The two of them were actually in the background. The dancing children were the subject of the picture, which probably explained how she and Anthony had been able to fly under the radar this whole time.

Still.

Their little cat was out of the bag now, wasn't it?

She slumped against the wall, her head spinning because she knew that, no matter what happened between her and

Anthony now, life as she'd known it up until three minutes ago was over.

O-V-E-R.

"Dr. Harrison?" A female airline employee hurried around the corner and craned her neck as she scanned the crowd. "Is there a Dr. Harrison here?"

Melody cringed, privately debated whether to make a run for it or raise her hand and finally decided on the latter.

"I'm Dr. Harrison."

"Oh, thank goodness." The woman's expression cleared as she beckoned Melody over, shook her hand and set off walking at a brisk pace. "I'm Bridgette. Your escort. Let's get you out of here."

Escort?

"I'm a little confused," Melody said. "I thought I had a driver to pick me up."

"Oh, he's here as well, ma'am—"

Ma'am?!

"—but the press are all congregated outside baggage claim like jackals around a carcass. So you need the escort. Here we are."

And she stopped in front of one of those golf cart things that Melody had only ever seen used for the disabled and the elderly. Oh, and there'd been that one time out of JFK, when she'd been on her way to a medical conference in Miami and she'd sworn she'd seen Denzel Washington zoom by with his handlers, but she couldn't be sure.

Stifling a burst of hysterical laughter, Melody reached for her overnight bag—"I'll get that for you, ma'am," Bridgette said, snatching it from her before she could exert herself—and climbed aboard.

Bridgette whisked her through customs. Whisked her through the airport. Whisked her through baggage claim. All of it went like clockwork to Melody's stunned mind, making her wonder what the big freaking deal was and why she couldn't just grab her bag and go like all the other passengers were going.

But then Bridgette whisked her through some side door, to where "the car," which turned out to be a brand new gleaming black Range Rover that had evidently driven straight from the factory assembly line to pick her up, idled at the curb.

"This'll all be over in a jiffy," Bridgette said with a deep breath and a supportive squeeze to Melody's arm. "Do you have sunglasses with you? Why don't you go ahead and put them on? There you go. Right, then. Someone will grab your bags for you. Don't you worry about that. All right. On three. One...two...*three*."

They hurried through the doors and outside to where a bright London morning, a cool breeze, a couple of airport security guys, the car and—*oh, shit!*—five or six shouting photographers waited to swarm her. One of the security guys took her arm and frog-marched her to the car, which was good because stunned paralysis had set it and she probably would have stood there gaping at the unfolding scene if not for them.

"Melody!"

"Over here, pet! Keep your head up!"

"Has he proposed, then?"

"Will you be meeting the Queen at the investiture?"

"Where did you meet?"

"Move your hair out of the way, Mel. Let's get a picture of that scar."

Melody reached up to smooth her hair and make sure it *was* covering her scar—

"There it is. Isn't that the Queen's spoon ring, Mel?" The

shutters clicked even faster. "Did he give it to you? Is it a promise ring?"

"Pretty little thing, aren't you? Why don't you give us a smile? Start things out on the right foot on this side of the pond. Go on, then. It won't hurt you to help us out a bit. We're only doing our jobs, Mel. No need to be a bitch."

Melody hurried faster, resisting the strong urge to swing on *that* guy. She wished she'd bothered to brush her hair and take a bit more time with her makeup now that her picture was going to be splashed all over the place. Wished she'd worn something other than her favorite weathered jeans and white peasant shirt.

Wished she'd had just a *bit* more advance warning that her life was about to blow the fuck up.

"Mel…Mel…*Melody!*"

The paparazzi jostled closer, the shutters of their fancy cameras clicking furiously as they tightened the ring of bodies surrounding her and made it all but impossible for her to walk the twenty feet or so to the car. One of them was an older man with more salt than pepper in his hair; one had an arm sleeved with colorful tattoos; one smelled like her grandfather's sporty aftershave from back in the day. There were no police nearby, which made her wonder what would happen if things really got out of control. It wasn't hard to picture them knocking her down, possibly trampling her. Nor did it strain her imagination to envision one of them with a gun or other weapon if he wanted to hurt her.

Arctic water ran through her veins at *that* thought, turning her blood to ice.

The hand on her arm tightened. The security people elbowed their way through and deposited her in the back of the car, quickly slamming the door shut behind her. The paparazzi converged on the car, straining to aim their lenses at her through the window the way she'd done in the past when she tried to get good shots of the pandas at the National Zoo. The trunk slammed. Someone smacked the car twice, a signal.

And they zoomed off, quickly merging into traffic as the photographers disappeared behind them.

Melody slumped back against the cushions, shell-shocked and, she realized for the first time, trembling.

"You all right, ma'am?" The driver glanced at her over his shoulder, another jolt because he and the steering wheel were on the right side of the car. "That was a little hairy, wasn't it?"

"You can say that again," Melody said shakily. "Thanks for the rescue."

"My pleasure. Get yourself settled. We'll be there in no time. Water bottle?"

"I'm good, thanks."

"All right. Buckle up, then. I'll just radio ahead. Let them know we're on our way."

"What's your name?"

"Hank, ma'am."

"Do me a favor, Hank. Call me Melody. You're adding ten years to my age every time you call me ma'am."

He chuckled. "I'll try, ma—I mean Melody. No promises."

"Thanks, Hank. For everything."

He nodded, eyes twinkling at her for a second in the rearview mirror before he focused on driving.

She, meanwhile, buckled up and pulled out her phone, dread congealing in her belly and backing up all the way to her throat. There were two new messages from Anthony wanting to know whether she'd landed safely and if the escort had connected with her, but she couldn't bring herself to answer him just yet.

She had some reading to do.

As best she could tell, the *Daily Universe* had broken the story of their romance. Honestly, the article was such a trope-filled caricature of the tabloid culture that she would have laughed if she hadn't been so stunned. There were references to their *romantic getaway,* the way they'd *gazed lovingly into each other's eyes* and seemed *deeply in love* as cited by *sources close to the couple*. There were actually several grainy photos of them laughing together in the receiving line, a couple of which were filled with so much veiled heat and longing on both their faces that she had to marvel that their story hadn't broken until now.

And that was just the beginning of the fun, folks.

There were *more* articles. More tropes.

There was one about her status as a science-y smart girl that included the picture from her hospital bio, the one that had led Anthony to want to meet her in the first place.

And there was one of the ones she'd dreaded most, right on top:

The noble burn victim.

Because she'd *overcome a tragic childhood accident* that left her *horribly disfigured despite her lovely eyes and hair* and had *bravely soldiered through years of horrific treatments* and *built a life to be proud of* while she *inspired others with her bravery and toughness* and hoped for *surgical advances that might make it easier for her to look in the mirror one day*.

The only good thing? There were no accompanying close-up pictures of her scar, but it was early yet. With her luck? She'd just provided the paps the shot they needed for the next round of articles.

Melody fumed in silence for a moment, longing to roll her window down and hurl her phone to the pavement as the car sped along at sixty miles an hour. As if she'd had a choice to do anything other than keep her chin up and put one foot in front of the other after her accident! What were her other options? To curl up into the fetal position under her blankets and never come out? To kill herself?

The smug SOBs who made up this shit didn't know *anything* about her. It was so galling to see her entire life, everything she'd ever done, been or experienced, reduced to a few hundred poorly written words by some "reporter" who'd never even met her.

What gave them the right to write and sell this garbage?

Angry tears burned the backs of her eyes. She swiped them away and kept reading.

A body language expert had been trotted out to opine that the color in Anthony's cheeks and the tilt of her head indicated that they were both equally besotted with each other and therefore well matched.

Ah. And here was the other storyline she'd really been dreading.

An expert on the royals had weighed in with his dog whistle opinion that *a woman like Melody* with *her unusual background* would *present a delicate challenge to the courtiers* who had *certain expectations and traditions* in mind for Anthony. But, he decided on a determinedly upbeat note, *A modern woman like Melody, who is capable of rising above her humble urban beginnings, may well be the breath of fresh air needed to bring the monarchy into the twenty-first century.*

Translation? The royal white folks in the palace weren't ready for a hood rat like Melody to invade their hallowed inner sanctum and get fried chicken grease and watermelon juice on their silk drapes.

Melody dropped the phone into her lap and made an involuntary and incoherent sound of rage.

"You okay, ma'am?" the driver asked, glancing at her in the rearview mirror.

Melody reined herself in, manufactured a smile and picked up the phone again.

"I'm great. Thanks."

"Let me know if you need anything."

"Thanks," she said again, scrolling through more articles.

You had to love the twenty-four-hour news cycle, boy.

You hopped a flight as a private citizen, went to sleep and woke up as a viral sensation.

There was an article about her clothes and hair, with photos culled from her social media and some fancy-schmancy stylist offering her two cents on how Melody could benefit from some smoothing serum to tame her unruly ringlets. That particular article also referenced the pants and shirt Melody had worn in Tanzania, as though she showed promise as a fashionista in the making.

Melody dropped her phone again in utter disbelief.

Those clothes were from TJ MAXX, people! She'd bought them on sale! They didn't signify anything other than they seemed airy and cool and offered protection from being bitten by nasty African bugs!

She rubbed her forehead, took a couple of deep breaths, wishing she had a Guinness or three, and dove in again.

Let's see…let's see…

Well, this article was nice. Sort of. It mentioned her education and career, stating that she'd be the first royal wife with such a high-powered career although she would, sadly, have to curtail it in favor of charity work.

She snorted. As if anything could induce her to scale back her career now that she'd finally finished her training and was a full-fledged surgeon. Please. No one ever expected the men to make the grand sacrifice for their relationship, did they?

Nothing like hopping into a time machine and finding yourself back in 1953.

And there was... hang on, what was this headline?

The Earl's Future Sister-in-Law?

The article included—*oh, my God!*—a mug shot of her sister Carmen, aka the Perfect Princess!

She quickly scanned for the details. Carmen had—*oh, my God!!!*—been arrested for a DUI this past Friday night. Well, that certainly explained why she'd been acting so weird during the video chat the two of them had with Samira at Java Nectar on Saturday, didn't it? The charges were still pending...she'd spent the night in jail and pled no contest...her career as a top NYC dermatologist was in question...her boyfriend Leonard, the junior senatorial candidate, had issued a statement:

"Although Dr. Carmen Harrison and I have ended our relationship, I wish her nothing but the best in the future and hope that she gets the treatment she needs."

Treatment? Carmen wasn't an alcoholic! She rarely, if ever, had more than a second glass of wine at dinner! She didn't need *treatment*! That lying rat bastard! Stringing Carmen along all this time, then dumping and disowning her when she got into trouble! Ditching her like a rat leaving a sinking ship, all to protect his own worthless hide from scandal as he ran for political office!

Melody pressed a hand to her heart, trying not to hyperventilate. Her life had exploded in the last hour or so, sure, but poor Carmen. She didn't deserve *this*.

Melody dialed her number and held the phone up to her

ear so the driver couldn't hear, watching the London skyline go by but seeing nothing—

"Hello?"

"Hey," Mel said quietly, noting the strain in her sister's voice. "Can't really talk right now, but I just wanted to check in. How's it going?"

There was a long silence that quickly turned brittle.

"Well, I don't know. Let me think….let me think…oh, there was that *one* thing." Carmen snapped her fingers. "I've kinda had a tough week. I've been arrested, fired—"

"*Fired?* Oh, no, Carmen."

"—and dumped. Oh, and I've also been *outed* in a huge way about all of that because it turns out my sister the saint is dating a freaking *prince*! And she never said *anything* about it to me."

"'The saint'?" Melody echoed, stung. "Where'd *that* come from?"

Disbelieving snort from Carmen.

"Nowhere. Listen, I gotta go. Between hiring a criminal lawyer, polishing my résumé and joining all the online dating sites so I can get married and have a couple of kids before my last remaining egg shrivels up like a prune, I really don't have time for chatting on the phone."

"Fine. I just wanted you to know that I had no idea things would unfold like this. I would have given you a heads-up. And I, ah…I'm sorry things didn't work out with Leonard—"

"No, you're not! Why are you such a freaking hypocrite? You *never* liked him. You *never* thought he was right for me. You *never* thought he would propose. And now you expect me to believe you're *sorry* that it didn't work out and he bailed on me at the first whiff of trouble? Is that what's going on here?"

"Oh, my God." Melody tried to keep the rising frustration

out of her voice. Carmen was hurt and upset. She was lashing out. Melody knew that. It was, therefore, her job to be the bigger person and not rise to Carmen's bait. No matter how impossible a task that turned out to be. "I wasn't his biggest fan, no, but I'm sorry that you're hurt. I want you to be happy. That's all I meant to say."

"Yeah? Well, I want *you* to be happy, too, so here's what *I* mean to say: you're not going to be happy packing up and moving to London and living in some gilded palace where you can't say what you really think or come and go without the Queen's permission and a bunch of security guys to escort you from point A to point B. You're not going to be happy wearing, I don't know, spectator hats and white gloves while you do charity work and go to Ascot and the opening of Parliament and shit instead of focusing on your career and trying to save little kids' lives in the operating room. And if you think that falling in love with your Prince Charming is going to override all of *that,* then you are sadly mistaken. And you deserve what you get."

There was a long and poisonous silence while Melody pressed her lips together to hold back what was either going to be a roar of rage or a sob of despair. She wondered why she'd bothered to call her sister in the first place.

Most of all, she wondered why sisters always insisted on telling the truth in all its brutality.

"Mel?" Carmen finally asked.

"Wow." Melody took a deep breath and tried to even out her wobbly voice. "That's quite a list. Anything else?"

"Look, Mel." Carmen's voice acquired a conciliatory tone that didn't do much to soothe Melody's scalded feelings. "I didn't mean to—"

Melody's other line beeped.

"I need to go," Melody said, eagerly seizing the opportunity to exit this excruciating conversation and not bothering to check the display. "I'll talk to you later."

"Come on, Mel—"

Melody hung up on her, savoring a moment of petty triumph before she clicked over to the incoming call.

"Yes, hello?"

"Miss Melody?" boomed a male with a Texas twang that probably carried a fat silver belt buckle, a pair of crocodile cowboy boots and a longhorn steer with it. "Tony Scott here. You're having a hell of a day, aren't you?"

Melody froze.

Anthony's father!

She hadn't spoken to him since her bout with the flu several months back, and now didn't feel like the ideal time to start. But what could she do?

"Truer words were never spoken. How did you get my number?"

"Honey, I've got folks on my payroll who could build me a spaceship and fly me to the moon by supper if I asked them to. Getting your phone number ain't exactly a superhuman challenge. Where are you?"

"On my way in from Heathrow."

"Good. I'm already here, installed in my old digs at KP. So we'll be neighbors for the next couple days, but there won't be much downtime, will there? Glad I caught you on neutral turf where you can talk a minute. Before you walk through those golden gates and get swallowed up by the machine."

Swallowed up by the machine.

Now *there* was a term guaranteed to make her run screaming from the room. Not that she planned to admit it.

She frowned. "Excuse me?"

"Don't get your hackles up and act all bewildered. It's just me and you having a quick chitchat. One outsider to another. You know damn good and well what I'm talking about."

She supposed she did. She was about to step onto the grounds of Kensington Palace and into a world as foreign to her as Outer Mongolia. A place where issues surrounding the Queen's authority, Anthony's sense of duty, class, race, wealth and protocol were, quite possibly, about to chew her up and spit her out.

That being the case, a tiny part of her appreciated having an ally on Team Outsider.

Was she suspicious of Tony? Of course. She'd heard more than enough about him from Anthony to be wary of the older man's motives.

Still. She wanted to hear what he had to say and prayed he might have some useful advice for her.

Something to take the edge off of Carmen's dire pronouncement just now.

"What's up, Tony?"

"Now, listen." Tony's voice dropped. Acquired a conspiratorial air. "The thing you don't want to do right now is give up your judgment and let yourself be railroaded into something that's not right for you. I don't care who's doing the railroading. If something makes your stomach hurt, don't do it."

Very sensible. Melody breathed a sigh of relief and felt some of the tension ease through her shoulders.

"Okay…?"

"I want you to benefit from my hard-earned experience. There are days when I think that, if I had it to do all over again, I'd go back to the beginning and pass on the whole adventure. Stay in my lane back in Houston and never meet Lou-Lou. Never get married. Never have Anthony. Save myself the worst heartache a man can have and still live."

Melody put her elbow on the armrest, pressed her forehead to her hand and let her eyes roll closed. Which was a better option than, say, roaring with frustration and punching her fist through the window.

"How is that helpful?" she asked wearily.

"Patience, Miss Mel. But if I chose that option, then I'd have missed out on the greatest joys a man can have. Never have met the love of my life. Never have Anthony." Harsh sigh. "And there's never any percentage in taking the coward's way out, is there? You're never going to win big if you hide from life."

Melody raised her head. Frowned thoughtfully.

"The thing I really regret—and here's the part that'll help you, if I haven't put you to sleep with the rambling—is that I didn't stand and fight. I let myself be run off. Let outside factors come between me and the woman I loved. Lost sight of the big picture. And here's what I want you to know."

Melody found herself sitting up straighter and listening harder.

"You're at a fork in your road right now, aren't you? You can take the easy way out and head on back to Journey's End. Tell yourself that this life isn't right for you. That's what I did when I signed off on a divorce I didn't want. You'll be nice and safe that way, but you'll have to live knowing that you had it all, or almost had it all, but threw it all away because you decided that fighting for it was too hard. And take it from me." Tony cleared his throat. "That's a mighty bitter pill to swallow."

Melody hesitated, trying to digest all that, and looked out the window just in time to see another gaggle of paparazzi swarm the car and try to snap her picture as they made the final approach to palace grounds.

But she was already in the car this time and they were quickly relegated to the rear-view mirror.

And then there was the quiet tree-lined street full of stately homes that seemed to belong in some regency romance novel and were so different from the quaint and cozy Cape Cods and colonials that she was used to back home. The wrought iron gate, guard station and security presence at the end. The breathtaking grounds.

The unmistakable red brick facade of Kensington Palace, the place where Anthony had grown up.

Her heart didn't know whether to explode with excitement or expire from terror.

All she knew was that, for better or for worse, she'd now slipped through the looking glass with Alice.

Or maybe she'd left Kansas and entered Oz with Dorothy.

Either way, she was a big-ass fish out of water swimming into the unknown.

"Miss Mel? Any of that make any sense to you?"

"Yeah," she said quietly, just as the car rolled to a stop in front of Anthony's current home, Loxley Cottage, a cozy ivy-covered and white picket-fenced red brick structure that felt much more manageable to her than ye grand olde palace over yonder. "It makes perfect sense."

"What're you going to do?"

"Hell if I know," she admitted.

"You'll figure it out. Least I think you will. Otherwise, you're not the woman I think you are. And I may be a lot of things, but a bad judge of character is not one of them."

She laughed until she saw the cottage door open and her pulse began to pound.

"Gotta go," she said quickly, just as Anthony stepped out with his phone pressed to his ear, his expression tight and anxious as he looked for her. "Thanks for the advice. I appreciate it."

"Anytime, Miss Mel," Tony said, chuckling. "You'll let me know how this fairy tale turns out, won't you?"

"As soon as I get it figured out myself."

17

Mindful of Hank, who busied himself with her bags, Anthony gave her a subdued "Hello, darling," and peck on the cheek. Then he led her into the cottage's sitting room, which was a window-filled slice of English country chic heaven. With its expensive navy-patterned upholstery and high-end antiques, it wasn't exactly the sort of leather-drenched man cave/bachelor pad she might expect to see back home, but she was betting it was also a far cry from the grandeur next door at KP. She checked it all out with keen interest, well aware of Anthony's watchful and concerned attention on her the whole time.

"I think that's everything, then," Hank said after he'd taken her bags down the hall to the bedroom. "Give a shout if you need anything. Pleasure to meet you ma—I mean, Melody."

"You too, Hank," she said, shaking his hand. "Thanks again."

Anthony frowned. "You didn't just call Dr. Harrison *Melody,* did you, Hank?"

"I didn't want to, boss," Hank said, holding his hands up. "She told me to."

"Well, you'd better do what she says," Anthony said with a resigned sigh. "She'll make my life a living hell otherwise."

"That's what I figured. You don't want to mess things up with this one. She classes the joint up," Hank said, winking at her as he ducked out the front door and quietly shut it behind him.

Alone at last.

Melody raised her brows and looked across the room at Anthony.

"Welcome to London," he said in that dry voice she loved so much. "Good flight?"

She burst into startled laughter, but he didn't look amused.

He didn't look amused at all.

"Come here," he said, opening his arms for her.

They hurried toward each other, coming together in front of the sofa for one of those joyous rib-splitting hugs that always made her feel as though she couldn't breathe and (conversely; simultaneously) as though she could finally breathe again.

The smell of his peppery and sophisticated cologne was embedded deep into his starched white shirt. She reveled in the scent that now meant home to her, whether they were in Tanzania, London or Journey's End. He whispered her name, his voice husky and urgent. She answered him with her own whispers. They swayed together, his hands delving deep into her hair to cup her head and anchor her for his fervent kisses.

Forehead…cheeks…eyes…nose…

Mouth.

She'd had a long overnight flight and a rough morning, yeah, but things would have to get a damn sight worse than this before she stopped melting when he kissed her. The kissing tapered down to a few lingering nuzzles before Anthony pressed his nose to her hair and breathed her in as though his life depended on it.

When he finally loosened his grip and pulled back enough to see her, his eyes were a thrilling blaze of blue. Bright enough to stop her heart.

"This seems like a good time to mention that I love you." He cleared his hoarse throat, color flooding his face. "I'm crazy in love with you."

Joy erupted from her on a startled laugh.

"Well, I would hope so after all *this*."

He ducked his head and laughed with her, his complexion turning even redder.

"About damn time," she grumbled, sitting on the sofa and pulling him down beside her.

"Sorry about that," he said, tugging an earlobe and trying to contain his grin by pressing his lips together. The effort deepened his dimples and made him look delightfully boyish and vulnerable. "It's best not to rush into these things when one can help it."

"Really?" She arched a brow at him. "So it wasn't until this very second that you realized you were in love with me?"

That sobered him up.

"No," he said, his smile slipping away and leaving raw adoration shining in his face. "I've loved you since the night we met. As I'm sure you probably know. But that seemed like a lot to spring on you on top of everything else."

"Hmm," she said, now running her thumb across his bottom lip, mesmerized by its lush tenderness. "Well, thanks for telling me. It would be really embarrassing if you didn't love me now that my face is splashed all over the Internet."

Another thrilling grin.

"You're very welcome," he said, leaning in for another lingering kiss.

She looked down at her spoon ring when they pulled apart, wiping away a fingerprint that marred its brilliant shine. When she looked back up at him, he was alert and waiting.

She felt her heart rise into her throat. She opened her mouth, but took her time, wanting to tread carefully.

"One of the photographers said that this is your grandmother's ring. That's not true, is it?"

Long pause.

"My mother made the pair of them when she was at some summer camp as a teenager. Granny has the other."

"Your *mother* made this ring?" she echoed, the room spinning around her. "Didn't that seem like the kind of thing you should mention when you gave it to me?"

He shrugged, a shadow passing over his expression.

"I might have. But it wasn't the right time, was it? Not when I couldn't even convince you to visit me here until now." He hesitated. "I didn't want to scare you off. And there was time. I'm not going anywhere."

Her heart swelled, making it harder for her to speak.

"So…you gave me your mother's ring when we'd only been together about a month?"

Another shrug, his gaze steady and warm on her face.

She studied him hard, not certain what she was looking for, but determined to find it.

"Quite a gift to give your new girlfriend," she said, trying to lighten things up.

"I thought you understood." Unsmiling, he stared her in the face. "I wasn't giving it to my girlfriend. I was giving it to my future wife."

A tidal wave of emotions surged through her, too many

and too fast to identify.

Relief. Gratitude. Excitement.

She took a deep breath, working hard to keep her butt on the sofa and not soar away like a balloon overfilled with helium. "Can I tell you something?"

He reached out. Took great care about wrapping one of her spiral curls around his finger, then letting it spring back into place. Flicked his sober gaze back to hers, his eyes everywhere, seeing everything.

"You can tell me anything, darling."

But he seemed to know already. His eyes crinkled at the corners, encouraging her.

"I love you, too."

His breath hitched.

"I was hoping you did," he said, leaning in a kiss that was tender. Infinitely persuasive.

But they couldn't live in that moment, much as she wanted to. Too much had happened today.

"I'm sorry," he said when they pulled apart again. "I'd hoped we'd have more time to get things figured out."

"It's not your fault. It was going to happen sooner or later. I'm just wondering why it happened *now*."

"That much I know," he said, his expression souring. "I was speaking to the press office when you arrived. All the interest in my ennoblement tomorrow has made photographers comb back through their photos to see what they can sell." His lips quirked. "And you weren't exactly subtle with the way you were looking at me that day in Tanzania, were you?"

"That's on *you*," she said, smacking his arm. "No one told you to make cow eyes at me."

"I can't help it! What do you want me to do?"

They laughed together for a delicious moment, but then

all her newfound fears and insecurities caught up with her again. Especially when she thought of the jostling throng of shouting men and the way she'd been just an object to them, no more sentient or worthy of consideration than a Porsche they might have photographed for a magazine ad.

It must have all shown up on her face, because Anthony noticed.

"How bad was it?" he asked, his jaw tightening. "I know they cornered you at the airport. And I expect they were waiting for you outside the gate just now."

She spent a couple of beats in a private battle between two parts of herself: the part that wanted to be perceived as Wonder Woman, a cape-wearing phenom capable of saving children's lives while also laughing off something as trivial as being photographed on the street when she wasn't expecting it, and the part of her that wanted to be safe and protected from people determined to stare at her.

"On a scale of one to having third-degree burns on my face?" She tried for an ironic smile that never quite took hold. "I'd give it a six."

Anthony looked murderous now.

"The press office is working on a statement asking for your privacy. We'll put it out later."

Her jaw dropped. "A statement? From who?"

"From *me*."

Thus commenced another private battle: the part of her that secretly yearned to be protected by a powerful man and the part of her that yearned to tell the press to go fuck themselves while she held her head high and went about living her regularly scheduled life regardless of what anyone thought of her.

"But...won't that make things worse? By drawing attention to it?"

"No. A statement will indicate the seriousness of our relationship, which will in turn indicate to the paparazzi that they need to give you a respectful distance and time to become accustomed to your new role and circumstances. My cousin's spouses were all given that consideration. It will also allow us to begin working on your training and visit the hospitals and see which ones you might like to apply to. I'm sure you'll have your pick, but still."

Melody gaped at him, her mind slowly replaying all of that and trying to come up to speed.

As someone who had completed her residency in the not so distant past, the idea of training for some new thing was enough to make her nauseous.

"Training?"

"There's a certain amount of protocol one has to get used to. And also security, of course. Self-defense training. Don't worry. We have people to help you with all of that."

Protocol? Security?

She'd thought about them, of course, but in the abstract. As something she and Anthony might one day have to discuss the same way they'd have to one day discuss where they'd live and when to have children. She hadn't thought the issues would be staring her in the face this quickly.

"I'm sorry it happened this way, but it's something of a relief that we're out in the open now rather than tiptoeing around our feelings," he continued. "It was like we'd taken a vow of silence or something. That was making me mental, to be honest, pretending there wasn't this big elephant in the room. Now we can begin working on putting our lives together here."

She nodded shakily.

"And you wouldn't be too unhappy living here for now, would you, darling?" He swept his arm wide to encompass the entire cottage. "They remodeled it a few years ago, before I moved in, but you can make whatever changes you'd like. The kitchen has been updated, though, so we won't have to worry about that. And Jameson Hall comes with the earldom. It's in Norfolk, near Sandringham. About two and a half hours from here. And it *will* need remodeling."

She blinked. Wished she had a Bloody Mary.

"I've actually started on a list of things we might—Melody? Are you okay?"

"Yeah. Of course."

But her fake smiling skills had only ever been sketchy at best. And she discovered she couldn't quite meet his eye.

He focused all that intensity on her.

"Tell me what's going on in that clever brain of yours. I've been doing all the talking."

She opened her mouth and discovered, way too late, that her words didn't want to line up in any sort of a coherent manner. Nor did she want to say or do anything that dimmed the light in his eyes or rubbed the joyous sheen off their confessions that they loved each other.

But…

She closed her mouth. Ran her fidgety hands up and down her thighs because she had to do something with them. Became irritated with the rubbing noise they made with her jeans and crossed her arms instead. Forced herself to look him in the face (he seemed vaguely concerned now), opened her mouth and tried again.

Probably best to just throw it all out there.

"I love you. I want to marry you."

He broke into that ecstatic smile that made her heart sing. Nodded encouragingly.

"But…I think it makes sense for us to live together for a while and see how that goes first. Because absence makes the heart grow fonder and we've probably been benefitting from honeymoon periods every time we get together again. You need the chance to see how bitchy I can be when I come off a long shift and want to barricade myself alone in my room without speaking to anyone for a while. See if you still want to stick around."

His expression cooled off. Just a bit.

Flattened out just a bit.

"No bitchier than when you're miserable with the flu, surely."

She hesitated, knowing that this conversation, already a dicey trek through a minefield to begin with, would not benefit from them getting irritable with each other.

"Maybe not, but back then we were in our own little bubble. We didn't have to deal with security and protocol and reporters jumping in my face and calling me a bitch when I don't smile for them or give them a better shot at my scar. Which is what happened earlier. So maybe we need a stronger dose of reality for a while before we start printing the invitations."

He stiffened. Stared across the room for a moment, a muscle working in his jaw. Looked back at her.

"You need an adjustment period," he said soothingly. "I completely understand that. I do."

She seriously doubted that anyone who'd grown up with this level of opulence and scrutiny could understand what a civilian needed to do to get used to it, but she gave him an A for effort. Somehow resisted the urge to snort.

"But I can't help feeling like this is some further test of my feelings for you. And as far as I'm concerned, the last several months—almost a year now—have been test enough already."

"I'm trying to use common sense. But you make it sound

like I get off on making you jump through hoops," she said, stung.

"Not at all. But you need to understand that if we'd been doing things my way, that would have been an engagement ring I gave you back in Tanzania. Not my mother's old spoon ring."

Melody stared at him, astonished, searching his face for signs of exaggeration and finding only steady honesty.

"Don't look so surprised," he said. "I told you back then that I wanted you to come to London and see how you liked it. What did you think that meant?"

"I don't know," she said, rubbing her heart. "I guess that you thought things were moving in that direction. Not that you were already sure."

"Well. Now you know. And you should also know that watching your face lose color while we have this discussion is particularly painful. Because I've been certain about what I want from this relationship since the beginning. And you're *still* not sure even though you just sat there and told me you loved me."

"It's not that I'm not sure about our relationship," she cried. "That's not it at all."

He went very still. "Enlighten me, then."

"It's moving to London and all of *this*," she said with a sweeping gesture at the room and KP next door. "I'm not sure I want to move to London. And I want you to think about moving to Journey's End."

18

Anthony cocked his head, looking as though she'd suggested a move to Atlantis's final resting place at the bottom of the sea.

"Excuse me?"

She hitched up her chin. "You heard me. You love Journey's End; you've told me a million times. You have Baptiste there. We'd have less press intrusion there."

"I made a commitment to my grandmother," he said, his expression turning stony. "I have engagements booked *here* for the next six months, if not longer."

She shrugged. "After that, then."

He emitted a disbelieving snort as his brows shot up.

"And what would I do for work in Journey's End, pray tell?"

"Practice law. You could take the bar in New York. Practice in Journey's End or Manhattan. Do the human rights work that's so important to you."

There was a poisonous pause.

Then his face closed off as though a switch had been thrown.

"I'm not licensed. I thought we'd been over this."

"I thought we could reopen the topic," she said evenly. "Remember when I gave you those study books over Christmas? I don't feel like you've really given the idea a fair shake."

"*A fair shake?*" Disbelieving laugh. "What, like you've given London?"

Well, he had her there, not that she planned to admit it.

"See, this is one of those moments that married people tend to run into. Where they have to see if they can work things out. Preferably without getting ugly about it," she said calmly.

His lip curled. He took a deep breath.

"We've talked about this, darling. I made a promise to my grandmother to help out when my grandfather died."

"But that was years ago, Anthony. And you're not a senior royal. You're so far down in the line of succession that you should be allowed to live your own life and do what you want to do."

His dimpled chin suddenly seemed to have a lot more stubborn in it.

"I gave my word."

"I know you did," she said soothingly. "You're an honorable person. You keep your word. And I love you for that."

He looked slightly mollified.

"But I don't think this is your calling. It might be your grandmother's calling, but it's not *yours*."

"How would you know?" he said, his voice brittle as he got up from the sofa and strode to the window, where he paced and cracked his knuckles.

"You can get angry at me all you want, but I'm going to tell you the truth."

"The truth as *you* see it."

"The truth as a person who loves you and wants the very best for you."

"Ah." Crooked smile. "Which is living in Journey's End. Where I've been traipsing nearly every week for nearly a year whilst hoping you would meet me halfway one day and show me half as much commitment."

She froze.

"What's wrong darling?" That crooked smile widened. "Isn't it acceptable for *me* to tell the truth as well?"

"Tell all the truth you want," she said, determined to stand her ground at this crucial juncture. "As long as you understand that as far as I'm concerned, we have two issues to work out: where we're going to live and what you're going to do for your career."

"I already have a career!"

"No, you don't! You have something you fell into when your grandfather died and you tried to do the right thing by your grandmother because you love her and she needed you."

"Well, what did you expect?" he roared, his voice booming through the room like a clap of thunder. "*You* weren't here! *You* didn't see what she did for me when Mum died!"

Melody froze, knowing he was about to give her a glimpse into a sacred emotional place he normally kept locked tight.

"Why don't you explain it to me?"

"*She* kept me together! *She* made me get my arse out of bed, take a shower and go to school when I would have preferred to die with my mother! *She* let me cry myself to sleep with my head in her lap! *She* forced me to rejoin the living and to really *live* because Mum would have wanted me to! And the least I can do now is return the favor and live up to my word."

In the ringing silence that followed, he tried to catch his breath while she tried to gather her words.

"I don't know your grandmother. But from everything you've told me, she's a wonderful woman who wants you to be happy. Maybe your debt is paid by now. And maybe she never even saw it as a debt."

He snorted. "That's not how things work round here. You don't just clock out when you've had enough."

"You make it sound like the Mafia."

"There are some startling similarities, I'll admit."

"Have you ever even discussed it with her, Anthony?"

"Discussed *what*?" he asked, flaring up again.

"Discussed that you want to be a lawyer. Told her that you read every legal biography and thriller you can get your hands on and watch every courtroom show and movie. And I'm betting you *have* been reading those study guides I got you even though you've never said a word about it to me. Am I right?"

He hastily turned away, his cheeks flooding with color.

"You look so unhappy and uncomfortable every time you have one of your charity events or speeches or meetings. It's all over your face in the pictures. You'd rather be having dental work done. I know it. Why won't you even consider—"

"And why won't *you* consider moving here to be with me? *My* life is here. *My* family are here. *My* work is here."

"I *will* consider it. I am considering it."

He gaped at her. "You are?"

"Oh, my God," she said, smacking her forehead. "Have you not been paying attention for the last few months? I *love* you. I swore off men and made peace with being a slave to my career and dying alone with only my twelve cats to notice. And then *you* came along."

His expression softened.

"I've never been happier," she said, fighting off a sudden surge of happy tears. "In my entire life, I never knew I could be this happy. You're everything I need in a partner. If you said you wanted to get married tomorrow and live in Journey's End with me, I'd say *yes* in a heartbeat. I would do *anything* to be with you."

"Melody..."

He reached for her, but she held up a hand to keep him at a distance for now.

"But you need to think about what you're asking me to do, Anthony. Don't ask me to uproot my entire life based on an obligation that you may or may not even need to fulfill."

"Uproot your entire life?" He looked stricken. Outraged. "Haven't we just established that *we* are the most important things in each other's lives?"

"The most important things? Yes. The *only* things? No." Her voice grew husky with all the day's overflowing emotion. "I *love* Journey's End. I love the shops and the river and the mountains. I love the leaves in the fall and the fact that I can walk everywhere. I love Samira and my other friends. I love that my parents are just a few hours away in Chicago and my sister is just a couple hours away in the city. I love my hospital and my colleagues and knowing that my mentor, Dr. Muhammed, is right there when I need her. I can't wait to get back there and see what's going to come through the doors on any given day." She hesitated, but, screw it, she'd come this far and might as well put it all out there. "I love the house that Raymond told me about the other day. It's my dream house. I've been wanting to buy that house for a while now. And I finally have the money and the opportunity."

His face turned purple.

"I can give you a *palace!*" he shouted, flinging an arm

toward where KP loomed outside his window. "I can make you a countess! I'm to be worth nearly a billion dollars when I come into my trust! What more do you want?"

Did he really not see? Was that it?

"It's a cage, Anthony! A gilded cage is still a cage! Over here, you don't have the freedom to come and go without security and paparazzi. You need your grandmother's permission to live here or to move into an apartment in KP. And you want me to move into the cage with you. You want me to give up my country, my town, my hospital, my friends and family, all my support system, my dream house, my freedom of movement *and* my privacy."

"It's a *privilege* to live here. To have the wealth and the opportunities."

"It's also a tremendous personal sacrifice. Don't deny it."

He opened his mouth as though he wanted to deny it, but wound up muttering a curse instead.

"And that's not all," she continued. "You're asking me to subject myself to photographers waiting to ambush me and tabloids waiting to make snide comments about my clothes and my *face* and my background." The beginnings of a dry sob rose up to choke her, but she ruthlessly swallowed it back down. She would *not* fall apart. "And you know what? I'll give them my clothes and my face. I *don't* wear designer clothes and shoes, and I *do* have a messed-up face—"

"Don't say that!"

"—but I will *not* stand around for this veiled racism about my *unusual background* and my *urban beginnings*. My parents are both Ivy League trained doctors like I am. Do you get that? They worked their asses off to put themselves through school and to put me and my sister through school. But I guess we're all less than because my father is black and we weren't smart enough to be born into posh families like the ones who live near here. I guess the press gets to say whatever the hell they want to say and I'm supposed to keep my head up and smile because that's protocol. Well, that's *bullshit.*"

"I'm so sorry, darling. But we all have to learn to ignore it as best we can—"

"Well, I don't have a switch I can turn on or off, Anthony! How am I supposed to ignore it when they reduce my entire life to the color of my skin and my noble victimhood because of my scar? And when they get up in my face to keep me from walking to the car, then call me a bitch when I don't smile for them?"

"Christ."

"Yeah, that happened today. Welcome to London, Mel. Oh, and my sister had a DUI. Did you see that *that* made the news as well? They're saying you have a *drunk* as a future sister-in-law. Just so you know." Outrage flared anew. "My sister may have made a terrible mistake by drinking and driving, but she is *not* a drunk."

"I'm sorry about all that. It's killing me that I can't protect you any better than that."

She could see that. The guilt and shame were written all over his shadowed face.

"It's not your fault," she said. "You did the best you could. You're only human."

He ran both hands over the top of his head, rubbing until she wondered if he wasn't yanking his hair out by the roots. Then he blew out a breath.

"I don't know what to say. You've caught me completely off guard. I never thought of leaving London. It's my home. Everything I know is here."

"You're asking me to leave everything *I* know, yet *you* won't even take a hard look inside yourself and ask whether *you're* happy with your work. You won't take the time to see about getting your license to practice law, which we *both* know is what you really want to do. If Nelson Mandela were here—"

"Don't you bring him into it!"

"He'd tell you that it's not right to play small and settle for a life that's less than what you're capable of. And you *know* that."

Anthony glared at her, jaw tight and nostrils flaring.

"That's quite the speech. Anything else?"

She took a deep breath, determined to say all of her piece.

"Yeah. Don't get it twisted. *You* are the prize here. Not KP or your title or your money."

He stared at her, his expression turbulent, until his flaring nostrils and wobbling chin forced him to turn away and swipe his eyes with the backs of his hands.

She didn't blame him. She felt a little teary herself.

"The thing is, if you said that you wanted me to move here so you could become a barrister, I'd do it in a heartbeat. I *want* you to be happy with your career. I could find a new hospital and make new friends. I could work on toughening up my skin and ignoring what the press says about me. I could get used to security trailing me around. But you want me to give up my entire Journey's End existence and everything I know so that we can live here and you can keep doing something that makes you miserable just because you're too stuck or too afraid to make a change and reach for what you really want. And I don't think that's right."

They gave each other hard stares for several beats. She had the despairing thought that a hungry crocodile and a gazelle getting a sip of water at a river's edge had a better chance of coming to a workable resolution than she and Anthony did in that moment.

"The press can find us in Journey's End, too, Melody."

"Yeah, but I can handle it better there. All of my emotional support group is there. And the thought of moving here and having you be my whole world terrifies me." She paused. "And it should terrify you, too."

He turned away, a muscle throbbing in his temple, and refused to meet her gaze.

19

Bloody coffee, Anthony fumed as he left the cottage and made the short drive to Buckingham Palace a few minutes later.

What was the *one* thing Anthony needed to plunge his flagging morale into subterranean level? Coffee with his grandmother and father, two people who harbored as much affection for each other as Henry VIII had for Anne Boleyn in the final days of their marriage. But Granny was determined for the two of them to mend their fences ahead of the investiture tomorrow—actually, *mend* was probably too strong a word; more like put a patch on and pray it held long enough for them to remain civil during the ceremony and reception afterward—and Anthony was the necessary third party to prevent them from coming to blows over their scones.

But in his current mood? He doubted he'd be much help to anyone.

Hell. He couldn't even help himself.

As evidenced by the lashing he'd just received from the lovely Dr. Harrison.

He rubbed his roiling gut, which seemed unlikely to take kindly to any food or drink at the moment.

For the life of him, he couldn't begin to understand how he'd so badly misjudged the situation with Melody. And to think that this whole time, he'd thought he had it figured out.

Maybe he was delusional. That would certainly explain a great deal, wouldn't it?

It had all gone so smoothly in his mind—their entire relationship, from beginning to end.

Step 1: They got to know each other and fell in love.

Step 2: Melody moved to London, where he proposed.

Step 3: They got married, had a family and lived happily ever after. In London.

Up until now, it had all gone according to plan.

Step 1? No problem.

So he'd thought that they were happily moving on to Step 2 (she'd admitted she loved and wanted to marry him a little while ago, for God's sake) only to discover that she hated Step 2.

She had, in fact, pretty much told him to take his stupid Step 2 and go fuck himself.

He wouldn't have been any more astonished if she'd announced she wanted to turn the Tower of London into a supermarket.

How on earth had he got things so wrong? It was as though he'd gone to Las Vegas to make his fortune on the blackjack table and lost all his money only to discover that he should have been aiming for nineteen rather than twenty-one.

Well, no. He knew, didn't he? He wasn't a mind reader (clearly) and they'd never discussed their long-term next steps in detail. They'd been so determined to get their courtship right that they'd tiptoed around the elephant in the room, which was how they'd manage the logistics of merging their lives on the same continent.

Now that ignored elephant had gone and shat all over their room.

And what was he doing? Was he back in the cottage, pleading his case and making sure that Melody wasn't packing her bags and heading back to Journey's End without him? No. He was headed to this bloody coffee that he didn't even want, followed by the investiture that he didn't even want.

On his current trajectory? He'd find himself married to Annabella Carmichael, living in KP and being the honorary head of every obscure charity in Britain for the rest of his life if he wasn't careful.

The surprises continued when he arrived at his grandmother's private sitting room and discovered his father whispering in the ear of his grandmother's ancient retainer, Mrs. Brompton.

Anthony stopped dead in his tracks, taking a moment to scrape his lower jaw off the floor.

It was no surprise to see the old man flirting, of course. He took it as his righteous mission from God to charm, beguile and/or seduce every possessor of a pair of ovaries over the age of eighteen. No. The surprising thing here was that Mrs. Brompton, a woman who didn't suffer fools—or anyone else—gladly and had never smiled a true smile in Anthony's living memory, was blushing and giggling like teenyboppers had during Frank Sinatra concerts back in the 1950s. With her white teeth and dimples, she looked lovely. Almost luminescent.

"Mrs. *Brompton*," Anthony said, unable to contain his shock. "What's got into you?"

Startled, Mrs. Brompton looked around at him, her face

turning the vivid pink of little girls' rooms. She hastily cleared her throat and smoothed her hair, whisking that smile away to parts unknown, probably never to be seen again.

"Just having a word with your father, sir."

"You *laughed*."

She shrugged, all that color concentrating in her cheeks. "It's been known to happen."

"No, it hasn't," Anthony cried, pistons firing in his brain. "And...hang on, now that I think about it, this explains all the times Granny knew things about my father, here, and my father knew things about Granny. *You're* the grapevine, Mrs. Brompton."

Tony tried to look innocent, doing his usual poor job of managing his amused smirk.

"Of course I'm not," Mrs. Brompton said severely, making a minute adjustment to the elaborate silver service and pastries, which already sat in pride of place on the coffee table. "Stop talking such nonsense."

Anthony barked out an incredulous laugh and wagged a finger at her. "I've finally got you all figured out."

But Mrs. Brompton was far too old and had been around the block far too many times to let a young guy like Anthony give her the business.

"You've done no such thing," she said, smoothing the front of her dress. "And you'd best make sure nothing happens to any of these cakes before your grandmother comes. Or else I won't be responsible for the consequences."

Lobbing a final glare at Anthony and something that might have passed as a rueful grin at Tony, who answered with a tiny wink, she swept out, banging the mirrored door behind her.

"Gotta love Millicent," Tony said, chuckling as he

reached for one of the smoked salmon sandwiches on rye and popped it into his mouth.

Anthony's brain nearly exploded.

"*Millicent?* Mrs. Brompton doesn't have a first name!"

"'Course she does," Tony said around his mouthful.

"And you'd better leave Granny's sandwiches alone or your life won't be worth living."

"It won't be worth living without a little fortification anyway," Tony said darkly, retrieving a silver flask from the breast pocket of his dark custom suit and taking a healthy swig.

Anthony hated to be nosy but, given his father's track record with women, it seemed prudent to ask.

"You and Mrs. Brompton never, ah…"

Tony looked startled. "What? No. Of course not. She's a good twenty-five years older than me."

"As if age differences have ever stopped you before," Anthony said, irritated by his father's late display of romantic standards. "Although I suppose your moral code only applies when the women are *older* than you."

"Shots fired," Tony said, raising a brow and taking another swig from the flask. "Didn't take long."

"Sorry." Anthony sat in the nearest armchair. "Did *you* prefer to be the one to break the peace today?"

"There's no peace when your son hates your guts." Tony looked somber as he helped himself to a scone and sat on the sofa. "How's Miss Melody? She's had a rough morning, hasn't she? She sounded a little shaky when I talked to her."

When he—*what?*

Anthony hesitated, torn between his desire to answer his father's comment with another shot and his desire to talk about Melody, the topic most on his mind at the moment.

"You talked to her?" he asked sharply. "When?"

"Little while ago," Tony said blandly, now swiping scone crumbs off the front of his starched shirt. "When she was on her way in from the airport."

"And what did you say to her?" Anthony snapped, wondering why Melody hadn't mentioned their conversation and also if he had his father to thank for Melody's sudden reluctance to move to London. "If you've ruined my chances with her…"

Tony grimaced. "Ruined your chances with her? Why would I do that when you and I both know she's the best thing that's ever happened to you? Stand down, boy. If you can figure out how to do that around me."

Anthony relaxed marginally, caught squarely between his implicit and lifelong suspicion of anything having to do with his father and his flare of hope that he might have an unexpected ally on his side.

"What did you talk about?" he asked, forcing himself to be calm.

"I told her not to make my mistakes," Tony said, staring him in the face and giving Anthony a glimpse of the kind of emotional pain he'd never suspected his father could feel.

His driving curiosity got the best of him.

"What mistakes are you—"

Without warning, the door swung open. In swarmed his grandmother's pack of beagles, now joined by several puppies who had evidently already learned all they needed to know about yapping.

"What have I missed?" The Queen followed them in, clipping her syllables with a hedge trimmer. Today's twinset was a pale lilac colored one that turned her blue eyes more of an indigo shade, and she'd traded in her pearl necklace for a glittering diamond pin on her shoulder that probably cost more than the GDP of some of the world's smaller countries. She wore a black skirt and the chunky black heels she often favored. A particularly boxy and ugly black bag dangled from the crook of her elbow. "All the good gossip, I expect."

The men leapt to their feet.

"You're *late*, AJ," she said, offering him her hand.

"Your Majesty." He took it and gave her a kiss on each cheek before nodding sharply and kissing her hand. "I'm not late. I'm never late."

"You were late for tea when you were eleven."

"No, I wasn't. You've done something with your hair."

"You've done something with your hair," Tony said at the same time.

The men frowned around at each other. Then Tony focused on the Queen.

Her expression was narrow-eyed and flinty as she regarded her former son-in-law, but Anthony thought he detected a glimmer of amusement in her eyes as she stared up at Tony.

"It's customary to wait until one is addressed before speaking," she said, extending him her hand and letting him kiss her cheeks. "But of course you're a *Texan*. No more manners than my dogs here." She used her free hand to indicate one of the larger puppies, who wore a navy collar, had his paws on the table and sniffed hopefully at the bottom layer of cakes on the tray.

"Anna Regina," Tony said, flipping that hidden internal switch that activated his twinkling eyes, toothpaste commercial grin and dimples whenever a woman entered the room. Even his spray tan seemed to glow a little brighter. He nodded and kissed her hand. "Twenty years later and you're still the prettiest monarch I've ever met."

She hitched up her chin, a harder nut to crack than Mrs. Brompton had been.

"Yes, and you still fancy yourself Don Juan, I see. Have you found your fifth ex-wife yet? Recognizing that it's still early in the day, of course."

Tony's lips twitched. "Not yet, but I'm open to introductions if you know anyone."

The Queen glared at him.

"You've eaten one of my smoked salmon sandwiches. *And* you've been drinking. Some of your favorite Kentucky bourbon, I believe?"

Tony shrugged, unrepentant as ever. "A drink seemed indicated for this little soiree."

"You're right. You may pour me whatever is left in your flask. Use the tumblers over there."

Tony obligingly headed for the drink cart. "You got it, boss."

Anthony checked his watch and felt the strong urge to be the adult in the room.

"It's ten-thirty in the morning," he called after his father, outraged. "Am I the only one who's going to be forced to drink coffee?"

"Do sit down, Anthony," she said, perching on the edge of the sofa, divesting herself of her bag and snapping her fingers at the dogs, who collapsed at her feet. "I hear the cat is out of the bag with your Doctor Melody."

"Yep," he said, dropping into a slouch in his chair.

"The press office is helping you?"

"Yep."

"And how is she doing?"

"Not great," Anthony said, drumming his fingers on the chair's arm.

"How else would she be doing?" Tony came back, sat on the sofa and passed the Queen her drink. "Her whole life just blew up on account of her association with you folks. You think that's easy on a person?"

"Well, it was certainly more than *you* could handle, wasn't it?" she asked, sipping delicately.

Tony stared her down, some of his charm slipping away.

"Not everyone is cut out for having their face splashed all over the tabloids every day."

"Not everyone is cut out for *marriage,* either," she said pointedly.

Anthony listened with half his brain, indifferent to the snark. He had to be, didn't he? How else would he have survived that dark time before his parents' separation, when screaming, slammed doors and smashed china and crystal were the order of the day? Still. It was a wonder how they managed it without driving themselves to insanity. Funny how people who'd been apart for twenty years could lapse into old patterns and pick up in the middle of their last conversation, wasn't it?

"Was I supposed to stay married to a woman who didn't want me?" Tony asked her, his twangy voice turning loud and brittle.

"Not at all, dear." The queen poured a cup of coffee from the heavy silver pot, her brows doing a slow creep toward her hairline while her voice dropped down into the range of a hissing cobra in a velvet pouch. She added a splash of cream. "I simply expected you to fight a bit longer and harder for—what did you call her? It was such a touching sentiment. Ah, yes. Your *soulmate*. These things often take longer than a cricket season. I'm sure that's what threw you. You're not used to that level of commitment."

"If my marriage to your daughter meant that much to you," Tony said, nostrils flaring, "seems like you wouldn't have signed off on the divorce back in the day."

"I disagree. If people are determined to self-destruct, who am I to stop them?" She gave Tony a poisonous smile before turning to Anthony. "Drink your coffee, AJ. Have a scone. That'll cheer you up."

Anthony leaned forward and took the cup and saucer from her, secretly longing for those simpler times when a good tea service with cakes had, in fact, cured most of the things that bothered him. Then he re-slouched with his drink carefully resting on his belly, putting his head on the chair's back and crossing a leg over his knee.

"I don't think I can expect Melody to move to London for me," he said quietly, frowning, the idea fully forming just as he spoke it. "It's too much to put on a person."

"Self-destruct?" Tony snarled at the Queen. "Hard to *self-destruct* when you never had a chance to begin with, isn't it, Annie? Sort of like you accusing an elephant of *self-destructing* when the big game hunter's got his sights set in the middle of the dumb bastard's forehead."

"*You* said *dumb bastard*, dear." The Queen kept her eyes lowered and sipped her bourbon again, dabbing her mouth with a linen napkin. "Not I."

Tony made a strangled sound of outrage.

"The thing is," Anthony continued, "her entire community is there. Job. Friends. Family. I mean, think about it. It's one thing when one lives in, say, Connecticut, and the future spouse lives in New York. Adjustments can be made. There's no great sacrifice. On either party's side."

Tony shot a quick glance at Anthony, who was frowning up at the ceiling now, leaned toward the Queen and lowered his voice.

"I guess *dumb bastard's* the right term for a husband who doesn't ask too many questions about his wife's whereabouts. *Dumb bastard's* the term for a husband who says his *I dos* expecting that his wife means her vows as much as he means his."

The Queen set her tumbler onto the silver tray with an angry clink.

"*Dumb bastard* is *exactly* the term for a man whose stubborn pride forces him to let everything he needs in life slip through his fingers without putting up a fight, then spends the rest of his life foolishly marrying women half his age and pretending none of the aforementioned bothered him."

Tony goggled at her, his face turning purple.

"Oh, I'm sorry, dear. I keep forgetting you don't like big words. Let me put it in Texan for you." She cocked her head and thoughtfully tapped her lips with her index finger. "What is the phrase? Yes, I have it." She cleared her throat and adopted a credible drawl that would be right at home anywhere in the Lone Star State. "You're so dumb, you carry your brains in your back pocket."

Anthony cracked his knuckles and chewed the inside of his cheek. "But I don't want her coming here and, I don't know, maybe starting to resent me—"

Veins popped in Tony's neck. "How dare you?"

"Oh, I dare," the Queen said icily.

"—one day when she misses her parents or her sister or her friends too much." Anthony took another sip of his coffee. "And what about when we have children? A woman needs her mother nearby for—"

"You think this is a joke? Your precious daughter took my heart and walked all over it with her spiky heels and you think this is a *joke*?" Tony demanded of the Queen.

"—advice and whatnot. And I'm an American citizen, aren't I?" Anthony nodded grimly. "I can live there as well as here. Perhaps better, to be honest. No one on that side of the pond snipes quite like we do over here."

"No," the Queen told Tony, a tinge of sadness creeping into her expression. "It's a *tragedy*. Because my daughter was as big a fool as you were when it came to doing the right thing by her marriage. Yet she never loved anyone the way she loved you."

Bitter snort from Tony. "That's the biggest load of bullshit you've ever tried to shovel in my direction, Annie."

"Oh, for *God's* sake," the Queen muttered, now angrily breaking up her scone and tossing bits to the dogs. "Like I said, you're your own worst enemy, Tony. You make it impossible for me to reach out to you no matter how much I might like to. For Anthony's sake, if nothing else."

At the sound of his name, Anthony felt the first flare of annoyance. He sat up straight and set his cup and saucer on the table. "Has anyone heard a word I just said? Because I could use a bit of advice here."

Evidently they hadn't heard what he'd said, because all their attention and venom remained laser-focused on each other.

"Oh, you want to talk about *Anthony*?" Tony looked slightly unhinged, with a wild-eyed sneer solely for the Queen's benefit. "By all means. Let's talk about how you've always been determined to control the boy's life. How about that? Let's talk about how you forced him to go to boarding school over here—"

"I didn't force that boy," the Queen cried, outraged. "He made his own choice. Which I supported."

"*That boy* is right here," Anthony said, his stretched nerves making him louder than he'd meant to be.

"Thirteen-year-olds don't make their own choices," Tony said with a derisive snort. "They're not capable."

"Yours was," the Queen said coolly. "Which you would have known if you'd been half the father—"

With that, Anthony slammed headfirst into the limits of his patience and control.

"That is *enough*!" he roared, smacking his palms on the table and making the coffee service jump. "Do you think I want to be trapped in this room while you two take each other's heads off over things that haven't mattered in twenty years?"

Ringing silence with two stunned faces turned in his direction.

Hell, he'd even surprised himself.

"Anthony Thomas Scott," Granny said in her most imperious voice. "You will apologize."

But Anthony wasn't fifteen years old anymore, and that realization had fully hit him for the first time.

"The pair of you should apologize to *me*," Anthony said, thumping his chest for emphasis. "My personal life is circling the drain, which I just confided in you, yet my two remaining parental figures are too busy hating each other to take a moment and listen to what I'm saying, let alone help me figure out how to make things work with Melody. I mean… Wasn't the purpose of this bloody coffee to make peace before tomorrow? For *my* benefit?"

The Queen and Tony exchanged a guilty sidelong look.

"And what is the point of this sniping?" Anthony continued, glaring at each of them in turn. "Do you even know why you're arguing, or is it just habit? Is it going to rewrite history? Is it going to save your marriage to my mother? Is it going to prevent her from skiing into that tree after the divorce and resurrect her from the dead?" He paused to catch his breath. "Or maybe you think it'll ease your consciences. Well, let me help you with that. By all means."

He turned to his father.

"You and Mum did the best you could at the time, but you

were both shit at being married to each other. It didn't work out. It's over."

He turned to his grandmother.

"Granny, you did the best you could to talk them into giving their marriage another chance, but they were stubborn. It didn't work out. It's over. None of this matters anymore. It hasn't mattered in ages. Now will the pair of you kindly stop flagellating yourselves and each other? It's bloody exhausting."

His grandmother and Tony exchanged another sidelong look, wary now.

"Why not take a moment to realize that you both love horses and dogs and me? What have you got to lose? Another twenty years of bitterness? Just let it go. For *God's* sake," Anthony concluded.

Tony recovered first. "*Let it go?* What, like you let go of all your hard feelings toward me for cheating on your mother? Like *that*?"

Anthony cringed. Nothing like being shoved face-first into irrefutable evidence of your hypocrisy.

Well, why not own it?

He smirked. "Actually, my most recent hard feelings toward you have to do with you denying me my trust fund. In fairness, I haven't had time to get over *that* yet, have I?"

But Tony wasn't having it. "Don't try to gloss this over! Why deny it? You think I cheated on your mother and broke her heart, and you draw a straight line between that and her death. You always have. You think I was a shit and she was a saint. Bottom line. Why not be honest?"

Sudden pain and loss gave Anthony a big whack in the chest, making it hard for him to speak. Staring into his father's bleak expression, he felt a wave of nostalgia that insisted he remember the good times they'd shared when he was younger. The fishing, skeet shooting and horse riding they'd enjoyed at the ranch. The times Tony had sworn him to secrecy before letting him drive the Jeep up and down the gravel roads. The music festivals in Austin. Their joint love of spicy barbecue and spicier Mexican food.

Anthony glimpsed his father's heartbreak over the loss of his son's love.

He didn't want to see it, but he did.

"Mum wasn't a saint any more than you were," he said tiredly. "But she was *my* saint. You made her cry herself to sleep. That's not easy for me to get over."

The Queen pursed her lips.

Tony ducked his head and swiped his eyes.

"On the other hand..." Anthony cleared his hoarse throat. "On the other hand, she took up with her riding instructor. I imagine that's not easy for you to get over."

"You knew about that?" his grandmother and Tony both asked, looking astonished.

Anthony nodded. "I saw them kissing in the barn before one of my lessons. They didn't know I was there."

Tony wiped his eyes again, murmuring something indistinct.

With an aggrieved sigh and thinning lips, Granny shook out a napkin and handed it to Tony, who used it to blow his nose.

"Look," Anthony said, studying his hands as he slowly rubbed them together. "Maybe we've all been living in the past. Focusing on things that no longer matter. And on that note, Granny..."

"What?" the Queen snapped, glowering at him. "If this is about your investiture tomorrow, you can just forget it. You're not weaseling out of it. You've given your word and I'm holding you to it. One's word means something."

Anthony's heart sank. He'd been afraid she'd say that.

But Melody was worth fighting for and the things that were important to her were crucial to him.

"Nothing like that," Anthony assured his grandmother. "But…the thing is…"

She stiffened.

Tony, much to his surprise, gave him an encouraging nod that she thankfully didn't seem to notice.

Much to Anthony's further surprise, the encouraging nod gave him strength.

He took a deep breath.

"When Pa died," he said, referring to his grandfather, "I promised I'd come home and help out. And I have done. For years now."

One of her brows shot up.

"But, Granny, maybe you've noticed that I'm not exactly setting the world on fire with my speeches to gardening clubs and my patronage of recycling programs and the like. And I think you can probably find someone else to christen your new ships for you. I'll be around for big events, of course, but I'm fairly confident that the world will continue to turn if I were to, say…practice law in New York instead."

"What's this insubordination all about?" she asked sharply.

He hesitated, not wanting to make Melody the object of Granny's ire.

But, on the other hand, anyone who'd ever had a passing acquaintance with him could surely see that he was happier than he'd ever been in his life, and the cause was obvious.

"When a man gets married, he has to do what's best for his wife and children. As you know."

Tony, still out of the Queen's line of sight, gave him a thumbs-up.

Anthony blinked furiously, trying not to smile at this crucial juncture.

"I *do* know," Granny said in her craggiest voice, eyes glinting as she watched him closely. "Too bad you have neither wife nor children at the ripe old age of thirty-five."

"That's about to change."

Granny's lips twitched with a smile that didn't seem to want to be repressed as she dabbed her mouth, wiped her hands, grabbed her handbag and stood, forcing the men to surge to their feet with her.

"About bloody time," she said, heading for the door. "Come, dogs. We've got to meet Dr. Harrison."

The dogs jumped up and streamed after her, the blue-collared puppy yapping the loudest in his excitement.

"Hang on," Anthony said, overtaken with a vague feeling of horror at the thought of an unsuspecting, un-showered and jet-lagged Melody opening the door and being presented with the Queen. "What about protocol? Aren't there rules for this? You can't just pop in on her, can you?"

"Oh, I'm sorry," she deadpanned. "Has she got some previous engagement that's more important?"

"Well, no, but…" Anthony stammered as she swept out, looking at Tony with a desperate but silent plea for help.

Tony held up his hands and backed up a step. "Not getting involved, son. I'm just glad old Annie's decided to terrorize someone else for a while."

From out in the corridor came the unabashed sound of the Queen's cackle of amusement.

"What else do you expect?" she called. "I have so few pleasures in life."

20

A few minutes later, Anthony let himself back into the cottage and left the door ajar, taking off his jacket and tie and rolling up his shirtsleeves as he went. He felt an unsettling combination of nerves and euphoria. Now that the dam had broken, things were moving at a breakneck pace. Which was of course the pace he'd have chosen for his relationship with Melody if he'd been in charge this whole time, but still.

This all seemed a bit too good to be true.

The dogs swarmed in after him, tails wagging as they yapped at each other and generally made nuisances of themselves tearing about the sitting room and exploring. It might have been his imagination, but he swore he saw that troublesome blue-collared puppy lift a leg and pee on one corner of a rug that, if not priceless, was certainly worth more than Anthony's hide, at least as far as Granny was concerned.

Ah, well. He had bigger fish to fry at the moment.

There was no sign of Melody.

He cleared his throat and sent up a silent prayer for the best.

"Melody?"

"Hey!" He heard her hurried footsteps down the hall. She sounded wide awake, which was good. He'd been half afraid she'd be buried deep in bed in a jet lag-induced coma. "You're back!"

"And I've brought company," he said darkly.

Melody appeared in the doorway, looking bright-eyed, pink-cheeked and good enough to eat.

Having showered, she'd piled her wet hair into one of those sexy trailing ponytails that left tendrils around her face and changed into a casual but lovely blue dress that thankfully skimmed her knees. God only knew how many times he'd listened to Granny chastise his female cousins for showing the world their *wrinkly little knees*. Granny probably wouldn't be wild about Melody's strappy open-toed sandals, but queens who unexpectedly showed up on people's doorsteps could not be choosy.

"I see that," Melody said with delight, stooping to greet the beagles as they bounced over to say hello. The blue-collared puppy, having satisfactorily emptied his little bladder, now leaned his front paws on Melody's shins and stared up at her for a closer look. "And who are *these* little guys?"

"Granny's dogs."

"And how was your coffee with Granny?" she asked, now squatting to scoop the dogs closer. A couple of them tried to jump up and lick her face, making her laugh.

"Very interesting." He opened the front door wider, with the desperate hope that what he was about to do wouldn't ruin his relationship with Melody forever. "But don't take my word for it. Why don't you ask her yourself?"

And in swept Granny.

She really played it up, too, giving her chin that regal hike she always favored when she opened Parliament in full regalia every year and settling her boxy black bag into the crook of her elbow. The twinkle of amusement in her eyes was a dead giveaway that she was enjoying herself, but he didn't expect poor Melody to realize that this first time out of the gate.

"My grandmother," he told Melody. "Granny, this is my girlfriend. Dr. Melody Harrison."

Granny held out one bejeweled hand. "How do you do?"

Melody's expression cycled through paralytic shock, horror at being caught letting dogs lick her face, punishing fury at Anthony for letting her be caught unawares like this and then, finally, gracious resignation and excitement during the time it took for her to rise, smooth her dress back into place and smile as she pressed Granny's hand.

And then Melody, to his utter delight, executed a ramrod straight and graceful bob of a curtsy.

"Your Majesty," she said, towering over the petite queen. "How do you do?"

Granny looked around at Anthony, her raised brows echoing Anthony's surprise.

"She curtsies," Granny said in a stage whisper.

"Who knew?" he said wryly with an approving wink at Melody, whose cheeks flushed with pleasure. He'd been a hundred percent certain he wanted to marry her for a long time now, but if not, the curtsy would have sealed the deal.

"One never knows with Americans," Granny said. "Some of them feel that a bow or curtsy is tantamount to reverting to colony status with Britain and paying taxes on their tea shipments."

Melody grinned. "Well, I *am* staying in your house and you're the only queen I've ever met. Seems appropriate."

Granny beamed at her. "And where did you learn to do it so well? I have several family members who could do with a lesson from you."

Melody laughed, then tilted her head as she thought it over. "I have no idea, now that I think about it. Probably *Downton Abbey*."

Granny exchanged another excited glance with Anthony before turning back to Melody.

"You're a fan?" Granny asked.

"Who isn't?"

"Favorite character?"

"Lady Violet, of course."

"Oh, I don't like her," Granny said, nose crinkling with distaste. "She's far too imperious. Who does she think she is? The Queen?"

They all burst into laughter. Anthony watched his two favorite women with great excitement and tried to blend into the background while they got to know each other.

Granny eased closer to Melody and put a hand on her arm. "You're a doctor, I believe?"

"Yes, ma'am. Pediatric surgeon."

"And your parents are doctors as well?"

"Yes. My father is an orthopedic surgeon and my mother is an OB/GYN."

"Well, at my age, I've closed up shop down there, so your mother is of no use to me, but perhaps your father could take a look at my knee one of these days. It's never been right after I took a nasty fall hunting a few years ago."

"I'm sure he'd be thrilled, ma'am."

"Your sister has had a bit of trouble this week, I believe?"

Melody hesitated.

"Yes. She's going through a rough period right now, but I think it's temporary."

"We all have our rough spots, don't we?" Granny said ruefully. "My great-uncle Rupert took forty years with his."

"At least," Anthony said.

Granny spared him a quick glance before refocusing on Melody. "You've met the dogs, I see. I'd heard a nasty rumor that you were a cat person."

Melody shot Anthony a quelling look. "Have you been running your mouth?"

"Constantly," Granny interjected before he could say anything. "You're all he can talk about. It's quite remarkable, really."

Anthony ducked his head, the better to hide his burning cheeks.

"*Now* who's running off at the mouth?" he muttered.

The women laughed.

"Let's just say that I see the benefits of both dogs *and* cats," Melody said.

Granny nodded with tremendous satisfaction.

"A true diplomat. You should fit in nicely. I'm thinking of giving the pair of you the little male, there, when he's a bit older. With the blue collar. The one who's currently chewing on the leg of that priceless end table. Every good home needs a dog or two. And I understand that you have a very fine dog park in Journey's End, so he should be happy there."

There was a long pause while Melody looked dumbstruck and Granny waited.

Then Melody's breath hitched and her questioning gaze flew to Anthony.

He shrugged, doing his best to remain a cool cucumber until the conclusion of the interview.

Melody blinked back a tear or two and smiled at Granny.

"That's incredibly generous, ma'am. Thank you. We'll take very good care of him."

"See that you do. Don't get so busy with your growing careers that you forget to feed him. There's nothing worse than a dead puppy lying about the place. His name is Winston Churchill. You must promise not to change it."

"Wow. That's quite a name for a dog."

"He's the pick of the litter, so he needed a strong name. It was either that or Harry Potter. And I thought he needed a bit more gravitas."

"True," Melody said, laughing.

"And I'll expect regular updates on his progress. And pictures. They've given me a smart phone, so you can text me. Here. Let me show you."

Anthony smothered a laugh while his grandmother pulled out her phone and Melody oohed and aahed over the bedazzled case with the royal crest on it.

"Well, dear," Granny told Melody, putting the phone away and shutting her little handbag with a conclusory snap. "I'll get out of your hair and let you go about your day. I hope you'll forgive me for popping in unannounced, but my curiosity got the best of me. I had to come and meet the woman who's had such an extraordinary effect on young Hamlet, here."

"I'm not *Hamlet*," Anthony said, frowning. "If anything, I identify much more with Macbeth. *He* was someone who knew how to deal with a troublesome monarch."

They all laughed.

Then Granny took Melody's hand, sobering.

"You mustn't be a stranger. We expect to see you both very often."

"Yes, ma'am."

"And I'm sorry about your not coming to the investiture tomorrow." Granny made a face. "But protocol must be observed with these things and you and I haven't officially met yet. Which reminds me. I'm going to issue a formal invitation to tea. And when you come, you must pretend we've never met. Otherwise my private secretary, Tommy, will never let me hear the end of it. And I have so little joy as it is. I snuck over here just now. He thinks I'm napping with a headache."

"I completely understand, ma'am," Melody said gravely.

"When we meet again, none of this ma'am stuff. You must call me Granny. And I shall call you...*Mellie*. After my mother's favorite beagle when I was a child. I hope you don't mind. But at my age, I don't really care if you do."

"I don't mind at all," Melody said, laughing. "I'm honored."

"We kiss each other on both cheeks when we see each other for the first time. People accuse Brits of not being affectionate, but that's not the case."

"Well, I hope you'll forgive me if I slip up and try to hug you one of these times. I know I'm on British soil, but sometimes my American exuberance slips through."

"I'm aware," Granny said dryly. "It's a terrible trait. Bubba does it all the time, despite my best efforts to discourage it."

"Bubba?" Melody shot him an incredulous look. "That is *quite* the nickname. I may have to use it."

"You will *not*," he told her with as much dignity as he could muster with his cheeks and ears burning.

Melody turned back to his grandmother. "I will try to keep control of my American exuberance and not hug you too often."

"Well." Granny gave Melody a long and thoughtful look, dimpling up at her. "I might overlook it this one time. As you're new."

Melody started to reach for her, then seemed to think better of it. "What about a kiss? Would a kiss be too much?"

Aggrieved sigh from Granny. "If you must, Mellie."

Grinning widely, Melody bent, kissed Granny's cheek and pulled her in for a true hug, which the Queen returned with interest.

Watching them, Anthony almost expired with happiness.

When they pulled apart, Granny patted Melody's cheek. "I'll see you soon."

"I'll see you soon."

Granny cocked her head and cupped her ear.

"Granny," Melody added, color flooding her cheeks.

Crisp nod from Granny, who turned and snapped her fingers.

"Come, dogs. Anthony, you may walk us out."

Shooting Melody a silent raised-brow look, he followed Granny to the threshold, where she snapped her fingers again and turned back to Melody. "I'm glad you enjoyed the tea. You write a very fine thank-you note."

"Thank you for sending it," Melody said. "I feel so special. I didn't know what I was missing this whole time. Now I'm a tea snob. I refuse to use any old tea bags anymore."

"There's plenty more where that came from."

"Good," Melody said, grinning with delight. "I'm going to hold you to that."

"And there's something one should always remember when the press gives one a hard time, Mellie. An Eleanor Roosevelt quotation. Perhaps you know it?"

Melody looked startled, but quickly mastered her quivering chin as she nodded. "'No one can make you feel inferior without your consent.'"

"*Precisely,* dear," Granny said with tremendous satisfaction.

Another nod, then Granny and her furry entourage went to the door, where she stood and waited for Anthony to swing it open for her. Then they walked outside and down the gravel path to where her unmarked car and security officer were waiting. The dogs leapt inside and took their places at the windows.

Granny paused, eyes twinkling. "She's an exquisite choice. I'm very pleased."

Anthony breathed a huge sigh of relief. As someone at the bottom of the line of succession, he didn't need his grandmother's permission to marry, but it certainly didn't hurt.

"So am I. Only pray I can get her down the aisle before she comes to her senses and realizes she's far too good for me."

"This should help you out, dear," she said, handing him something from her purse.

By now, Anthony felt quite overcome. He opened his arms and started to pull her in for a hug, but she prevented that by holding up her hand for him to kiss.

"That's enough American affection for the day," she said, pressing her lips together to quash her smile as she patted his cheek. "One mustn't overdo."

21

Anthony hurried back inside, his overjoyed brain buzzing with half-formed plans about how to proceed from here. A checklist. He needed a *checklist*.

First off? He needed to wrap up the charity events he'd already committed to, which were scheduled for the next several months. He needed to sign up for the New York bar exam, sign up for a review class to help him pass said bar exam and see about getting a job. He and Melody needed to discuss where they'd live and make an appointment to see her dream house, which was probably perfect for their needs at this point. He needed to select a date to actually move so that he and Melody no longer had to endure any more of these excruciating good-byes and separations, bearing in mind that he couldn't very well pack up all his stuff and check it with the baggage when they went back for Baptiste and Samira's wedding, much as the idea appealed to him at the moment.

All important considerations, no doubt.

But one item in particular loomed large, knocking everything else to the side:

Making Melody his *wife*.

Honest to God, he felt his soul grin at the idea.

The proposal would have to wait a bit, obviously, what with his investiture tomorrow and the quick fly-back to Journey's End for the rehearsal dinner and wedding at the end of the week. And while he was no genius or professional when it came to romantic gestures, even *he* knew that one couldn't go around getting engaged and thereby trampling on someone else's big day. Plus, some of his married friends had regaled him with their proposal extravaganzas, which often included weeks of intense planning culminating in grand gestures that often involved things like doves, butterflies, decoy cars and surprise getaway weekends to exotic locales.

So...

What to do? What to do...what to *do*...?

Their one-year anniversary was coming up in a couple of months, wasn't it? Maybe he should plan the proposal around that. He could take her to, say, Bali or Fiji for a quiet weekend in one of those luxury huts on the water. She'd love that. Or he could do it over the holidays, which of course opened up a whole new can of worms in terms of whether to spend the holidays at Sandringham with Granny and his family (his soul gave a big thumbs-down at the idea of enduring another singalong with Uncle Dicky) or in Journey's End with Baptiste, Samira and the baby, who would be experiencing his first Christmas. That sounded *much* more fun, as far as he was concerned.

Well, they'd figure it out. They had time.

They had all the time in the world.

He discovered her sitting on an ottoman looking dazed, her hands on her cheeks and her eyes wide.

"Oh, my God," she said on a giggle tinged with hysteria. "I just met the Queen of England. Your *grandmother* is the Queen of England. I can't believe it."

He would have laughed with her—it was always amusing to witness people meeting Granny for the first time—but a sudden surge of emotion made that impossible.

It overtook him sometimes, threatening to wipe him out.

Melody was glorious. Her eyes...her skin...her amazing smile, which always seemed to collect all the joy in the universe and concentrate it on her face. With the late morning sun shining through the windows and catching streaks of gold through her tumbling curls, she looked as though she had a halo. Which only made sense, because God knew she had to be an angel capable of miracles to bring about the sorts of changes his life had undergone since he met her.

She was a mere mortal. He understood that. Just an average-sized woman with workaholic tendencies, a stubborn streak a mile wide and a spine made of titanium. Yet she was such an outsized force in his life and loomed so large when he thought of her that there was something triply endearing about seeing her take such girlish delight in something.

He slowly walked closer, hoping to get his unexpected tears on lockdown and give his throat a chance to loosen up enough to say something by the time he arrived at the sofa and sat opposite her, but no dice.

"Anthony," she said as she got a good look at him, love shining bright in her eyes even as her smile slipped away. "It's okay, Blue Eyes. Don't cry. You're breaking my heart."

He could only shake his head and press his lips together.

A manly tear or two was one thing.

Sobbing was out of the question.

Yet he couldn't quite get it together when she scooted to the edge of her ottoman, ran her soft hands through his hair and pressed fervent kisses to his face. By this point, she knew him as well as anyone did, but he didn't have the words to tell her how far she'd brought him since they first met. How different these tears were from the despairing ones he'd cried in the days and months after his mother died. How his body was far too small to contain all the swelling joy inside him.

She pulled back a little and wiped his tears away, her brown-eyed gaze steady and warm.

Strong.

He stared at her as they held tight to each other's hands, wanting her to see the magic she'd performed. Hoping to cobble together enough of an explanation for her to understand that he wasn't insane.

"Do you have any idea what you've done?" he asked her.

She looked down and shook her head, wiping away a quick tear of her own.

"It would have been..." Hoarseness forced him to stop and clear his throat. "It would have been enough for you to come along and smile at me. To make me laugh. To challenge me. To drive me mad in bed. To *enthrall* me."

Shaky laugh from Melody, who wiped away another tear as it traced down her cheek.

"But for you to see inside me and know I need my career and my freedom when I didn't even know it myself...for you to charm my grandmother like that..."

He shook his head, incredulous, and rested his elbows on his knees so he could rub his temples and get his act together while another wave got him. She said nothing, giving him both the time he needed and her silent support, which was *everything*.

When he was ready, he used his shirtsleeves to wipe his face (oh, how Granny would love *that* if she could see him now) and took Melody's hands again.

"You have to marry me," he said urgently, his voice rough. "Only think of all the ways I can muck things up again without you here. You don't want that, do you?"

She laughed.

And speaking of mucking things up...

It occurred to him, far too late, that he'd sprung this on her with none of the romantic gestures he'd had in mind. He'd just blurted it all out there, which was only to be expected because he was an idiot where these things were concerned. But it wasn't too late for him to do one thing right.

So he slid to his knee in front of her.

"Please marry me."

She laughed again. A tear or two fell. He wiped them away, savoring the warmth of her skin.

"Oh, I don't know," she said, her smile slowly fading. "It's such a hard decision. I was looking forward to being alone with my career to keep me busy during the day and my medical journals and a cat to keep me company at night."

He wiped another of her tears, waiting.

"And now, the greatest man I could ever hope to meet shows up on my doorstep. And he brings all *this*"—she swept her arm wide— "with him. I wonder what I should do?"

"You don't have a choice. You said you would marry me today if I agreed to move to Journey's End, and now that's a done deal. I even got Granny to sign off on it. So you should say yes."

"Yes."

He felt a wild swoop of euphoria. "Yes?"

"Yes."

He grabbed her face and started to kiss her to make it official, then thought better of it and reached into the pocket of his slacks.

"Anthony."

"Patience, darling. You need your ring, don't you?"

"There's a *ring*?"

He pulled out the black velvet box granny had just given him. Opened it to show her.

She gasped and put a hand over her heart, which he took as good signs.

"Granny let me choose a couple of things from her collection," he said, pointing. "The emerald-cut diamond in the center there came from my great-grandmother's tiara, which is the one my mother wore to the first state dinner after she got married. I thought about giving you her engagement ring, but that seemed like bad luck for us, given how their marriage turned out, don't you think? And the baguettes on the sides came from one of Granny's favorite necklaces. But that thing's got so many diamonds no one will ever know it's a couple short."

"It's amazing," she said, breathless, as she presented him with her left hand. "It's exactly what I would have chosen for myself."

Grinning, he slid the ring onto her finger. It was a perfect fit.

"How did you—"

"I rummaged through your jewelry box while you were sleeping and traced a couple of your rings."

She gave him a suspicious look. "You're *sure* you weren't trained by MI6?"

He laughed. Kissed her hand. Looked up and found himself startled by the blinding glow of happiness in her expression.

And the sudden startled heat as he traced a thumb over the inside of her wrist.

He hesitated, his heart thudding in his chest.

Then he kissed her mouth. It was dewy. Sweet.

Her smile receded in favor of the hard glitter of desire in

her eyes and the harsh sound of their breath as anticipation built between them.

His paused, his attention dipping to those lush lips he loved so much, which of course made him lick his own lips.

She gasped.

He knew and loved that needy sound. So he kissed her again, harder, employing the shallow sweep of his tongue to make her just a bit hotter as he experimentally trailed his fingers down the outside of her breasts to see if he could spark enough electricity to make her jump.

Ah. There it was.

It occurred to him that he might not be the one for grand romantic gestures or charming chitchat at cocktail parties like, say, Baptiste and Nick. His name would be on nobody's suggestion list if the occasion called for someone to be eloquent and insightful with his feelings.

But when it came to driving the lovely Dr. Harrison out of her fucking mind with lust, then he was The Man.

Oh, yes, indeed.

So he broke the kiss just as she began to squirm and surge to get closer to him, thrilled that he possessed the power to make her eyes glaze over like that.

"I wonder if I might have a word with you in the bedroom, fiancée," he murmured, surging to his feet and hooking his fingers through her dress's belt to pull her up with him.

"I suppose," she said, her color deliciously high now. "But I'm not sure what you could say to me in there that you couldn't say out here."

He glanced around at the sitting room while his hands went to work unknotting her belt. "I'm not sure Granny's furniture is equipped to handle harsh language. And I wanted to mention that I plan to fuck you into next week."

"Oh, thank *God*," she said, heaving a dramatic sigh. "I was afraid you'd start to call it *making love* or some other euphemism now that we're engaged."

He frowned down at her, incredulity getting the best of him.

"You really *are* the only woman for me, aren't you?"

"You'd better believe it," she said, hitching up her chin.

And that was enough with the talking.

He grabbed her hand and all but yanked her poor arm out of its socket as he tugged her down the hall to the bedroom.

"Take off your pretty dress," he said, turning her loose long enough to yank the heavy drapes closed before they gave some passing gardener the shock of his life. Then he went to work on his own clothes. "Wouldn't want to wrinkle it."

Happy to oblige, she unwrapped the thing and let it slither down her arms and drop to the floor, revealing all the luscious curves he could never quite get enough of. Today she wore a lacy white bra and panties set that highlighted her honeyed skin, lifted her breasts for his greedy hands and eyes and also revealed far more of her tiny dark nipples and pussy than they covered.

He paused, arrested.

"You've been shopping, I see."

She fluffed up her hair, then put a hand on her hip, meeting his gaze with an unmistakable challenge in her eye.

"Hope you don't mind. I wasn't sure what the dress code was in London."

He started to laugh, but his straining cock had only so much patience and it was about to run out. So he pulled her in and helped himself to big servings of her tight arse and rounded hips, her hair and breasts and *mouth*.

She was as starved and eager for him as he was for her,

urging him on by hooking him around the waist with one of her juicy thighs and planting her hands on his arse while she thrust against him and moaned with the thrill of it all.

When his skin felt hot and tight and the overwhelming lust locked all his breath in his throat, he broke the kiss and pushed her back enough to get a hand between them.

"How would you like it today, Dr. Harrison?" he asked silkily, skimming his fingers under the edge of her panties and along the creamy cleft between her legs. "Missionary? Cowgirl? Doggy?"

She'd groaned and let her eyes roll closed and her head fall back when he touched her *there,* but now she managed to stare him in the eye and focus as she nuzzled and nipped his mouth just enough to make him wonder if he'd come in his pants the way he'd done all those years ago with his first girl-friend, thereby going down in flames on the greatest day of his life.

And then it got worse.

"Against the wall."

He gaped at her.

"And don't break any of Granny's things," she added, standing on her tiptoes and kissing him again.

A wild combination of triumph and euphoria took over, guiding his hands and making him rougher than he'd meant to be. He told himself to be considerate on this day of days, but there was a serious disconnect between what his brain said and what his body heard.

All he knew was that his mouth was full of her tongue, his hands were full of her arse, her thighs were wrapped in a death grip around his waist and the room had four good walls that needed a workout.

He backed her against the nearest one and braced himself with one hand. Ever helpful, she loosened her grip enough for him to reach inside his boxers and get his cock in hand. They adjusted their angles.

"If you're not ready, speak now or forever hold your peace," he said, panting and trembling with the effort to keep himself in check.

"I'm *so* past ready."

He laughed, said a silent thank-you that they'd long ago dispensed with condoms since she was on the pill, and thrust inside her.

They both gasped. He may have cursed. He definitely saw stars as her tight little pussy clamped down and held on tight. They both needed a moment to adjust to the position and the delicious intimacy of staring each other in the face like this.

He shook his head, another surge of emotion catching him off guard.

Those brown eyes were there, seeing everything. Understanding everything.

"I *love* you," he said, his voice hoarse.

"And I love you."

They found their rhythm and picked up the pace. He thrust harder. Deeper. His legs and arms burned with the strain of exertion, but that somehow only enhanced the experience, making him all the more mindful of her earthy scent. The silkiness of her skin. The breathiness of her cries. The rawness of her voice as she called his name when she came.

He held her as she stiffened and then melted, wrapping her arms around his neck and resting her head on his shoulder so that her hair trailed down his arm. And when she'd begun to catch her breath again, he swung her around and laid her on the bed without pulling out.

His turn.

He pumped his hips and followed the spiraling sensations to the most explosive orgasm of his life, shouting her name as he came because he was far too full of her to keep it all inside.

And when it was over and they'd settled back to earth with him rolling over so she lay atop him, she kissed his sweaty chest and raised her head to look at him and grin.

"What?"

"I can't decide what the best part of my day was. Seeing the cottage and KP next door, finding out you love me and are willing to move to Journey's End, meeting the Queen or getting engaged. And it's barely noon yet!"

"It damn well better be the mind-blowing fucking," he said, glaring at her.

"There is that," she said, laughing.

"And what about the paparazzi?" he asked, smoothing her back. "Was that the worst part?"

She shook her head, the dreaded P-word not dimming her glow a bit.

"The good parts of my day were so amazing I don't remember any bad parts."

"Good," he said, twisting a strand of her hair around his finger for the pleasure of seeing it spring back into place again. "I can't promise to save you from all of that, but I can promise to always love you as hard as I can."

She leaned in for a gentle kiss before pulling back with the smile of a well-satisfied woman on her lips.

"That's the only promise I need."

EPILOGUE

"I don't know about you, but the sight of all these wedding preparations is starting to make me feel nauseous," Melody whispered in Anthony's ear that Friday night at Baptiste and Samira's gorgeous rehearsal dinner. They were in the park, where flickering lanterns adorned the tables, strings of fairy lights ran through the trees, moonlight glittered off the Hudson winding through the valley below and the rose-covered gazebo was all set for the ceremony tomorrow. Melody had just finished snapping several shots of baby Jean-Luc, who'd smiled for the first time, and most of the people at their table, including Baptiste and Samira, had headed off for a spin around the dance floor. "Let's have a show of hands. All in favor of eloping to Vegas?"

Anthony raised his hand along with her, much to her surprise.

"We could go down to the courthouse Monday morning, as far as I'm concerned," he said.

"Could you wear the uniform with all the medals that you wore to your investiture? I *love* a man in uniform."

He made an outraged sound. "Well, why not mention it? I

would've been parading around in the bloody thing this whole time."

They laughed.

"So are we meeting on the courthouse steps?" she asked hopefully.

"We'd better not. Granny would have my head. She loves weddings. She's made some noises about St. George's for us."

Melody grimaced. "How can she be making noises? We've only been engaged for thirty seconds."

"You've no idea," he said grimly. "She loves helping with the flowers and the music, according to my cousins. You've been warned."

"And where's St. George's?"

"Windsor."

"As in Windsor *Castle*?" She felt a vague flare of panic. "Isn't that a bit much for a non-heir like you?"

"One might think. I raised that very point with Granny. She says it's quite small and intimate."

"Good." Her lungs loosened up enough for a relieved exhale. "How many people does it hold?"

"Only eight hundred," Anthony said blithely, disappearing behind a sip of his Guinness.

"Eight hundred?" she cried. "Are you serious?"

"Granny is."

"What if we wanted to get married here in Journey's End? Couples get married in the bride's hometown, don't they?"

"*You* tell her."

Melody opened her mouth, gearing up for a semi-hysterical rant about keeping their wedding to an intimate and manageable affair, like Baptiste and Samira were about to have, when he subtly tipped his head to a distant point off to their right. A group of photographers, who'd been thwarted by Baptiste's security personnel and barricade, had their telephotos trained on them, a fact that Melody kept forgetting.

"Careful," he murmured. "The paps would love a shot of us fussing at each other. Think of what the body language experts on staff at the *Daily Universe* would make of *that*."

She rolled her eyes before leaning in a bit closer. "Wonder what they'll make of *this*?"

Grinning, he met her halfway for a lingering kiss that left them both a bit breathless and glazed. Melody was just debating whether she wanted to dive in again when a shadow loomed over their table.

"You two lovebirds engaged yet?" Tony asked, drawl mitigated a bit by the cigar clamped between his teeth. He'd brought a server with him. The man distributed a glass of champagne to Melody, whisky to Anthony and bourbon to Tony. Tony slipped him what looked like a hundred-dollar bill, much to the man's astonished delight as he hurried off. "I don't see the ring."

Melody kept her jaws firmly shut on that one as she tipped her head for Tony's kiss and watched him drop into the vacant chair on the other side of her. She also resisted the urge to finger the gold chain that was tucked into her bodice, at the end of which hung her precious ring. She and Anthony had of course decided not to upstage the wedding tomorrow by mentioning their engagement, but they hadn't made plans beyond that. Melody, for one, favored keeping their secret for a while longer, at least until Anthony had moved to Journey's End and passed the bar exam.

Anthony shot his father a disbelieving look as he toasted him in thanks before sipping his whisky.

"As if we'd tell *you* if we had."

"What?" Tony said, the soul of bewildered innocence. "I can keep a secret."

"Apparently you can't," Melody said, giving him the side-eye. "Did you wait a full hour before you blabbed to Anthony that you and I had talked on the phone the other day?"

"Oh, that." Tony flapped a hand and puffed a few smoke rings over their heads. "That wasn't *blabbing,* per se. That was me trying to nudge things in the right direction."

"I don't need *nudging,*" Anthony said, slinging an arm around the back of Melody's chair. "I'm smart enough not to let Melody get away. I think we can all agree on that."

"Can we?" Tony asked pointedly.

She and Anthony exchanged a quick glance during which their mutual adoration shone through. The more she tried to keep her smile down to a minimal level, the more her overflowing emotion seemed to escape through her overheated cheeks. Anthony, meanwhile, gave her a swift and possessive once-over that telegraphed his desire to swallow her whole. If the paparazzi snapped a shot of *that* look, the body language experts would stay busy for weeks to come.

"Yes," Melody told Tony. "You can."

"Well, thank God for small favors," Tony said, beaming as he raised his glass and they all toasted. "And I suppose it's too much to ask whether you are also getting your legal career back on track, son?"

"No, it's not too much to ask," Anthony snapped. "And allow me to mention that you are setting a new land speed record for nosiness tonight. Is it all the bourbon?"

"That's a distinct possibility," Tony said cheerfully, getting up again. "I just need to know what to tell the lawyers about your trust."

Anthony's face went blank. "My trust?"

"Yep. I'm thinking I might release a fourth of it to you lovebirds on your wedding day. Maybe a bit more when you pass the bar exam and the bulk when you pop out a kid or two. A man who's got sense enough to marry Miss Mel and get his career back on track has sense enough to manage his money and do something worthwhile with his life. How do you like them apples?"

He strode off without waiting for any response, waving over his shoulder at them.

She and Anthony looked at each other, neither quite knowing what to make of this sudden reversal of fortune.

"How do you feel about this?" she asked him, stunned. "Excited?"

Anthony cocked his head and thought it over for a minute.

"It's fine. I knew the money would come one day." He ran his hand through her hair, cupping the back of her head and bringing her in for a quick nuzzle under cover of whispering in her ear. "And I already have everything I need, don't I?"

"What a coincidence," she said, kissing him back. "So do I."

He stared at her, that wonderful hand stroking her nape.

"You know what's going to happen to you when we get home tonight, don't you?"

"I was hoping, but I don't like to *assume*."

His eyes gleamed at her in the candlelight. "Generally a good policy, but this is a sure thing."

"Good."

"And how would you like this sure thing tonight, Dr. Harrison?"

She pursed her lips while she thought it over. "I think I feel like a cowgirl tonight."

"Really?" he said with a flare of unmistakable interest.

"Really."

"Look!" Nick, looking triumphant, arrived at the table with Jean-Luc nestled in the crook of his arm and sat across from them. Though his earlier bout of smiling seemed to have abated for now, the baby gurgled happily and watched everything with an avid gaze. "I charmed the nanny into giving him to me. Baptiste and Samira are still dancing"—he tipped his head toward the dance floor, where the newlyweds-to-be were regarding each other as though they'd decided to move the wedding night up twenty-four hours—"but when they're done, you'll need to distract him for me. Otherwise, I'll only have the baby for thirty seconds."

Melody smiled indulgently at him. "I'm surprised at you, Nick. Wasting time with a little baby when there are all these beautiful women here tonight." She pointed to the dance floor, where she had no problem identifying a couple of unabashed and staring females who looked as though they'd love to make a Nick sandwich later on. "And I thought I saw at least one redhead in the bunch. What if they all get away?"

"Don't worry." Nick flashed his killer smile, all white teeth, grooved dimples and Latin charm. "I'll make up for lost time later. And of course the baby will help attract *more* women."

He smiled down at the baby, who studied him closely, seemed to decide he was an okay guy and smiled back. Nick laughed with delight. But then, without warning, his face twisted with what looked like quiet despair. Melody watched, riveted, as he hastily ducked his head, swiped his eyes and switched the baby to his shoulder, the better to press kisses to his fat cheek and cup his curly head.

Luckily, Nick was too absorbed with the baby to notice Melody and Anthony exchanging a worried look.

"Is he okay?" Melody whispered.

Anthony nodded sadly, leaning in to murmur in her ear.

"He was married out of school. His wife immediately

got pregnant. Right before she was due to give birth, she was hit by a drunk driver. She and the baby died. It was a boy."

"Oh, my God," she said, pressing a hand to her heart. "That's terrible."

"I know."

They watched Nick, who seemed to have recovered and was now bouncing the baby on his lap.

"I can't imagine him married, though," Melody continued. "He seems far too into women."

"He's got to do something to cope," Anthony said. "I've always thought that—"

"Hat's off to Samira for catching a billionaire who also makes wine," said a new female voice.

Melody cringed and glanced around in time to see her sister Carmen's unsteady arrival at the table. Carmen dropped into the nearest chair, sloshing some of the red wine from her goblet onto the pristine white tablecloth.

Anthony, who had just met Carmen that afternoon, shifted uncomfortably.

Nick watched Carmen, sudden shadows darkening his face.

"Baptiste knows what he's doing with a grape, doesn't he?" Carmen continued before sipping appreciatively. She reached the bottom of her glass in an alarmingly short period of time. "Maybe he has an extra billionaire friend he can introduce me to, now that I'm single again."

"Why don't you take it easy on the wine?" Melody asked her, trying to keep her voice low and pleasant.

"And why would I do that?" Carmen said. "We're at a party, aren't we?"

"You wouldn't want to get yourself into any trouble," Nick said before Melody could answer, his jaw tight and his lyrical Italian accent a bit thicker than usual. "There are less destructive ways to blow off steam."

Carmen looked startled, although whether it was from being called out by a complete stranger with a baby or being confronted by one of the sexiest men present, Melody couldn't say.

Carmen, being Carmen, recovered quickly enough.

"Who the hell are you?" she demanded.

Nick's gray-eyed gaze swept her up and down as he absently patted the baby. "Domenico Rossi. My friends call me Nick. Who the hell are you?"

"Carmen Harrison."

"My sister," Melody supplied apologetically, embarrassed to have any association at all with Carmen at this drunken moment.

"Ah." A flare of recognition crossed Nick's face. "A lovely Italian name for a beautiful woman. You should think of other ways to pass the time, Carmina. You can't handle your alcohol."

Carmen barked out a bitter laugh. "Truer words were never spoken, *Domenico*. That's probably why I got that DUI after just one glass of wine at dinner last week. But now that everyone thinks I'm an alcoholic anyway, I may as well act the part."

Nick's heavy brows sank lower, threatening to engulf his entire face.

"Or you could find another hobby to keep your mind off your troubles. As I say."

"Like what?" Carmen snapped, bemused.

Nick shrugged. "Sex works very well for me."

Carmen made a strangled sound.

Melody and Anthony exchanged raised-brow looks.

Unsmiling, Nick stared Carmen dead in the face.

Until she recovered enough to surge to her feet.

"Fuck you and your sorry advice," she told Nick. "What do you know about me and my troubles?"

"Nothing at all," Nick said smoothly, still patting the baby. "But I know about troubles."

Melody and Anthony sat there, frozen inside their astonishment.

Carmen and Nick seemed to have a tough time tearing their eyes off each other. But she finally managed it, blinking and turning to Melody.

"Anyone else want more wine?" Carmen asked, picking up her glass with a crooked smile. "Speak now, or forever hold your peace."

She swept off without waiting for any response.

"Sorry about that," Melody muttered, wishing that *she* had another glass of wine.

"Your sister isn't what I expected," Nick told Melody, eyes flashing as he watched Carmen work her way through the crowd, to the bar. "I thought she'd be more like you."

"Don't let *her* hear you say that," Melody muttered.

"Is she all right?" Nick asked.

"No," Melody said. "And I plan to find out exactly what's going on as soon as I can."

"I think she needs you, darling," Anthony said with a sympathetic rub of Melody's shoulder.

Baptiste and Samira returned from the dance floor just then, looking flushed and happy. Until Baptiste looked down and realized that Nick was now Jean-Luc's BFF.

"I see you've kidnapped my son," Baptiste said, putting his hands on his hips and trying to look severe as he glared down at Nick. "Luckily, no harm seems to have befallen him. Otherwise I would have to kill you. And I would hate to do that because getting thrown in jail might make me late for my wedding tomorrow."

"I'm allowed to hold the baby," Nick said defiantly. "As an honorary uncle and a member of your wedding party. Ask Samira."

"It's true," Samira told Baptiste. "It's all in his contract."

Chuckling, Baptiste took the baby, raised him up high, took a whiff of his diaper and made a face before offering him back to Nick. "Let's see how committed you are to Jean-Luc now that he needs to be changed."

Nick grimaced, stood and put up his hands as though being held at gunpoint.

"Jean-Luc? Who is Jean-Luc?"

They all laughed.

Nick checked his lap and his cuffs, smoothed his hair and gave himself a couple of spritzes with his breath spray.

"I think I *will* see what kind of mischief I can get into tonight," he told Melody with a wolfish grin.

"Knock yourself out," Melody said, laughing and shaking her head.

"Just make sure you're not late for the wedding," Samira and Baptiste both said.

More laughter on all sides as Nick waved and strode off.

Baptiste hitched the baby on his hip and turned to Samira, his eyes filled with sensual promise. "Let's find Mrs. Smith so she can put the baby to bed. You and I have some consummating to do."

Samira squawked with mock outrage as she smacked his arm.

"Kindly do *not* put our business out there in the streets!"

"What?" Baptiste, to no one's surprise, remained entirely unrepentant. "What do you think *they'll* be doing before the night is over?"

"He's got us there, darling," Anthony told Melody, one brow raised.

"And don't think you're fooling anybody," Samira warned Melody as she linked arms with Baptiste and they turned to go. "There's a ring dangling at the end of that little chain there. I know it."

Anthony stiffened, managing to look like a mask-wearing bandit sneaking out of a house with a bag of loot slung over his shoulder, but said nothing.

Melody, meanwhile, worked hard to maintain her poker face as she fingered her chain.

"What, this? Why can't it just be a pretty gold necklace?"

"You are no Viola Davis," Samira said, shaking her head and rolling her eyes as they walked away. "Make sure you keep your day job."

They headed off, leaving Melody to blow out a relieved breath. "I think they fell for our clever denials, don't you?"

"Not in the slightest."

"Yeah, I pretty much sang like a canary. I feel like I've been interrogated by James Bond."

They laughed together for a beat or two, until the music changed and the sound of Joe Cocker's gravelly voice came over the speakers as he launched into "You Are So Beautiful." And suddenly there was no room in Melody's world for anything except her fiancé, how much she loved him and how far they'd come since they first danced to this song on the magical night they met.

Apparently she wasn't the only one feeling this way.

Anthony stood and extending his hand.

"Dance with me."

She stared up at him, pausing for effect.

"I thought you didn't dance?"

His dimples deepened.

"The old me didn't dance. The old me also didn't smile much, didn't think about what he was doing with his life and doubted he'd ever fall in love and get married." He shrugged as he took her hand, pulled her up, tugged her to the dance floor and reeled her in. "Times change, don't they?"

"Oh, I don't know." She trailed her fingers along his nape for the thrill of feeling him shiver. "You're still everything I could ever hope for."

He pressed his lips to her temple for a lingering kiss.

"And you're everything I need, Dr. Harrison. You've always been everything I need."

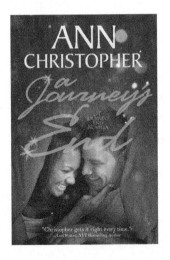

Read A JOURNEY'S END Now!

THANK YOU FOR READING *Everything I Need*! I hope you enjoyed watching Anthony and Melody fall in love as much as I enjoyed writing their story!

QUESTION: Do you have any other contemporary romance series?

ANSWER: Yes!

If you love small towns, family sagas and sexy brothers, you'll want to read *A JOURNEY'S END*, the novella that began my Journey's End series, today! And it's **FREE!**

Here's a teaser:

Can two wounded people find happiness together?

Meet widower and loner James Harper, who avoids romance like the plague.

And vivacious single mom Miranda Lowe, whose nasty divorce blew up her life.

What happens when they're stranded together one dark and stormy night? Come to Journey's End and find out…

If you enjoy sexy and emotional contemporary romance novels, read *A JOURNEY'S END* now!

And if you enjoy reading stories about rich and powerful men falling crazy in love, then don't miss my Warner Family series. The first book, ***TENDER SECRETS***, is available for FREE! Download now!

Want to stay up to date on all my news about upcoming book releases and deals? Sign up for my **newsletter** and **Facebook** page.

Finally, thank you in advance for helping me spread the word about my books, including telling friends, mentioning them on your social media and/or leaving reviews on the retailers. Word of mouth sells more books than anything else, and I appreciate your help.

Turn the page for an excerpt from *A JOURNEY'S END*…

Chapter 1

"Hit me. Hurry."

Grinning, Miranda Lowe passed the oversized cappuccino mug across the counter to her friend Zoya, who was red-nosed, bleary-eyed and hunched inside her puffy jacket looking distinctly the worse for the wear.

"Here," she told Zoya. "Drink some quick. Before your hands start shaking."

Zoya took a grateful sip, her eyes rolling closed. "One of these days, I'm going to get you drunk so you'll tell me what you put in here that makes it so addictive. It's chicory, right?"

"Nope. Crack."

"I knew it." Zoya eyeballed the glass cases on either side of the counter, her gaze skimming over the pastries. "You'd better give me a caramel scone, too."

Miranda grabbed a fat scone. It was still warm from the oven and gooey with icing. "For medicinal purposes?"

"Yeah. Let's go with that. Why don't you come sit with me and have one, too?"

Miranda wiped her hands on her apron, ignored the temptation of something sweet and buttery, and tried to look happy with the cup of peppermint tea she'd been nursing for the last hour.

"I'll sit with you for a minute, but I'm not eating a scone. I'll let you get fat by yourself, thanks."

Zoya, who was an effortless size six—skinny witch—frowned as they headed to a small table near the picture window facing the street and sat. "You can't have any more to lose, Randi."

Miranda slapped one hip. Thanks to her religious and endless calorie counting and treadmill walking, it was now merely curvy rather than meaty, and she wasn't taking any chances. "One scone and it's all over for me. I'm not trying to lose. I just want to maintain my size twelve. So you sit there and say a prayer of gratitude that you were blessed with a"—she scowled and made quotation marks with her fingers—"fast metabolism."

Laughing, Zoya took a big bite.

Miranda watched, trying not to hate her.

Not that she ever could, of course.

They'd been close since the day Miranda opened shop here in town and Zoya showed up with a warm batch of chocolate chip cookies to welcome her to the neighborhood. Since then, they'd bonded over their shared love of hiking, baking, wine-tastings and pretty much everything else.

"I know I keep saying this," Zoya said, chewing, "but I really love the holiday decorations. It's so cozy. I could stay here all day."

"Thanks."

"Will you come decorate my shop for me?" Zoya ran the quilt and yarn arts boutique a couple doors down. "I think it needs something else and we've got two whole days till New Year's. Plenty of time."

"The fifty Christmas quilts you have hanging on the walls aren't enough?"

Zoya sighed. "I don't know. It looks better here."

With a swell of pride and satisfaction, Miranda surveyed her small domain, which was empty now that the morning rush had quieted down. Java Nectar was everything she'd wanted it to be when she moved here to Journey's End two years ago. Fresh from her nasty divorce after ten years of marriage, she'd poured her heart—and her settlement money—into making her small business a success.

The location—for her new life and her new career—had

been crucial, and she'd chosen carefully after spending time in several towns north of Manhattan. Journey's End, which was nestled between the Hudson River and Emerald Lake, was quaint but upscale and only about an hour and a half outside the city. As such, it was a favorite destination for people with disposable income and an urge to spend time out of town, and Miranda liked to think that her little coffeehouse was the heart of it all.

With an indigo awning and matching market-umbrella-covered tables in the warm months, it was midway down the storefronts on DeGroot Avenue, between the antiques shop and the outdoor gear shop. The inside was cheery, with sky blue walls, weathered tables, chairs, benches, and reading areas around the stone hearth, where she kept a roaring fire stoked all through the winter. She normally kept jazz classics playing, but she'd switched to holiday songs promptly on Black Friday.

Since December was her favorite time of year, especially this year, when her seven-year-old twin boys would be with her rather than her ex in Brooklyn, she'd gone a little overboard with the decorations. There was a fresh Christmas tree, of course, strung with golden beads and glittering white lights and decorated with the painted wooden candy canes the local kids had decorated on her last crafts and coffee day. More white lights—could you ever have too many white lights? — and fresh pine garlands wound their way around the counters and doorframes. Bowls filled with cinnamon-scented pinecones served as table centerpieces. Carved wooden nutcrackers and Santa Clauses lined the stone hearth and mantel, and a large brass menorah had a special place in the front window.

The overall effect was, Miranda hoped, welcoming and comforting.

"So did the boys like their quilts?" Zoya asked, snapping her out of her thoughts.

Miranda had stashed a holiday lap quilt under the tree for each of the boys this year. She'd made them during the December sessions of Zoya's quilt club.

"They loved them." Miranda grinned as she remembered their delight the first time they snuggled down with their gifts to watch a movie on the sofa. "They've been dragging them everywhere they go, all around the house. Those poor abused quilts need to be washed already. It's great."

"That's awesome! When're they coming back?"

The twins had spent the weekend in the city with their father. Miranda had spent her alone time wallowing in the peace and quiet, but only for ten-minute increments. Then she'd swung the other way and missed the boys' nonstop chattering and bickering.

Yeah, she was a mess.

"They're getting back tonight," she told Zoya. "We're going to do our usual—watch *Toy Story,* fall asleep on the sofa, then wake up in time for the ball drop and a glass of sparkling grape juice. We're big partiers. You know. "

"Every day is like a day in Vegas at your house—uh-oh." Zoya suddenly spied something out the window. Trying to hide her growing smile behind her mug as she took another sip of coffee, she tipped her head toward the street. "Here comes your favorite person."

Miranda stilled, but her pulse kicked into overdrive. Worse, prickly heat crept over her cheeks until she felt as vividly fluorescent as the night-lights at Yankee Stadium.

Zoya watched her with narrowed eyes and keen interest, which didn't help the situation.

Making a valiant stab at casual indifference, Miranda shrugged, turned her head and glanced out the window in time to see the only pebble in the shoe of her new, post-divorce, single-mom existence here in idyllic Journey's End:

A huge black truck, spotlessly clean despite the recent snowfall and resulting sludge in the streets, pulled up to the curb, executed a perfect parallel park, and went quiet. The driver's side door opened. A man unfolded his tall body from the cab and, unsmiling, headed for Java Nectar.

Miranda's breath hitched.

James Harper had arrived for his morning cup of coffee.

Chapter 2

"He's not my favorite person, so I don't know why you say that every time he shows up. And I don't hate him, either. I don't think about him at all, okay?"

Painfully aware that she was dissolving into a babbling bundle of nerves, Miranda tried to shut up. Zoya continued to watch her, brows raised. Miranda smoothed her hair behind her ear. Zoya waited.

The babbling resumed.

"He's a customer, I serve him coffee, he pays, he leaves, end of story," Miranda added, now fidgeting in her seat. "And he's the boys' troop leader, but that's it. We had one date months ago. Big deal. Who cares? I'm over it. I am so over it." She waved a hand. "His loss. He's still not over his wife's death, I guess. Whatever."

Zoya stopped trying to hide her amused grin. "Whatever. Right. So why is your face all red?"

Miranda got up and blasted Zoya with a gaze as frigid as she could make it. James was almost to the front door now, his limp barely discernible and his booted feet crunching on the salt-covered sidewalk, and Miranda didn't have time for this conversation. The last thing she needed was for James to realize they were talking about him.

"If my face is red, it's probably because you won't let it go. I'm sorry I ever told you about the date—"

"The best first date of your life, you said, if I recall correctly," Zoya continued, unabashed.

Wistful memories of that magical night, never very far away, drifted back to Miranda.

The boys had been with their father the weekend that James finally—finally—asked her out. He'd said they'd do dinner, so she'd dressed in her prettiest LBD and waited for him to pick her up, giddy with anticipation in a way she hadn't been since her first date with her ex.

When he'd shown up with arms loaded with groceries, she'd been charmed and intrigued. When he'd made her sit, nibble on cheese and olives and sip red wine—a delightful Malbec she'd never tasted before—while he whipped up the most delicious shrimp linguine a girl could imagine, she'd been mesmerized. When they sat down at her dining room table to eat, she'd been enthralled as they'd talked and laughed and laughed and talked. About books and current events, his big family, which included several brothers, all of whom sounded as interesting as he was, her boys, their mutual hobbies (fishing for him; quilting for her) and their tastes in music (classical for him; hip-hop for her).

The one thing they hadn't talked about was how he lost his wife two years ago, around the same time she'd gotten divorced, but that hadn't bothered her. They'd get to it in time, she figured.

On that first night, though, it was all about fun and laughter.

After a three-hour dinner, he'd taken her to a little DeGroot Avenue dessert and wine bar (he didn't bake), where they'd eaten carrot cake and she'd wondered: a) if it was possible to fall in love with someone in one night; and b) if it was always a bad idea to sleep with someone on the first date.

Deciding that it was, especially for a divorced single mom living in a small town, she'd happily looked forward to their first kiss at the end of the night.

Except that he'd gotten progressively quieter and more withdrawn on the ride back to her house and dropped her off at her front door with a peck on the cheek and a shifty-eyed promise to call her.

He'd called the next day, all right.

To tell her they had "bad timing."

Just like that. After all the fun they'd had the night before and after she'd glowed under the warmth of his gaze the entire time, as though his eyes doubled as some sort of high-powered tanning bed—now, suddenly, they had bad timing.

Well, whatever.

Bastard.

Since then, she'd gamely pretended that it was all the same to her. That he hadn't tap-danced all over her tender heart with the spiked crampons for ice climbing he sold in his stupid little shop next door.

Not that she was bitter.

"Best first date ever?" Miranda managed a carefree laugh, a difficult feat considering she was lying through her teeth. "I'm positive I didn't say that."

"Those were your exact words," Zoya reminded her. "If I recall correctly. Which I do."

"Drop. It."

All but snarling now, Miranda turned away from Zoya's soft laughter and marched back to the counter. She made it just as the front door swung open with a jingle of sleigh bells and a sharp gust of wind.

And there he was, striding into her coffeehouse with that quiet confidence—James Harper, the most appealing guy she'd met in years.

Otherwise known as the guy who wanted nothing to do with her.

After holding the door open to admit his sidekick, a forty-pound, blue-eyed husky named Frank (for Sinatra), he paused at Zoya's table. This gave Miranda a second to arrange her features into an expression that was welcoming but otherwise disinterested.

And to stare at him, of course.

As always, he looked as though he'd been ripped from the pages of the latest L.L. Bean or Land's End catalogue, with his well-worn jeans, a black long-sleeved knit shirt, and one of those plaid, fleece-lined flannel shirts on top. Today's plaid? Black Watch. Despite the weather—and today it was a sinus-clearing nineteen degrees Fahrenheit in the sun, if you could find any sun—Miranda had never seen him in a true winter coat. He either had a layer of walrus blubber miraculously hidden beneath his broad-shouldered, hard-edged body, or else he was impervious to cold, unlike the rest of the normal folks around town.

She was betting on the latter.

As the owner of Open Sky Outfitters next door—the must-stop shop for hikers, hunters, skiers, campers, dog-mushers, birders, fishers, and anyone else who had a thing for communing with insects, cooking over a fire and/or breathing copious amounts of fresh air while engaged in an enterprise that was uncomfortable in one way or another—he looked like he'd been sent over straight from central casting. Miranda doubted there was any manly activity he couldn't handle with ridiculous ease. Fell a hundred-year oak with a chainsaw? No problem. Build a log cabin by lunchtime?

Make a gourmet meal from dragonflies and toadstools? Catch a trout with his bare hands?

Check, check and check.

It probably had something to do with a surplus of testosterone. He was drenched in it. Like Achilles, who'd been held by his heel and dipped into the River Styx so he'd become invulnerable. James here had probably been soaked in a vat of testosterone to make him irresistible to women.

Right now, for example, Zoya was simpering.

"Hey, Zoya," he said in that deep murmur of his. "You staying warm today?"

Zoya grinned and ran a hand through her hair, tossing it over her shoulder. "I'm working on it."

Since no one was looking at her, Miranda figured it was safe to roll her eyes.

Frank, tags jingling, started to trot over to say hello to Zoya, but froze when James frowned down at him. "Did you wipe your paws, man? Go wipe your paws." He snapped his fingers and pointed to the mat just inside the door. "Go."

Frank, muttering, dropped his head, went back to the mat, and wiped his four paws.

"Got some news from California," James told Zoya.

Zoya stiffened, her smile sliding off her face. She shrugged, making a valiant stab at looking nonchalant. "Oh?"

"Daniel's moving back," James said.

"Oh," Zoya said faintly, color rising over her cheeks. Then she abruptly stood and grabbed her coat, abandoning her coffee. "Well. I'd better get back to the shop. I'll see you two later."

"But—" Miranda began.

"I'll call you later," Zoya told her. "Bye."

With that, she hurried out.

Miranda picked her bottom jaw off the floor and looked

to James, whose expression was grim as he approached the counter. "What the heck was that all about?"

"She and my brother have a, ah, history. I thought I should give her a heads-up."

Miranda frowned, disgruntled. She hated being out of the loop. "She's never mentioned it. I'll have to punish her severely when I get the chance."

Dimples bracketed his mouth, although his smile never quite took hold. It never did with her. "Have at it. So. Morning."

As always, he gave her a crisp, impersonal nod.

"Morning," Miranda replied.

Their gazes connected and held. Predictably, any other thoughts she had, including curiosity about Zoya and Daniel, flew right out of her head.

That was what being close to James did to her.

For the billionth time, Miranda wondered why he had such a powerful effect on her. He was sexy, yeah, but so what? Lots of men were sexy, including a couple guys she'd briefly dated in the city right after the divorce, but they blew it the second they opened their mouths and actually said something—often something ill informed or narcissistic. Maybe that was the issue. With the notable exception of the night of their date, James never spoke two words when one would do, and he never spoke when silence was an option. He'd've been a good choice to teach, say, Gary Cooper or John Wayne something about strong and silent.

So, yeah, she'd probably hate him if he ever opened up and started talking to her again.

Plus, he wasn't even handsome—not in any traditional sense. He was ...striking. Arresting. His sleek brown hair, which never received much attention from a brush, invariably curled around his ears, nape and forehead. His straight nose had a ridge in it, and one of his thick brows was always higher than the other, giving him a perpetual look of skepticism. His cheeks were too severe, and his full lips didn't do much smiling, at least when she was around.

His eyes . . .

"Did you save any coffee for me?" he asked.

See? There he went again. Looking at her. With those gleaming brown eyes that revealed little and seemed to hide everything.

Yeah. It was the eyes that got to her.

"I think I can scrounge something up," she said, turning to the machine.

"Thanks."

This was where things got awkward. When she poured for other customers, it was easy to lapse into banter about kids, the weather or the Jets. But James didn't talk much, especially to her, and she was determined not to be chatty with him—"Our timing is bad," he'd told her; oh, *please*—so that didn't leave much middle ground for small talk.

She always had a thrill of awareness between her shoulder blades, as though he was staring at her.

Except that when she pivoted back around with his to-go cup, he was checking his smart phone.

"Here you go," she said. "Coffee. Large. Black. Hot."

He glanced up, nodding his thanks. And then, to her utter astonishment, he said something ...more.

"I'm afraid you'll slip me something with whipped cream in it one of these days."

That unlikely image got a snort out of her, but she wrestled it into submission before it became a laugh.

"You? No way."

He almost smiled.

Flustered, she passed the cup across the counter to him.

Their fingers brushed.

The brief contact shouldn't have been that electrifying. It shouldn't have made sparks of heat shoot up her arm. She shouldn't have jerked her hand away under the pretense of straightening her ponytail.

"So," she said, now running her hand over the top of her head. "Anything else?"

"Yeah." He hesitated. Something flickered in his expression, disappearing before she could analyze it. "How about ...one of those."

He pointed to a brownie, the first he'd ever requested even though he came for his morning coffee every weekday morning.

Her jaw dropped, and she spoke before she could stop herself. "You don't eat brownies."

"You didn't know I eat brownies. There's a difference."

On that enigmatic note, he reached for his wallet and handed her the money. She took it, making sure there was no skin-to-skin contact this time. He didn't immediately turn to go, and she felt the weight of his gaze on the top of her head as she grabbed his brownie, which meant that another awkward moment was in the making.

Luckily, Frank saved her. He trotted over to the edge of the counter, sat back on his haunches facing Miranda, and raised a paw to shake. Frank considered this an ironclad deal: if she shook, she owed him a treat.

She shook. "Hi, Frankie. How's the good boy? Huh? How's the good boy?"

Frank leaned his head back and did a husky *ooo-ooh* sound, reminding her that he wasn't that far removed from his wolf cousins. Laughing, she took a treat from the dog jar she kept for such occasions (she made a mean biscuit, with oats, honey and peanut butter) and tossed it to him. He caught it with a quick snap of his jaws and gulped it down with barely a crunch, his tail wagging happily.

"He's such a good boy. Yes, he is." The smile was still lingering on her face when she raised her gaze and discovered James looking at her. Really looking in a way that no one else ever did. Focused. Intent. Unwavering.

Her thoughts scattered like the snowflakes beginning to drift outside.

"I hate to sound like a broken record, but Frank's a, uh, great dog."

"Thanks." Blinking and pointing his thumb over his shoulder, James reeled in whatever he'd been thinking and locked it safely away. He took a step or two toward the door, Frank trotting after him. "Gotta open the store."

"Bye," she said.

He paused long enough to look back over his shoulder. "You should close up early. Snow's coming."

That didn't jibe with what the forecaster had said this morning. She glanced out the window, where a couple of wimpy flakes were trying to fall.

"What, that? It's nothing."

He tapped his left thigh. "The leg never lies."

Curiosity got the best of her. The story behind his limp was a topic of endless speculation around town, especially with her boys and the others in his scout group. The latest outlandish rumor? He'd been bitten by a shark while scuba diving in Australia.

"How did you hurt your leg?"

"I'm afraid I can't tell you that." Those dimples grooved down his cheeks again, softening his harsh features and framing his perfect mouth.

"Just so you know? I plan to keep asking until I wear you down."

He cocked one of his heavy brows. "If anyone can wear me down, it'd be you."

The husky note in his voice sent a shiver rippling down her spine as she watched him leave, the door swinging shut behind him.

**If you enjoyed this excerpt, read
A JOURNEY'S END today!**

ABOUT THE AUTHOR

A recovering lawyer, Ann Christopher has been published since 2006 and writes contemporary romance and romantic suspense.

When she's not writing, Ann likes to do the following, in no particular order: read; cook; eat; hang out at Target looking for new stuff she doesn't need; play with her 2 rescue dogs and 2 rescue cats; and travel the world with her family. She lives in Ohio with her family.

If you'd like to recommend a great book, share a recipe for homemade cake of any kind, or have a tip for getting your teens to do what you say the *first* time you say it, Ann would love to hear from you!

Stay in touch with Ann!
AnnChristopher.com
ann@annchristopher.com

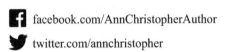

facebook.com/AnnChristopherAuthor

twitter.com/annchristopher

Made in the USA
Middletown, DE
06 November 2024